DR. CYCLOPS

BearManor Media
P.O. Box 1129
Duncan, OK 73534-1129

Phone: 580-252-3547
Fax: 814-690-1559

www.bearmanormedia.com

Dr. Cyclops by Will Garth first published:
New York: Phoenix Press, Publishers,1940
The short story by Henry Kutter first appeared
in *Thrilling Wonder Stories*, June 1940
Released as a film by Paramount 1940

First BearManorMedia Edition 2012

Edited and book design by Philip J. Riley ©2013

The Nightmares Series is being published to preserve original movie tie-in novels that were printed in the 1950s and 1960s on the old style pulp paper. We hope these reprints will allow them to last into the new century.

Other books in
Philip J. Riley's

NIGHTMARE SERIES

"Brides of Dracula" by Dean Owen
"The Revenge of Frankenstein"
(Based on script by Jimmy Sangster)
"The Raven" by Eucice Sudak
"The Bride of Frankenstein" by Michael Egremont

DR. CYCLOPS

by
Will Garth

Includes the short story
by
Henry Kuttner

Philip J Riley's

NIGHTMARE SERIES

BearManor Media

Will Garth

"HEY! YOU UP THERE!! YEAH YOU!!!!! BIG BALD UGLY DUDE!!!!!"
By Richard A. Ekstedt

Big giant bald guys chasing little normal sized people. Normal size bald people chasing little peanut people…

Ok! I get it!!! Works fer me!!!! I get it!!!!!

And it doesn't even have to be people in the 'chaser' role, either! Remember the Cyclops in the movie, "The Seventh Voyage of Sinbad" (or, even in the movie, "The Cyclops"?)? Big ugly one-eyed creature, licking its chops, as it decided to cook up fresh barbecued Persian sailor (hold the hot sauce).

But when it comes to the image of a 'Giant' (granted, the people he was after were a little shorter than you would normally meet at a fast food joint), for me, at least, would be a huge, maniacal, chortling bald and spectacled abhorrent vision. Sweaty, gleeful and sadistic: an amoral monster that would casually snuff out a human life with the same disinterest as swatting a buzzing fly. His name is Doctor Alexander Thorkel, originally immortalized in Technicolor on the huge silver screen with demented glee by veteran Hollywood actor, Albert Decker.

But to the rest of the world, known as the diabolical "Doctor Cyclops"!

The story of the evil Alexander Thorkel had been called forth, born to hellish life, from the mind of the famed fantasy writer, Henry Kuttner.

Henry Kuttner was born on April 7, 1915, in Los Angeles, California. His parents, who originally came from Prussia and Great Britain, arriving in the United States, had decided to settle in San Francisco. He grew up in poverty, following the death of his father. As a young man, Henry worked in a literary agency, run by his uncle (Laurence D'Orsay), in Los Angeles. He sold his first story, entitled "The Graveyard Rats", to "Weird Tales" magazine in 1936. He then met writer C.L. (Catherine Lucille) Moore (January 24, 1911-April 4, 1987), who was part of the famed "Lovecraft Circle" and eventually married her. They worked together on several works, usually using pseudonyms (Lewis Padgett, Laurence O'Donnell) that spanned the 1940's and 1950's. Famed fantasy writer, L. Sprague de Camp, a close friend, said that their collaboration was so intense, that, after a story was finished, it was often impossible for Kuttner and Moore to recall who had written which part of the stories worked on.

Henry Kuttner's friend, Richard Matheson, dedicated his novel, "I Am Legend" (1954), to Kuttner , as Ray Bradbury did with his book, "Dark Carnival" (which would end up being reprinted as "Something Wicked This Way Comes").

The strain of writing finally caught up with Henry Kuttner by the 1950's and, while working on his Master's Degree in the field of Psychiatry, it was reported he died of a heart attack or stroke, on February 4, 1958. One of his final projects, it appears, was the story for the television pilot, with Curt Siodmak, "Tales of Frankenstein" (from Hammer Films).

"Thrilling Wonder Stories" published Henry Kuttner's short story, "Doctor Cyclops", a tale about a Nazi scientist who has perfected the ability to shrink organic matter, but alas, has not the means to keep the organisms alive. Tricking a group of scientists to come to his isolated jungle compound , in South America, the insane scientist- Doctor Thorkel- has them find the solution and then turns his shrink ray upon them. A cat and mouse game begins, between the scientists (who have discovered they are slowly growing back to normal) and the murderous Thorkel. Popular Library reprinted this story, part of a fantasy collection, in 1967, under the Kuttner short story title.

There is now some misconception on the history of the short story and the novel, which we will return to in a moment. Let us first look at the motion picture version, filmed by Paramount Pictures in 1940.

Paramount Pictures was no stranger to the fantasy genre. Cecil B. DeMille had considered a film version of the Edwin Balmer/Philip Wylie novel, "When Worlds Collide" in 1934 and an adaptation of H.G. Wells's "The War Of The Worlds", in 1935 (of course, Paramount did both films, later, under producer George Pal).

The studio had created such gems as "Doctor Jekyll and Mr. Hyde" (1931), "Island Of Lost Souls" (1932), "Alice's Adventures in Wonderland" (1933), "Supernatural" (1933), and of course, "Death Takes A Holiday"(1934). It was only a matter of time for Paramount to once again pool its creative talent and dip down deep into that bottomless well of the fantastic!

Written by Tom Kilpatrick for the big screen, directed by "King Kong" driving force, who took control in the canvas chair, Ernest B. Schoedsack, the film production of "Doctor Cyclops" became the *first* fantasy thriller shot in three-strip-Technicolor   (the earlier Warner Brothers features, "Doctor X" and "Mystery In The Wax Museum" were filmed in the, by this time, obsolete 'two-tone Technicolor' process).

"Doctor Cyclops" was, upon completion, released to theatres on April 12, 1940 to very good reviews and box office.

The plot deals with the insane Alexander Thorkel (Albert Decker), who has developed a process of shrinking organic matter by use of radium. After the brutal murder of his colleague, Dr. Mendoza (Paul Fix), Thorkel summons the world renowned Dr. Rupert Bullfinch (Charles Halton). Warned by his friend, Professor Kendall ("King Kong" 's very own 'Captain Englehorn', actor Frank Reicher), who say's Thorkel is 'very difficult' to work with, Bullfinch decides to travel to the South American stronghold of the strange scientist. Doctor Mary Robinson (Janice Logan), Bullfinch's strong willed co-worker, decided to go with him. They are joined, eventually, by Bill Stockton (Thomas Coley) and Steve Baker (Victor Killian). What follows is a horrifying adventure of death and near madness.

"Doctor Cyclops" was special for fans of the fantastic that still holds up to this very day. The cast was an excellent group of actors, spearheaded, of course, by Albert Dekker. Born December 20, 1905, and an active Broadway stage star from 1927; the 6'3" star made his film debut in 1937. He was a graduate of Bowdoin College and served, politically, in the California legislative from 1944-1946 (Democratic Assemblyman, 57th District). He appeared in many films during the 1940's and 50's, with a excellent performance in the Ralph Meeker film version of "Kiss Me Deadly". His final film, before his death on May 5, 1969 was in "The Wild Bunch" (as a railroad detective).

Thomas Coley, in the role of Bill Stockton, was born on July 29, in Bethayres, Pa. He made his film debut in "Doctor Cyclops". The actor carved out an excellent career on television, appearing on such shows as "Lux Video Theatre", "Armstrong Circle Theatre", "Kraft Theatre", "The Doctor", "Center Stage", Robert Montgomery Presents", "Gunsmoke", "Perry Mason", "Death Valley Days" and "The Loretta Young Show". He died on May 23, 1982.

Janice Logan, as the strong and independent Dr. Mary Robinson, was born on May 29, 1915 in Chicago, Illinois. She made her film debut in 1939 in "Undercover Doctor" and this followed by such motion pictures as "Undercover Doctor", "What A Life", Opened by Mistake", "Summertime Hotel" and "El as Negro". She died on October 23, 1965.

In the role of the outspoken Dr. Rupert Bullfinch, Charles Halton, who made his a career as irritating bureaucrat characters, was a respected stage actor since the 1920's. Born on March 16, 1876 in Washington, D.C., he was best known as Carter, the bank examiner in "It's A Wonderful Life" and having a roles in "Room Service" (with The Marx Brothers), "To Be Or Not To Be" (with Jack Benny), "Across The Pacific" (with Humphrey Bogart), and "Enemy Woman" He died on April 16, 1959.

Victor Kilian, in the role of Steve Baker, was born on March 6, 1891 in Jersey City, N.J. He made his Film debut in "The Wiser Sex" (1932). This was followed by "Banjo On My Knee" (1936). In the 1940's, the actor appeared in "Virginia City" (with Errol Flynn), "Young Tom Edison" (with Mickey Rooney), "Sergeant York" (with Gary Cooper), and "Reap The Wild Wind" (with John Wayne and Ray Milland). The actor, while working on "Reap The Wild Wind", suffered an accident, damaging his eye while doing a fight scene with John Wayne. During the 1950's, he was Blacklisted during the McCarthy era but The Actor's Guild would not go along with the ban. He continued, instead, to work on stage.

It was later he became famous for his role as Grandpa Larkin (aka "The Fernwood Flasher") on the spoof soap series, "Mary Hartman Mary Hartman". He was murdered on March 11, 1979 just after his 88th birthday. His final performance was on "All In The Family", in the episode titled, "The Return of Stephanies's Father".

Italian American actor, Frank Yaconelli, who played "Pedro", Thorkel's kind Hired Man, who helps Bullfinch and company, was born October 2, 1898 in San Biagio, Italy. His family came to the United States a year later and settled in Boston. He quit school at age 12 and helped to support his family. When World War 1 broke out, he lied about his age and joined the army and then was assigned to the 92 Aero Squadron. During World War 2, and later, Korea, he worked as a USO Director (and performer). He was given a Senate Resolution (posthumously) for "devoting a lifetime to unselfish service and entertainment to people all over the world and areas of conflict that our service men were stationed." He died November 19, 1965.

Paul Fix (as Doctor Mendoza), best known as Marshall Michah Torrance, on the television series, "The Rifleman", was born on March 13, 1901. He appeared in dozens of movies and television shows in over a 56 year career, spanning from 1925-1981. He was a veteran of the United States Navy in the First World War and later, became an actor. He first performed in New York and later, Hollywood. He became friends with John Wayne, coaching him in acting. His roles included a judge in "To Kill A Mocking Bird" (with Gregory Peck) and in the films, "El Dorado" and "Sons Of Katie Elder" (with John Wayne). For fans of fantasy, Paul Fix played Dr. Mark Piper in the original Star Trek television pilot, "The Cage" (with Jeffrey Hunter). He also appeared on "Twilight Zone", Voyage To The Bottom Of The Sea", "The Time Tunnel" and "The Wild Wild West". Many fans of cult movies will remember him for his appearance in "Night Of The Lepus". He died at age 82, on October 14, 1983.

You are now holding in your hand a double treat, two for the price of one! The original short story and now, the expanded novel, of "Doctor Cyclops".

Thanks to Mad Scientist (who works part-time as Film Historian) Philip J. Riley (and I, as his blundering lab assistant), have brought back from the steaming jungle of Doctor Alexander Thorkel, a tiger's (or jaguar's) tail…er… tale… of adventure that will *never* shrink in size!!!!!

Richard A. Ekstedt
Somewhere on a mountain in PA!!

CHAPTER ONE

The broad blue waters of the Pacific lapped on the beach below Trujillo, in Peru's province of Libertad. To the east the climbing slopes of the Cordillera Central rose up thousands of feel in the air and hid the mystery and menace that is the interior of Peru.

In the roadstead, offshore there swung at anchor a small coastal steamer that had connected with the Grace liner at Guayaquil to the north. There was quite a stir among the native boatmen who were moving cases of expensive scientific equipment ashore in their small craft, for the passenger list of the coastal steamer was made up of a visiting American party of world renown

One of the Peruvians, more educated than his fellows, pointed with some awe to the dominant figure of Dr. Rupert Bulfinch, where he stood at the low rail of the coasting vessel, looking toward the rising mountains with a far-seeing stare that seemed to penetrate beyond the bustling Trujillo to the jungle depths. Dr. Bulfinch was close to six feet in height, rather burly, and his firm hands, closed over the wooden rail, indicated that he was capable of handling most of the problems that came his way. His eyebrows were of the overhanging type, and shaded his deep grey eyes.

He paused for a moment. His fingers closed over the edge of his tropical kepi, and he removed the helmet from his head. Then a soiled handkerchief mopped his brow. Replacing the helmet. Dr. Bulfinch turned to his young feminine assistant, Dr. Mary Phillips.

Dr. Phillips was on the vivacious side, with a trace of seriousness such as seems to come to most women who enter the scientific field. Perhaps it is a defense mechanism so that their male colleagues will take them seriously. Perhaps it is a natural reaction to the far-stretching vastness of scientific research and its results.

"How do you like the place?" Dr. Bulfinch asked slowly.

Mary Phillips was conscious of the fact that her blonde hair was straggling down over her forehead, and that beads of sweat were forming on her nose and along her forehead. But nevertheless she said:

"It looks all right to me, even though it isn't exactly chilly."

"I wonder how Thorkel is making out." Dr. Bulfinch referred to the object of their journey. "Fellow didn't say much of anything about why he wanted us. But it must be something to do with mining. He insisted that he needed a biologist and a geologist. We ought to be able to form some sort of a conclusion from that."

Mary Phillips nodded.

"What was Dr. Thorkel working on before he left New York?"

Dr. Bulfinch shrugged. He looked past the ship over the crude lighters. Here and there in the waters of the roadstead young boys were swimming. Some of them came close to the boat, and looked up at the white-clad Americans. One of them signalled for a silver coin, offering to dive to the bottom of the bay to retrieve it.

"Unfortunately, Dr. Thorkel and I weren't on very good terms when he was in New York. He did give some scientific papers at the annual meetings, and people seemed to think a lot of him. But I always had the idea that he was a bit crazy.

Aren't we all?" Mary laughed.

Then, as the last of the crates that had been loaded in the waist of the ship was lowered over the side in a rope net, the conversation took on a more serious note.

"What are we going to do about Dr. Handy?" Mary inquired slowly.

"William has become something of a problem," Dr. Bulfinch admitted. "Let's go in and see whether he's up. I'm sure the captain wants to get out of here. He won't want to delay any longer than necessary."

They crossed the deck, pushed open a cabin door, and stepped inside. The third member of their party, Dr. William Hardy, well known geologist and mineralogist, was seated on the edge of his bunk.

"How do you feel, William?" Dr. Bulfinch inquired solicitously.

"Not so good," Dr. Hardy replied. "I'm afraid I have a touch of this blasted fever, and my heart's been acting up since we left Panama. I didn't realize that we were going to have to go up into the Cordilleras for ten or twelve thousand odd feet. My lungs just won't stand it."

"We're ready to go ashore," Dr. Bulfinch declared slowly. He did not think it was necessary to comment on the fact that Dr. Hardy should have considered his health before leaving New York.

"I'll be able to make it," the mineralogist decided. "But I'll have to stay in Trujillo until you folks come back from the interior. If Thorkel has anything in the way of minerals that need expert analysis, you might send them down by messenger."

Mary Phillips was helping Dr. Hardy with his linen coat. The garment seemed to hang on his gaunt shoulders like a piece of sacking that had been cut on rather voluminous lines.

"Maybe Thorkel won't like that," Dr. Bulfinch replied to Dr. Hardy's suggestion. "You know how he is about such things."

William Hardy shrugged as though the matter had been taken out of his hands. Then he quivered as the whistle on the front of the coastal vessel's single funnel let out a weird shriek.

"Captain's getting impatient." Mary declared. She picked up Hardy's handbag and carried it out on deck where the other cases of Dr. Bulfinch and herself were waiting transshipment to the last native boat.

The trio took leave of the smiling native captain, and he wished them luck on their scientific expedition. Then the Americans were in the bobbing lighter and lusty Peruvian was poling them toward shore.

As they moved in toward Trujillo with its white buildings shining along the street that edged the water, Mary dragged her hand in the water, felt the little ripples that ran through her fingers, then looked up at Dr. Bulfinch with an expression that was half smiling, half haunting.

Dr. Bulfinch returned her glance with a knowing nod of his head. Dr. Hardy was curled up on some gaily colored blankets in the stern of the boat, and was already nodding wearily.

"How long do you think we'll be down here?" Mary asked.

"Rupert Bulfinch shrugged his shoulders, then replied:

"Can't tell. We brought along enough supplies for a year, and have arrangements for Pan American Airways to fly down additional equipment if it's needed. But Thorkel has been here for something like two years."

"Maybe I could learn to fall in love with one of the Incas in two years," Mary laughed. Then she became conscious of the glance that the boatman was directing toward her, and she subsided. The quay was close by now, and other lighter men had their boats tied up beside it, and were hoisting the packing cases of equipment to the pier. Smiling, uniformed native officers were supervising the job, and when their own craft came up along side the stairway, Dr. Bulfinch mounted the stone steps, took out his wallet and handed it to the head of the officers.

The copper-colored official glanced over the documents, saluted the doctor, and tipped his hat to Mary Phillips. Dr. Hardy was still in the boat. Minutes later he aroused himself enough to get out of the craft and join his companions on the pier.

A low-wheeled dray was commissioned to cart the equipment up-town in preparation for the journey to the interior. Then the three Americans climbed into a taxi. The native driver waited expectantly while the Americans held a consultation.

"Where do we go from here? Mary inquired.

"I think the American Consul ought to be the first stop," Rupert Bulfinch declared. He consulted a printed list that he had in his pocket, and said: "That will be Fred Harper." He gave the name to the driver. The taxi motor burst into life, the car started up rather abruptly, throwing them all to the back of the seat, and then wheezed off the pier and headed toward the American Consulate.

Inside the Consulate there were the usual preliminaries, then the party was ushered into the private office of Consul Fred Harper. Harper was a young, lively American, still a bit short of thirty. He had once had Dr. Bulfinch as an instructor at college and when the professor confronted him, a look of genuine pleasure lighted the eyes of the Consul.

"Good day, Doctor," he said. "I must say, I never expected to see you down here. Thought you'd pulled out of active service and buried yourself in a laboratory with your biology.

"Something to that, all right, Fred," Dr. Bulfinch admitted. "But there are lots of things to be learned about biology outside the laboratory. I'm down here to help Dr. Thorkel."

Fred Harper nodded. He seemed to be trying to recall the name. Finally he said:

"Oh, yes. He's the fellow up in the jungle near Iquitos. Been away from here quite a while. I'd rather expected him to be back in the United States . . .What can I do for you?

"Several things," Dr. Bulfinch declared. They talked for a while about necessary permits for the scientific party to go up country with its equipment, and Fred Harper agreed to provide these documents and to see that anything else arriving by later boats was taken care of and moved along with the greatest possible dispatch.

Then the Consul offered them rooms in the Consulate until they should be ready to take their departure. This hospitality the three Americans willingly accepted. They broke up and went to their various domiciles to prepare for supper.

But Mary Phillips had other thoughts in mind, and she had hardly closed the door behind her before she was again opening it and returning to Fred Harper's office.

There was no denying the fact that the young American Consul had been favorably impressed by Dr. Bulfinch's young and attractive assistant. He looked up happily when she came back to his sanctum and asked:

"Is there anything troubling you?"

"Yes," she replied, "there is. And the success of the expedition may depend on it. I'm surprised that Dr. Bulfinch didn't mention it." Mary paused and, while she was trying to frame her next question, gazed around the high-ceiled room.

"You've seen Dr. Hardy," she went on. "he isn't fit to go inland. He seems to think he can do his work right here, if we send him the samples from up in the hills. But as I understand it, this Iquitos place you mentioned is about five hundred miles from here. That means a one thousand mile round trip to send something down to Hardy. It wouldn't pay, especially if Dr. Thorkel wanted something taken care of in a quick time.

"You're right," Harper declared, leaning back in his swivel chair, and studying the perfect features of the girl with ill-concealed admiration. "But just what do you want me to do for you? I could wire the States, and have them send someone else down. Is that it?"

"That's one solution," Mary admitted. "But then we might get someone else who would develop asthma or the creeping meemies in the high altitudes. Isn't there someone around here who's accustomed to the weather and who might be willing to take on the job?

Fred Harper picked up a letter opener on his desk and drummed it on the corner of the mahogany table. Then he leaned back still farther and gazed at the patterns on the ceiling. Finally he came forward with a bounce and said:

"Maybe we can do something. It might solve several problems. Your man is up at Cajamarca on the Maranon River. That's on your way to Thorkel's camp. But whether he'll go along with your party is another thing entirely. Unfortunate case, that. I've wanted to help him out, and I have to a certain extent, but I'm not sure it's the right kind of help. Maybe *you* can do something."

There was no mistaking the importance of the personal pronoun.

Harper rose from his chair, went over to a file cabinet and pulled out one of the drawers. When he came back to his desk he was holding a batch of papers. Scrawled writing was visible on them.

"This fellow, Bill Stockton's his name, was doing all right for himself as an engineer and mineralogist down here in South America. Then he got into some kind of a mix-up because of a German or Jap outfit that was trying to get concessions here. People he thought were his friends let him down, and he decided to throw up everything and go native. He makes a few dollars here and there, but usually gambles it away. These are some papers concerning him that might be of help to you. You can study them while you're on the way up to Cajamarca."

Mary Phillips took the packet and thrust it into the pocket of her skirt. Then she smiled at Fred Harper and said:

"I think you're being a real pal. I'm sure Bill Stockton is going to come through."

"I hope he dies," replied Harper fervently.

CHAPTER TWO

As the little scientific party approached Cajamarca several days later, Mary Phillips began to have some misgivings about her forthcoming meeting with Bill Stockton. She had been able to strike up a conversation with several of the natives who were in the scientific entourage, and some of the stories they told her about Bill were anything but encouraging.

In Cajamarca itself, inquiry produced the information that Bill Stockton lived in the jungle about six miles from the settlement. Dr. Bulfinch agreed to take charge of the disposition of the equipment for the time being, and to make arrangements for the next few days' travel, while Mary Phillips sought to make contact with the disillusioned American engineer.

At first Mary didn't know exactly how to proceed. The idea of going six miles through the jungle with a couple of native guides who were more than casually occupied with the task of cutting down the bejuco vines, listening for the sounds of lurking jungle beasts, and snapping back at the chatter of the monkeys and the sounds of the gaily plumbed birds, was not particularly appealing . . .

But they finally came to a clearing that held Stockton's house and one of the natives touched Mary's arm and said:

"That Bill Stockton house. We wait here."

Mary Phillips nodded, and looked through the surrounding growth into the clearing. There was a rather primitive-looking dwelling of adobe in the center of the space that had been reclaimed from the jungle. A low stone wall was around the patio. Broken bits of furniture were piled at one corner of the place.

Several native children were playing around with a dog, and near them, working over a primitive washtub, were two or three women. In the doorway of the house was a younger woman, leaning against the jamb, and surveying her domain with all the air of a regal queen.

There was no sign of Bill Stockton. Perhaps he was off in the jungle somewhere. Mary Phillips circled around the clearing keeping in the shelter of the hanging vines and bulking trees. The guides followed her soundlessly. On the other side of the house, Mary spotted a small pile of broken bottles that gave evidence of the chief ingredients of Bill's diet. She sniffed with distaste and decided that she would be able to do a much better job of impressing Bill with his importance to the expedition if Dr. Bulfinch were along.

So she beat a hasty retreat, and two hours later was explaining the situation to Dr. Bulfinch. The middle-aged biologist shrugged his shoulders, then said:

"Maybe we're wasting out time. But Thorkel expects us to bring him a mineralogist, so I guess we'll have to go through with it. I'd rather hoped you'd be able to do the job, but if you feel you're not up to it—well, I guess two of us will be better than one."

Dr. Mary Phillips looked at the biologist, then said:

"I wouldn't ask you to do it, but somehow the surroundings don't seem to be the sort that a decent woman would want to visit—alone."

Dr. Bulfinch mulled over Mary's words for some moments, then agreed:

"Quite so, my dear, quite so. I know exactly how you feel. We'll go there together this afternoon, after we've had something to eat and our usual dose of quinine."

Mary grimaced, and replied:

"The mere mention of the stuff is getting me down. I certainly hope that Dr. Thorkel's retreat is one of those places that's above the timber line, where the snow has a chance to do some of its stuff. I understand that if you get far enough up toward the clouds you find things of that kind down here. Wasn't it Carveth Wells or one of those fellows, talking about the Equator, who called it 'Hell below Zero'?"

"That's right," agreed Bulfinch. "But he was talking about the Mountains of the Moon in Africa. Must be quite a place, that. I'd like to go there."

Just thinking about a place on the Equator that had a temperature below zero made Mary Phillips feel a bit more comfortable, and she set about the job of supervising the preparation of the midday meal. This meal, coming in the midst of the siesta period as it did, was seldom attended by any elaborate ceremony.

The Andean sun had begun its dive into the Pacific Ocean before Dr. Bulfinch and his comely assistant again rounded up the two guides and headed back into the jungle for the verbal foray with Bill Stockton and his menage.

Their progress was much slower on this jaunt, because Dr. Bulfinch seemed to be eternally entranced with the variety and color of tropical fauna, and inevitably paused every hundred yards or so to make observations and jot down material in his leather-covered notebook.

Finally, however, in just two hours, they had again reached Bill Stockton's abode. Mary Phillips watched as the two guides sat down on a rotting log and indicated that the rest of the job was up to the visiting scientists.

A sense of languor seemed to hang over the deep green of the jungles. Little rustlings in the grass and lush growth about them marked the departure of small animals and reptiles that fed on the teeming insect life of the tropics The sounds of larger animal and reptile life might have been discerned farther off in the jungle, where a fever-infested creek wound its way through the hanging tendrils that dangled from the overshadowing trees.

Mary noted that, while the women and children had disappeared from the once-whitewashed wall surrounding the Stockton compound, the comely Indian girl in the doorway still stood there like some primitive statue modeled in a strange shade of bronze. Dr. Bulfinch examined these surroundings more or less cursorily.

Another important change in this scene from that which Mary had observed was reclining chair.

In this lolled the rather sturdy figure of a white man. He was garbed in shabby whites that apparently had not been friendly with water for upwards of several months. On a small bamboo table within easy reach there was a bottle of liquor and a bunch of native cigars.

The stubble of beard that grew on Bill's face was mixed with a film of sweat and dirt, and the whole ensemble was anything but attractive. Involuntarily Dr. Bulfinch found his nose curling up, and his lips turning at the corners.

"Is that you scientist, mineralogist, or what did Harper call him?" he asked in a half whisper.

"Engineer, doctor," replied Mary Phillips. She tried to keep all traces of her own first impression out of her words.

"I don't know why Hardy had to go and pass out on us. This might have all been avoided."

Perhaps there is something about a woman that can see worth in a man, even when it is hidden under an outward shell such as marked Bill Stockton. Whether this is the case or not, the fact remained that Mary Phillips felt that there was something in Bill worth salvaging, and she was determined to go ahead with the task.

Conscious of the fact that Bulfinch would at least lend her moral support, Mary broke from the cover of the jungle, picked her way along the debris-laden walk that led to the tumble-down house, and finally passed through an opening in the low stone wall. Dr. Bulfinch followed along behind her like a well-trained St. Bernard. Bill Stockton heard the approaching footsteps, and vouchsafed a quarter turn of his head. When his eyes set on Mary Phillips, they immediately brightened, and Mary felt certain that the cloudiness of dissipation that had held them heretofore could readily be waved away.

"Good afternoon," Mary began.

"How've you been?" Bill asked languidly. His single look of admiration had faded into the grimy lines of his face, and he was again chiefly interested in his liquor and his cigars.

One corner of the patio consisted of a wooden frame that held up a roof of red tile. There were holes here and there where the tile had dropped off, and the whole structure appeared in imminent danger of collapsing, but nevertheless Mary Phillips leaned against one of the dilapidated-looking supporting pillars and surveyed Bill with mixed feelings.

Dr. Bulfinch came to a halt beside her.

"I'm Dr. Mary Phillips, Mr. Stockton," Mary announced. Then, pointing toward her companion, she said: "This is Dr. Rupert Bulfinch."

Bill Stockton nodded, sipped from his glass, then said:

"Lots of work up here for a good doctor; maybe for two of them. Some of these natives around here are in a hell of a mess. The government's been trying to help them out, but you know how it is.

Mary sensed that Bill was deliberately misunderstanding her, for there was a quizzical gleam in his eye, but nevertheless she set him right.

"We're not medical doctors," she declared. "We're biologists. You've heard of Dr. Alexander Thorkel. We're on our way to his camp."

"Is that so?" Bill was mildly interested, or seemed to be. "I've heard of Thorkel. He's the crackpot that's up in the jungle around Iquitos, piddling around with some sort of machinery. He's got all the natives afraid to go near the place. But that still doesn't explain how you happened to come here."

"That's what I'm about to explain," Mary replied. "Dr. Thorkel is apparently on the verge of a great discovery. He got in touch with the American Scientific Society and asked to have three outstanding scientists sent into the Peruvian jungle to assist him in the final phases of his work. Dr. Bulfinch here is recognized throughout the world as one of the leading biologists, and I have also had some small success in that direction."

"I see," Bill Stockton replied. "And what about the third gent—or is it another dame?"

"Dr. William Handy is back in Trujillo. We had to come along without him. He is a famous mineralogist."

"Mineralogist, hey? Then that stuff they've been telling about Thorkel is probably right."

Mary Phillips was puzzled, and the look on Dr. Bulfinch's face indicated his curiosity, too.

"I'm afraid I don't understand," the girl declared. Unknowingly she was turning on the full force of her glamour. Its very simplicity was having its effect upon Bill Stockton, even though her words were making little or no impression upon his studied carelessness.

"According to the natives in the district of Scaramento, your pal Thorkel is doing some kind of alchemy up there. He goes around dressed up in one of them Faustus outfits, makes all kinds of weird smoke columns, and talks to the devil. Like as not he's traded his birthright for the devil's help in locating the lost Inca gold mines. At least that would jibe with the stories I've heard.

For the first time since the dialogue had opened, Dr. Bulfinch took part.

"Sounds like native superstition to me," he said. "Dr. Alexander Thorkel is a scientist of reputation and ability. I'm sure he's had nothing to do with the black arts, and certainly is not consorting with the devil. It's preposterous."

Bill Stockton shrugged his shoulders. He tipped the bottle on the table, half filled his glass, and continued his libations. Finally Mary Phillips said:

"Fred Harper's a friend of yours, isn't he?"

For once Bill Stockton's aplomb was pierced. He straightened perceptibly, then asked:

"You got a message from Fred? Fine fellow, Fred. Doesn't belong down in this beastly country."

"You might call it a message," Mary went on. "He told us that you were a clever engineer, an experienced mineralogist, and might welcome the chance to—well—to pick yourself up by the bootstraps. You understand."

"I'm afraid I don't," Bill returned sternly. "It ain't like Fred Harper to meddle in anyone's affairs. And it looks like he's meddling in mine."

Mary was not to be turned aside. She pressed on: "Are you an engineer?"

"I was," Bill Stockton admitted defiantly. A swig from his tall glass punctuated the statement.

"—and a mineralogist?"

"I've handled some of the biggest mining jobs south of the Panama Canal," Bill declared. But after this admission he slumped back in his chair, and its huge depths seemed to enfold him like one of the jungle creepers that ruthlessly took possession of the firm boles of the trees all around them.

"This may be your golden opportunity," Mary continued. "You can't tell."

"You look as though you might be someone's guardian angel," Bill admitted with a touch of admiration.

"Dr. Phillips is offering you the job simply as a business proposition," Dr. Rupert Bulfinch declared. "There's nothing deeper about it than that."

Mary smiled. Dr. Bulfinch was now aligned beside her, and urged:

"Man, you've got to help us out. There's a considerable matter of honor involved, and you ought to be man enough to fight for your own decency."

While the biologist was talking, Mary suddenly felt that she had the solution to Bill's unwillingness to pull up roots and move eastward into the jungle, and thence back to civilization.

"Those Indian women who were washing with the children—do they mean anything to you?"

Bill Stockton looked at the girl, then cast a languid glance out toward the edge of the jungle. The women and children were not there. Finally Bill smiled a bit, and said:

"You're off the track there, lady. I ain't that sort of a fellow. They're relatives of my housekeeper. Seem to like the water down here. Also figure it's easier to wash in a washtub than on a rock at the edge of a stream."

"Your *housekeeper*?" Mary emphasized the second word.

"Definitely," replied Bill Stockton emphatically.

"Then that makes it much easier. You can't call these surroundings living. We're giving you a real chance to get back into your own way of life, to mingle with your own people to—well do I have to go on?"

Bill Stockton laid down his glass and picked up one of the native cigars. He bit off the end ruthlessly, clamped down his teeth on the stogie, then lighted it.

"I can see what you're aiming at," he replied. "But hereabouts people don't argue with Bill Stockton. He does what he wants to do, and what he doesn't want to do, he don't do. Is that clear?"

Mary Phillips felt rebuffed. She drew herself up to her full height to renew the battle, however. They were all sublimely unaware of the fact that the sun had long since disappeared over the tips of the jungle giants, and that the long fingers of black that closed around everything along the Equator were possessing themselves of the clearing.

The argument went on, waxing and waning: Bill Stockton was adamant. Finally the lateness of the hour prompted Dr. Bulfinch to say:

"This discussion has become quite pointless. We'd better rejoin our guides and head back to Cajamarca."

Bill Stockton looked from Mary to Rupert, then said:

"Guides? I haven't seen any guides."

"We left them out in the jungle," Mary explained. "We didn't know just how you would receive us."

"I'm afraid you're stuck here for the night, then," Bill declared. "Your boys probably headed back for town as soon as it started to get dark. The natives don't like to play around with the jaguars that haunt the creeks hereabouts after dark.

Dr. Bulfinch seemed to be disturbed at this delay, but Mary Phillips considered it a heaven-sent respite. Perhaps with the white company at his house, Bill's mood in the morning would be quite different. Mary hoped that it would.

CHAPTER THREE

When Mary Phillips awoke the next morning it was barely twilight. She lay for a while on the rather shabby cot, looking up at the patched mosquito netting and the sooty chimney of the lamp that had served as rather inadequate light the evening before. Her kit was folded neatly on a backless chair at one corner of the room.

She pushed aside the mosquito netting, and slid around until her feet found her shoes. Then she was walking across the primitive room, with its dirt floor, unpainted walls, and single window looking out on the patio. There was some sort of activity out there, and as she stood behind the makeshift lattice work intended to keep the tropical rains from coming through the window, she watched the activity with interest.

Bill Stockton was in the center of the patio. He was hoisting water from the well. As he brought up the bucket he spilled its contents into a cracked stone olla that was still whole enough to contain water. When he had completed this job, he placed a heavy china basin over the water jug and strode toward the house.

Mary was transfixed when she suddenly discovered that his destination was the very window at which she was standing clothed only in vest and panties. She moved back from behind the lattice work and flattened herself against the wall. There was a wooden bench just inside the window, and Bill pushed aside the lattice work, lowered the jug of water and the basin to the bench, then withdrew.

Whether he saw Mary cowering against the wall, or whether he cast a glance in the direction of her pallet and discovered her absence, the girl could not say. His thoughtfulness in the matter of the water was something that Mary considered somehow out of keeping with his usual character. She sensed that it was a definite victory for her.

Half and hour passed before she heard the voice of Dr. Bulfinch coming to her through the open windows. He was whistling snatches of his college alma mater song, even though his class was that of 1901, and he had long since left the sacred confines of the campus. This whistling accompaniment to his morning toilet indicated a pleasant view of the future.

Perhaps the night's sleep had lightened the tension of the three Americans.

Mary began to doubt this, however, when they were gathered on the porch again, and Bill had ordered the Indian girl to set out a rustic breakfast. As though by common consent, both Dr. Bulfinch and Mary returned to the job of pressing Bill Stockton into their service.

"I've thought about your proposition all night long," Bill cast a look at Mary, as though anxious to get her reaction. "I've considered other angles, too, besides the mineralogy business."

Mary flushed, then said emphatically:

"I'm glad you did."

For a moment it looked as though Bill Stockton might be wavering. Dr. Bulfinch said:

I'm sire Fred Harper is going to be disappointed, and I know Mary will be. She's been counting on you!"

Bill looked wearily at Dr. Bulfinch, then said:

"No, thanks. Or to make it plainer—just no." Then he turned to Mary, motioned toward one of the glasses on the bamboo table and said:

"Have a drink, Doc?"

Mary Phillips could not mask her annoyance.

"Mr. Stockton," she requested, "do you mind calling me either Dr. Phillips—or—nothing?"

If Dr. Bulfinch realized the meeting and battling of will that was going on in his presence, he did not indicate it, but merely pressed on with the matter at hand.

"My dear sir," he insisted, we have already come ten thousand miles. Please make an effort to grasp our situation."

Bill nodded pleasantly. He seemed to be enjoying himself.

"I can grasp the situation without any effort," he declared, bending his elbow, and starting another glass of liquor for his still bearded lips. "You man Hardy's heart couldn't stand this altitude, and I'm the only other mineralogist this side of Lima." He took a drink, and settled down in his chair. Mary looked at Dr. Bulfinch and shrugged her shoulders. Bill went on: "The answer's still no."

At this moment Mary became aware of the fact that the Indian girl was again at her post of lookout in the doorway. The door itself was slightly ajar, but nevertheless the piercing glance of the girl was visible in the semi-gloom of the house. There was evident happiness in the Indian girl's eyes.

Dr. Bulfinch, apparently unaware of the completeness of the defeat, went on with his argument.

"You have had a scientific training, Mr. Stockton," he said. "We are on a mission of great importance to science. We need your experience and training. Doesn't that mean anything to you?

"No," Bill replied sharply. Mary sat up a little straighter. She was holding what she felt to be a trump card, but thus far she had not wanted to use it. It might prove to be humiliating, and Mary was enough of a student of human nature to know that Bill was not the sort of a person to accept a humiliating situation gracefully.

"I don't understand your attitude," the girl declared.

"You would," he said listlessly, "if you realized that there was a time when my scientific education, my engineering degree, and all the rest didn't save me from any soul-searching. Then I found out that the natives were my friends—my real friends. They didn't ask questions about my intentions. They didn't feel that they were degrading me by helping out. They weren't Indians or Incas or natives—they were human beings—and I was another human being needing succor."

Somehow Mary realized that Bill Stockton was at the end of his patience, and decided that now was the time to strike. She adopted her most genial expression, cast a fleeting menacing glance in the direction of the Indian girl. then said:

"We were warned that any of the usual ways of offering you work would be likely to fail."

After having delivered himself of a serious analysis of his feelings, Bill was amused by Mary's declaration. He asked:

"Who did me that favor?"

"Why, Fred Harper, the American Consul, he merely admitted you were on an—extended—vacation." Mary paused meaningly, accented the word "vacation," then glanced around Bill's establishment again.

"But as your friend, he now admits that he has only been doing you harm in buying up your I.O.U.'s."

Mary was tempted to chuckle at the effect of this disclosure upon Bill Stockton, but she knew that this would only cancel the effect of her carefully planned psychology.

"Do you realize how much money you owe? she persisted.

"Never gave it a thought," Bill admitted haltingly.

"Exactly three thousand, nine hundred and six dollars," Mary told him. She snatched up her handbag from the table, opened it and took out a considerable sheaf of wrinkled checks and promissory notes.

"You pick up things quick—don't you?" Bill remarked, in an effort to lighten the situation.

Mary Phillips said nothing. Bill, seeing that his attempt at humor had fallen flat, moved back to his chair, and watched the girl with the expression of a trapped bird captivated by a snake.

"I own these notes and I.O.U.'s," Mary insisted. "I paid my good hard-earned money for them. And I don't intend to lose out. So now, Mr. Stockton, which would you rather do? Go to jail—or go to work?"

Dr. Bulfinch was leaning against the rail, his eyes stirring with ill-concealed laughter. Bill Stockton was squirming in his seat. Finally he bowed to the inevitable with some grace, and left them long enough to go in and talk to the Indian girl.

Dr. Bulfinch looked at Mary Phillips, winked, and then said:

"Probably giving the housekeeper instructions on how to take care of things until he gets back."

"I don't think he's ever coming back—here," Mary insisted with bewildering emphasis.

Half an hour later the three of them were on the way back through the jungle to Cajamarca.

CHAPTER FOUR

After a day of renewed organization in Cajamarca, Mary Phillips and Dr. Bulfinch were more than ever convinced that Bill Stockton was going to be a welcome and valuable addition to their entourage. He knew of routes to Iquitos that would take them along some of the automobile roads that were the modern prototypes of the old Spanish Military roads.

Over these highways it was possible for them to transport the more or less bulky equipment in rickety, but nevertheless navigable trucks. Their own journey was shortened by the use of automobiles that had not seen the assembly line for a decade or more. Nevertheless they seemed to roll along with a minimum of repairs and a maximum of jolting.

One effect of the final showdown with Bill Stockton that Mary had not foreseen troubled her as she drove along with him and the biologist. Bill had more or less retired into his shell, and left her with the distinct impression that their relations would be "armed neutrality" until he had been able to pay off the notes she held.

Mary Phillips ridiculed this a number of times, and in his blundering way, Dr. Bulfinch tried to come to her assistance, but he only seemed to succeed in making things worse.

When they were well up beyond Barranca near the Ecuador border, they were forced to exchange their automobiles, such as they were, for more primitive ox carts. These provided such a jolting ride that Mary and her two companions were more than willing to hike along beside the vehicles, particularly when they were covering an especially rocky part of the trail.

Several days with the oxen took them to a small native village on the upper stretches of the Maranon River, one of the tributaries of the Amazon. Here they were able to get makeshift flatboats that took them down through a rather wild section of the Peruvian Jungle to Iquitos.

Since leaving Cajamarca, more than two weeks had elapsed. In that time the relations between Bill and Mary had mellowed somewhat, and Dr. Phillips found it a bit difficult to conceal her pleasure at this fact. Perhaps there was something to this tropical influence on romance.

With the arrival at Iquitos, however, the scientific purpose of the expedition again surged to the fore Inquiry around the village brought mixed interpretations of the activities of Alexander Thorkel. Some of the natives confirmed Bill's original story regarding the black magic and flaming pillar legend. Others dismissed any inquiry concerning the eminent scientist with a shake of the head and a shrug of the shoulders. The group that aroused most interest, however, was made up of about a score of Indians from the Rio Napo. These threw up their hands, their eyes popped open with uncontrolled fear, and they fled from Mary, Bill and Rupert as though the mere mention of the name of Alexander Thorkel were enough to curse them.

Dr. Bulfinch shook his head slowly, then said:

"Now you can see what scientists are up against, trying to work in the back country, among superstitious natives. Thorkel's activities have a perfectly logical explanation, no doubt, but the minds of these people are too childish to accept it."

The practical-minded Bill was willing to forget about this angle, and said:

"How are we going to get up there with all these things?"

His survey included the piled cases of the supplies, and his own goods and chattels which made up quite a sizable pile in themselves.

"Can't we get hold of some llamas or something?" Mary suggested.

"Maybe," admitted Bill, "but I haven't seen a llama in a week or so, and those animals aren't freewheeling, you know. You have to have someone to drive them."

Dr. Bulfinch, as usual, was surveying his surroundings while Mary and Bill were prodding each other verbally. The streets that made up the suburb of Iquitos were winding and muddy, and the main thoroughfare was dominated by a rustic inn at the very edge of the trail leading into the hinterland.

The inn was built on one side of a courtyard. A stone wall about six feet in height went around the yard. One end of the enclosure, including the sheltered well and a portico, was roofed with the same sort of red tile that covered the main building in the jungle near Cajamarca, but it didn't seem to make Bill Stockton the least bit homesick.

But this was not the thing that had particularly attracted the good doctor's attention. It was the siesta hour, and most of the people in Iquitos were reclining in the shadows, or in their upper rooms taking their ease. What Dr. Bulfinch had discovered was a group of mules tethered along a rail in the courtyard of the inn. A few villagers were seated on benches, their huge straw hats effectively shielding their faces from the noonday sun, and oblivious to everything and everything going on around them.

"Llamas, nothing," Dr. Bulfinch declared. "We'll use mules. And there they are." He pointed in the direction of his discovery. Mary and Bill looked down the winding, rutted street, and then Mary sighed with relief.

The trio started toward the inn, and when they were in the shelter of the tiled porch, a beaming native proprietor came out to greet them.

"Good day," he greeted in a sibilant, musical tone. "You will have something cool to drink?"

"Sure, set them up," broke in Bill, before either of the other two had a chance to speak.

"The mules," Dr. Bulfinch finally managed. "Who owns them?"

The tavern-keeper had already gone for the drinks, and either did not hear, or ignored Dr. Bulfinch's query. But response came from another quarter. In the shadows of the portico a sturdy, well built, and sun-tanned white man stirred. He glanced in the direction of the trio, then asked:

"What do you want to know about the mules?"

The villagers under the portico also stirred, and watched the exchange between the Americans with some interest.

"We'd like to rent the mules," Mary explained.

"Rent them?" The bronzed muleteer didn't seem enthusiastic about the idea.

"What for?"

"Aren't they for rent?" Mary countered.

"Not that I know of," the owner replied. "I brought them up here for my own work."

Neither Mary Phillips nor Dr. Bulfinch had considered this angle. But nevertheless the feminine scientist went on:

"What is your work?"

"Sorry," laughed the Mule driver. "I'm Steve Baker. I'm a prospector. Looking for Inca gold."

Mary looked at him, then nodded in understanding.

"Mining it, or stealing it?" she inquired with a smile, anxious to put him at a disadvantage if she could.

"I'm a mining man," Steve Baker replied. "I don't have any truck with these adventurers that rob the natives."

Dr. Bulfinch was puzzled. Mary was still mistress of the situation, however, and she decided on a bold course.

"You didn't bring these mules all the way up from the coast, did you?"

"Of course not," replied Steve Baker. "I bought them after I got here. Anyone would be foolish to cart a string of mules all through this country."

Mary shook her head in evident satisfaction, then said:

"I thought so. Well, we hired these mules by cable more than a month ago."

Dr. Bulfinch joined in. "We certainly did," he insisted. "And we've brought all of this bulky material along with us on the assumption that the mules would be here, ready and waiting to carry our equipment further inland."

Bill Stockton was standing in the background, seemingly enjoying the argument that was taking place between Mary Phillips, Dr. Bulfinch, and Steve Baker. He was quite a different individual from the man who had been picked up at Cajamarca. A shave and a couple of days at the wash basin had worked wonders with his appearance, and under the careful attention of Mary Phillips his clothes had taken on something more of a resemblance to a tailor's conception of popular tropical wear.

At the present time, however, Bill seemed to be entirely oblivious to his appearance, and much more interested in watching another man undergo the ordeal of argument that he had already faced.

Dr. Bulfinch was opening his billfold and displaying a sizable sum in both American and Peruvian currency. He said:

"We are more than willing to pay a reasonable rental for the animals. They mean a great deal to us. We have had all kinds of trials in getting this far, and certainly don't want to feel that we can't cover the last twenty-five or thirty miles because of something like the rental of a string of mules."

Steve Baker shook his head. "Nope," he said, "I couldn't rent these mules to my own mother. I'd like to help you—"

Dr. Bulfinch broke in firmly with: We do not need your help. But we did hire these mules by cable more than a month ago."

"That's too bad," Steve told the biologist. "Since then I bought 'em. I'm a mining man and I got use for 'em.

"Will you please listen, while I endeavor to explain our position?" Dr. Bulfinch asked in his best scholarly manner.

"Sure."

"I'm a biologist," Dr. Bulfinch began, as though the presence of a scientist like himself in the Peruvian Andean country definitely demanded some sort of an explanation.

"I know all about them," Steve declared. "You're a bug hunter."

Dr. Bulfinch appeared to ignore the comment, and went on:

"Dr. Alexander Thorkel, whom we are on our way to join, is also a bug—a biologist."

"Sure," agreed Steve blandly.

"Dr. Thorkel has been doing field work for the last two years in his camp on the Karana River."

Steve Baker looked at the scientist with renewed interest. Up to now he had been inclined to josh each remark of Dr. Bulfinch, but suddenly he was skeptical.

"That's tough country," he declared. "and a long time to chase butterflies."

Mary Phillips had been following the discussion with considerable interest.

She decided that Dr. Bulfinch was getting nowhere fast, and her own sense of scientific responsibility immediately came to the fore.

"Mr. Baker," she declared, "I'm sure you don't realize that Dr. Thorkel is the greatest living authority on organic molecular structure."

"Is that so?" Steve was mildly amused. I guess there's nothing like learning a trade."

As he spoke, he stroked his chin, eyed Bulfinch quizzically and then spat deliberately as he pondered the situation. While the two scientists were deadly serious about their predicament, Bill Stockton appeared to enjoy the inherent humor of the situation. He took hold of Mary's arm and, when she turned to him, said confidentially.

"You got me—now let's see you get him."

Mary was definitely annoyed, but she did not feel that any good would be served by arguing with Bill at this moment.

"Do you want more money for your mules, Mr. Baker?" she asked slowly.

Steve Baker seemed to notice Mary's eminent feminine lines for the first time. He turned to her admiringly, and after a brief pause, he asked:

"Are you one of these docs, too?"

Mary saw fit to overlook this remark, and plunged ahead with another question.

"If it isn't money—what is it you want?

"I want to go along," Steve Baker declared without delay.

Bill Stockton was the one most completely surprised by this statement. He straightened up, an astounded look on his face. His hands dropped to his sides, and his mouth formed a large O as he said:

"What?"

Dr. Bulfinch was only an instant behind him with his retort:

"That's ridiculous! What for?"

Steve shrugged his shoulders. His eyes roamed from Dr. Bulfinch to Mary, and then to Bill.

"Never mind what for," he declared. "Nothing else about this party makes any sense. Why do I have to?"

Mary was willing to accept the inevitable. Not so Dr. Bulfinch, however. He turned to Mary with true scientific aplomb and said:

"This is most irregular. Dr. Thorkel sent for three selected people, and three only."

Steve Baker definitely considered himself the master of the situation now, and said:

"Suit yourself, Doc. If the mules go, I go.

Mary was not in the mood to argue, and when Dr. Bulfinch saw that he wasn't going to get any satisfaction from her, he shook his head, shrugged his shoulders, then said:

After all, I guess the main thing is for us to get up to Thorkel's place with our equipment. He must be wondering what's keeping us."

Steve Baker shook himself out of his apparent lethargy for the first time since the argument had begun, then said:

"Fine. You're cutting yourselves in with a fine guy, and it'll save you some money. I'm willing to gamble with you folks, and if there's any profits, that's where we're going to be able to cash in."

Dr. Bulfinch was too surprised to make any response to this. Mary Phillips seemed to thing that this was a very amusing situation, and, for once in a week or ten days, she and Bill Stockton appeared to be entirely in agreement.

Steve Baker barked out orders to a half dozen Indian muleteers who were willing to go to work, now that siesta was over and the argument was settled. They began packing the mules with the expedition's baggage.

CHAPTER FIVE

It was soon evident, however, that the mule train wasn't going to get under way without further complications in Iquitos. These handicaps did not come from any outside or official sources, but rather from the group itself. While the Indians busied themselves around the mules, and Steve Baker was talking to the innkeeper about supplies for himself and his men, Dr. Bulfinch and Bill Stockton were standing alongside one of the crates containing electrical equipment.

Bill was more interested in his own pile of miscellaneous luggage than in the equipment of the expedition. On top of his baggage there was the huge rattan chair that he had been occupying when the two scientists had first encountered him in Cajamarca.

Dr. Bulfinch was giving explosive vent to his feelings.

"But this is preposterous!" he declared emphatically.

"What's preposterous about it?" Bill wanted to know. Mary had gone into the inn to keep cool, and was not on hand for the beginning of this new discussion. Now, however, she came bouncing back into the patio.

As she approached, Dr. Bulfinch replied to Bill's question.

"How can you expect me to jettison scientific equipment to make room for your easy chairs? The good doctor didn't give Bill chance to get a word edgewise, but rambled on: "What, that is manifestly absurd."

"Not as absurd as for me to be uncomfortable for the next six months."

Steve Baker came out of the inn, anxious to get started so that they could make a good part of their journey in the cool of the evening.

"Make up your minds, boys," he broke in. "There ain't enough mules for all of the stuff."

Dr. Bulfinch turned to Mary, feeling certain that she would be capable of understanding his position, and that she would undoubted add her influence with Bill to his own expressions of indignation.

"This is my entire X-ray unit," he explained.

Mary turned to Bill. "You're just trying to delay us. I don't know why, I should think you'd want to get this job done."

She did not elaborate on this statement. Bill looked at her with an expression that mirrored surprise and hurt, then asked:

"How can you say that? I'm already to go."

"You're enough of a trained man to realize the importance of Dr. Bulfinch's equipment on an expedition of this kind."

Bill immediately adopted an expansive mood, and said generously:

"I do."

Mary Phillips breathed with a sigh of relief. Then, as she watched him, Bill Stockton pulled the big chair down off the top of his pile of baggage, placed it under the portico, and settled in it comfortable. As he did so, he concluded:

"There is only one thing to be done. The X-ray kit goes. I'll wait here.

Immediately Mary's sense of satisfaction burst like a pricked bubble. She placed her hands on her hips in exasperation, then looked slowly from Bill to Bulfinch, and back to Bill again. She gritted her teeth angrily as she declared:

"Unhappily, Dr. Thorkel did not send for X-ray equipment. He did send for a mineralogist."

Dr. Bulfinch could do nothing but resign himself to this state of affairs, but his tone was icy as he said:

"Regrettable, but correct."

With this momentous decision reached, Steve Baker went on with the task of loading the mules. The Indians worked with increased acceleration. Finally, just before twilight fell over Iquitos, the mules were lined up and headed out through the village archway toward the trail.

The winding path present a labyrinthine appearance as it would along the eastern slope of the Andes toward the jungle in the distance below. At the base of the path there was a narrow gorge that cut into the now darkening green walls of the jungle.

Even though they had had several irritable moments while getting under way on the final lap of their journey, Dr. Mary Phillips and Dr. Rupert Bulfinch felt a new lightness as they marched into the eat toward their destination. They might not have felt so light of heart and step had they known something of the experiences that lay ahead of them.

Two days later they were approaching their destination. An old Indian, completely familiar with the Karana River country, and oblivious to the stories of his tribesmen, had volunteered to guide them, and they had made good time.

The Peruvian, carrying himself as proudly as one of his Inca forebears, was leading the party on foot over the winding and tortuous trail through the mountains. Steve Baker rode behind him on the first mule, while some distance separated Baker from Bill Stockton at the head of the scientific section of the party.

As the old Indian came out of the jungle to the bank of the river, a bit of action greeted him. On the opposite side of the river, hidden partly in the reeds, there was a strip of beach enclosed by a semi-circular bank over which hung the encroaching green-black cloak of the jungle. Drawn up on the beach was a small abandoned dugout canoe. Asleep beside the canoe was the form of a young Peruvian.

The sleeping Indian was Pedro Caroz, native servant of Dr. Alexander Thorkel. In anticipation of the arrival of his servant associates, Dr. Thorkel had sent Pedro to the river crossing to meet the party and guide them to his camp. Pedro had a companion in the form of his redoubtable canine friend, Paco, a dog of nondescript breed, but unswerving loyalty.

As the Indian guide came down to the bank of the river across from the beach, he spotted his countryman and the dog, and called to Pedro in native dialect. The call did not immediately arouse the native, but the sound of the tinkling bells on the mules, the noises of the train, and the cries of the muleteer's voice all combined to make a sound that aroused Paco the dog.

He awoke with a start, darted down to the edge of the water, then looked across the river to determine the source of the noises. And instant later he was running back to Pedro, nuzzling him to awaken him. The native servant sleepily pushed the dog away, but Paco was persistent until Pedro finally awakened. The old guide laughed at these antics, then turned to consult with Steve Baker as the latter rode up.

Before the guide could point out Pedro, the scientist's servant had scuttled to cover, obviously anxious to avoid being seen by the newcomers. Almost immediately, however, he retraced his steps and came back to the edge of the brush. His head popped out, and he watched the approach of the mules as they came down to the river and splashed into the water.

It was not long before the first animals in the train were on the sand of the beach that Pedro had been using for his nap. Satisfied that this train was the one for which he was waiting, because of the presence of the white men and the boxes and bales of scientific equipment, Pedro, with his dog at his heels, finally turned tail and hastened up a jungle path to report to Dr. Thorkel.

The old Indian guide had no trouble in following the trail that Pedro had taken, and as he moved along up the path, Steve Baker pulled his mule out of line and waited for Bill to overtake him.

As Stockton jointed the miner-mule owner, Steve said:

"The guide claims we'll be at Thorkel's camp in another ten minutes. You and I seem to speak each other's language. For the last time, are we pardners, or ain't we?"

Bill had been subjected to this pressure ever since Steve Baker had joined the party. Mary and Dr. Bulfinch had gotten something of a laugh out of these exchanges, but they were no longer funny to Bill Stockton. Finally Bill said:

"Partners in what? Nobody's looking for any lost mine."

"I know different," Steve insisted. "You're an engineer with mining experience. Dr. Thorkel sent for someone like you special. You were even willing to leave important scientific equipment behind so you could bring along your easy chair. You're not kidding me."

The American engineer merely laughed. There was no point in arguing with Baker. As the mule owner drove on ahead with his mules, Bill waited for Dr. Bulfinch and Mary to come up, and when they joined him, he said:

"About another half mile."

Dr. Bulfinch fixed him with a steady stare, then said seriously:

"There's no such measurement as 'about,' Mr. Stockton."

Before Bill Stockton had a chance to think of a suitable retort, Rupert Bulfinch had heeled his mule past him, and was on his way up the trail. Mary Phillips did not seem to be in any such hurry, however. She pulled her mule in beside Bill, and rested one of her hands on his. Then she said:

"Bill, do you hate me for making you come on this trip?"

"It's been all right so far," he replied gaily. "Maybe someday I'll write a book about it."

Mary studied him carefully for a moment. Traces of his dissipation were marked, partly because of the tiring trip, but somehow there was something more manly about Bill than when she had first met him. She went on talking:

"Are you upset about the load we lost this morning? Maybe I had something to do with it."

Bill shook his head. There was a new seriousness in his tone as he said:

"No, I'm not upset. I've had liquor jump into rivers by itself before. I'm sure you had nothing to do with it."

Mary Phillips felt almost like kissing Bill Stockton for this remark, but somehow she felt that Bill would not be likely to appreciate it. Instead she decided to change the subject.

"Aren't you curious about what's waiting here for us—for you—working with the two greatest biologists in the world?"

"Working on what?" Bill wanted to know.

"Well, it must be something important, or Dr. Thorkel would not have sent for us. You will do your part—" she murmured— "you will help us, won't you?"

Bill Stockton grinned a disarming grin, then said:

"You've made this menagerie tick so far, haven't you? Why start worrying now?"

With this reply, Bill Stockton rode on ahead. Mary was left flat-footed in the center of the trail. Her mind was in something of a turmoil as she tried to fathom Bill's real feelings. Her job in getting up to Dr. Thorkel's camp would certainly have been in vain, if he refused to cooperate with the famous scientist; and Mary knew that she, alone, would be to blame.

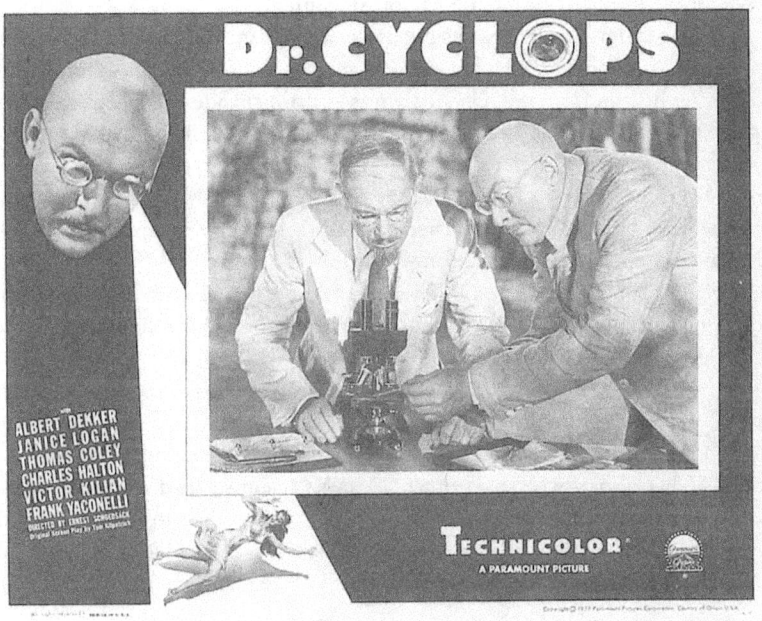

CHAPTER SIX

Dr. Alexander Thorkel's camp and experimental station on a knoll above the Karana River, on the headwaters of the Amazon River, was extremely primitive. But as long as the buildings and equipment were adequate to house his small staff and his laboratory, that seemed to be all that bothered the technician.

The main building was a small, mud-walled house. Adjacent to this there was an open, primitive mine shaft surmounted by an ancient, rude framework for hoisting. Around the building and the mine shaft there was a small expanse of open yard with several ruined huts along one side.

A bamboo plant fence shutting off the area immediately around the mine shaft also marked the limits of the rest of the yard, and beyond this, enclosing the whole clearing, was an eight foot high mud wall. The lush, green growth of the jungle pressed in on the little clearing on all sides, high reeds formed a first line of defense, then the taller growths and tangled lianas succeeded them to mould into a wall of turbulent plant growths.

The back door of the house led out into the mine yard which was surrounded by the bamboo fence. The end of the fence ran to the corner of the house. The balance of the area inside the mud walls was typical of a tropical compound. The side of the house abutting on the compound possessed a heavy wooden door which seemed to be always barred, and there was a single window in the wall. This was closed on the inside by heavy solid wooden shutters.

Dr. Thorkel was nowhere in sight as the mule team and party approached the house. But as soon as Pedro appeared in the gateway of the compound, out of breath after his run from the river, there was a stirring inside the dwelling. Paco the dog ran along in front of Pedro, now and then turning aside to give his attention to some of the small jungle rodents that raced before him, evidently aware of the danger from the dog, as a result of past experience.

The sound that came from inside Dr. Thorkel's house resembled the hum of a dynamo running, and had a sibilant undertone.

Even though he knew that Dr. Thorkel was expecting the arrival of the scientific party, Pedro was nevertheless cautious about his approach to the house. Instead of going to the door, he sidled over to the window hesitantly and pounded on the ledge. There was a break in the sound of the dynamo, then the sibilant tone dropped to a lower pitch.

Inside the house, Dr. Alexander Thorkel heard Pedro's rapping. In spite of the sounds of his laboratory, Dr. Thorkel, like most scientists, had very keen hearing, and was immediately conscious of the slightest sound alien to his surroundings. The doctor was standing in front of a switch panel. His capable fingers were manipulating several power switches on the wall. Before him there was a small, square window set with heavy mica. This small window was cut in the upper center of the ordinary crude wooden door which presumably led to some interior compartment in the house.

To the initiated the activity behind the mica window would have been a complete mystery. It was no wonder that the natives in the vicinity were inclined to make up all sorts of stories. The flames that quivered and rebounded in the room caused a weird fluctuating green light which decreased and increased in intensity as Thorkel manipulated the switches. The strange hum rose and fell in tone value with the changes in the green light.

Dr. Thorkel himself might well have impressed a superstitious Peruvian as being akin to the devil. His burly body was completely encased from head to foot in the lead laboratory armor used by workers in radioactivity.

When he turned around in response to Pedro's knock on the outside window, Thorkel's face added to the impression of unreality. He looked like some great, uncouth monster, whose eyes reflected the weird green light from the mica window.

Pedro's voice came to Dr. Thorkel through the wooden shutter of the window.

"Mr. Dr. Thorkel—"

Assuming that Pedro's return marked the imminent arrival of his colleagues, Dr. Thorkel's hands went to the switches. He threw them off. The hum ceased and the green light began to die away. Then Thorkel lifted the lower flap of his mask enough to permit him to speak.

"What is it? he asked impatiently.

"The people is come," Pedro informed him, wrestling valiantly, as usual, with the English language.

"Good!" replied Thorkel emphatically. "I'll be right out."

Even as he spoke, Dr. Thorkel was pulling the lead helmet off entirely. Even without the mask, his face was something to remain long in the mind of the beholder. One might almost have said that the face was a lesser counterpart of the helmet. His face was ebony, his head close-shaven, heavy and massive.

The doctor also wore heavy, thick, closely fitting glasses. One could not help being impressed with the fact that his face was the face of a man with equally great physical and mental powers. The ensemble, however, left the feeling that here was a man wholly ruthless, and accustomed to driving his physical and mental powers over every opposition.

From his mellow attitude, more or less out of keeping with his usual character, it was obvious that Dr. Thorkel had been counting the days since dispatching his message to the American Scientific Society, and was now as impatient and eager to receive his visitors as they had been to reach him.

As he opened the door he saw the mule train coming in to the compound. Several chickens and a big black cat were scratching in the dirt, and seemed only mildly interested in the arrival of the four-footed, long-eared animals. Pedro would act as the official reception committee while Dr. Thorkel got out of his laboratory armor. The Peruvian servant was already running from the house to meet Steve Baker, Bill and the others.

As soon as they were inside the compound, they all gathered around and looked at their destination as though it were a corner of the Garden of Eden. Curiosity shone in the eyes of all four members of the expedition. Dr. Bulfinch was curious not only about the surroundings, but about the happenings in the laboratory itself. Mary Phillips shared this interest to a considerable extent.

Bill Stockton and Steve Baker were more interested in the mine shaft, and exchanged winks with each other, as though to indicate that their suspicions had been well-founded.

As Pedro approached, Dr. Bulfinch cleared his throat and asked:

"Where is Dr. Thorkel?"

At the moment Pedro seemed to be more concerned with the activities of Paco, his dog. The little animal was running up and down the length of the mule train, sniffing at the mules from a little distance. Pedro slapped his thigh and called:

"Paco! *Vente!* The dog obeyed its master, although somewhat reluctantly. Then the Peruvian was beside Steve Baker, and asked: "Did you see on the trail a horse with spots?"

"Nope," replied Steve emphatically. "Didn't see no kind of a horse."

Pedro shook his head as though conscious of a grave loss. Paco began to run off into the jungle. Paco called to him: "*Vente!*" Dr. Bulfinch watched this little exchange impatiently. Pedro seemed to sense this, and said: "My dog, he must not get lost, too!"

"Then tie him up," Dr. Bulfinch ordered sharply. "I'm interested in finding Dr. Thorkel. Isn't he here?"

The Peruvian seemed suddenly aware of his responsibilities and, with a gesture toward the house, said:

"He is come—right now."

Mary and Bill were chatting in low tones. Steve was still appraising everything about the camp. Dr. Bulfinch pounded his fingers on his knee. At Pedro's words, the four of them glanced toward the house.

The door opened and Dr. Alexander Thorkel appeared. He had divested himself of his lead clothing, and was now dressed in slack, wrinkled, tropical linen. He advanced across the compound with an assured step. He was smiling a friendly, gracious smile.

At the approach of their host, the travelers dismounted from their mules. Dr. Thorkel immediately directed his steps toward Rupert Bulfinch, his hand extended.

"Dr. Bulfinch—?"

"Glad to know you, Dr. Thorkel," replied the biologist. They shook hands.

"You honor me in coming," replied Dr. Thorkel.

Dr. Bulfinch immediately dismissed the suggestion and said hurriedly: "The honor is mine—in being asked to join you, Dr. Thorkel."

The hermit scientist's attention was now turned toward Mary. He lifted his brows with interest as his appraising glance ran over her trim figure. She was conscious of the frank pleasure in his expression as he said:

"You must be Dr. Phillips . . . . You were brave to come . . . ."

"I was glad to," Mary replied without hesitation. Then she shook hands with the doctor.

Bill Stockton seemed to be getting a big kick out of these formal amenities among the scientists. He observed them rather cynically. A moment later, however, Bill was aware of the fact that he was the center of the scientist's attention, when Dr. Thorkel turned to him hesitantly, sensing the difference in type between the New Yorkers and the mining engineer.

"Dr. Hardy, I presume," Thorkel began. "You're rather younger than I expected."

Bill composed himself, to Mary's evident relief, and said simply:

"Sorry to disappoint you, but I'm not Dr. Hardy. I'm Bill Stockton."

Mary interposed an explanation at this point. "Dr. Hardy became ill, so rather than delay your experiments, we enlisted Mr. Stockton's services."

Dr. Thorkel looked from Mary to Bill, sensed something of the bond that had developed between them, then said to Bill:

"I'm sure you are qualified." He bowed graciously to the mining engineer.

"My past was well looked into—" Bill began. Then he grinned at Mary as Dr. Thorkel's attention shifted to Steve Baker. The miner was still gawking at his surroundings, and observed:

"Funny sort of a place to find 'way down here in the woods."

At this injuncture Dr. Thorkel raised his voice the merest tone as he said:

"I don't recall a fourth—"

Dr. Bulfinch stepped into the breach at this point.

"Mr. Baker owns and operates the mule train. He insisted on coming to look after the animals."

Dr. Alexander Thorkel nodded in understanding. He then focussed his attention on Bill and Steve and squinted through his thick lenses as he said:

"It was very kind of you to help us."

With this statement, he appeared to be dismissing them until their services would be required again. Then he turned to Mary and Bulfinch, placing an arm on each one's shoulder in a warm, comradelike manner. They started walking toward the house.

As they drew near the open door, Dr. Thorkel said:

"Bulfinch, your last work on the molecular structure of organic tissue convinced me that no one was so well fitted to collaborate with me at this stage of my labors."

"I am twice honored," Dr. Bulfinch declared.

Before they reached the house, Dr. Thorkel turned aside, and they began to angle across the compound. Mary looked apprehensively toward Bill, but he ambled along with them. Dr. Thorkel was enlarging upon the reasons for sending his message to them. When he had completed an outline of his requirements, he said:

"You can imagine how welcome you both are—" he paused— "when I explain that I sent for you because my eyes will no longer permit me to use a microscope."

"Shocking!" declared Dr. Bulfinch in amazement and surprise.

Mary was immediately the feminine, practical scientist.

"Couldn't something be done for them—if you went back to the specialists?" she asked sympathetically.

"I must stay here until my work is done," declared Dr. Thorkel, "otherwise all of my preparatory work would be in vain. You know how it is."

The two scientists were familiar with this devotion to duty in spite of the weaknesses of the body. Their estimation of Dr. Thorkel increased by leaps and bounds. Finally the doctor asked:

"Are you altogether too fatigued to attack our first problem at once?

Dr. Bulfinch looked at Mary, but the girl merely shook her head and said:

"Of course not."

It was evident that the hermit scientist was gratified with this wholehearted response, and he left them for a moment, to return shortly with a high-powered microscope and several slides in a case. He set up the microscope on a camp table under an awning.

Dr. Thorkel motioned toward Mary, and she approached the microscope. She manipulated the controls carefully. Bulfinch and Thorkel were leaning over Mary's shoulders, watching.

"Ready," she announced.

Thorkel removed a slide from the case. "We will call this specimen A." he announced. Mary took the slide from him carefully and placed it in position under the microscope. When it was adjusted, Dr. Thorkel turned to his colleague and said:

"And now, if you please, Dr. Bulfinch."

Bulfinch took Mary's place at the microscope, and Dr. Phillips drew back. She was flushed and excited. While she did not know the nature of Dr. Thorkel's experiment as yet, the fact that she was here on the ground, actually engaging in work with him and Dr. Bulfinch, was a thrill that stirred her to the depths of her soul. Suddenly she began to worry, and a couple of ridges wrinkled her brow. Reluctantly she left the two scientists and started away from the camp table and the shelter of the awning.

She sensed that Dr. Thorkel would probably want Bill Stockton before long, since he appeared to be anxious to lose no time in having the visiting experts check on his findings. Bill had drifted off with Steve when it became obvious that Dr. Thorkel was not going into the house.

Mary Phillips did not have much trouble finding Bill. He was comfortably settled in his big rattan chair in the shade. Mary breathed more easily when she discovered him. For a moment she had been afraid that he might have gone off into the jungle with the urge to depart. She hurried toward him with a glance backward toward Bulfinch and Thorkel. This was the critical moment when she would have to prove that she could actually deliver Bill's technical assistance.

"Come on, Bill," she began. "You must do your part. I brought you. I'm responsible for you!"

Bill Stockton stirred uneasily, looked at Mary through half-closed eyelids, then said languidly: "You ought to have a herd of sheep, or nine children. Then you could *really* worry."

It looked for the moment as though tears were going to dart to the eyes of the woman scientist. But she managed to contain herself, even as she realized that, whereas she had held the whip hand over Bill before, now she was completely helpless.

"Are you punishing me? she asked him warmly.

"Oh, no," Bill replied carelessly. "You're doing that yourself." He settled down deeper into his chair. His elbows found the most comfortable spot on the arms; then he said: "I'm just sitting here."

Mary was definitely exasperated, and she burst out: "I wish you'd get up off the back of your neck."

This was a signal for Bill to slide down even further into the chair, until he gave the impression of an overgrown St. Bernard striving to curl up and make himself comfortable in one of the seats of the gods. He looked up toward Mary with a twinkle in his eye, while he said:

"Don't you know that all great scientists worked on their backs? Columbus lay on the dock at Genoa and dreamed of the trip to the New World. Newton discovered the law of gravitation while under an apple tree—and Rip Van Winkle—there was a man—"

Mary decided that it would be best in the long run for her to try and match Bill's mood, so she asked:

"What did he discover?"

Bill yawned drowsily, then opined: "The Science of Sleep."

While Mary strove to get Bill onto his feet and headed in the direction of the microscope, Thorkel and Bulfinch continued with their work. As Mary turned to watch the progress of the microscopic study, he saw Dr. Thorkel removing the first slide from the instrument. He was thrusting a second into the microscope, and his whole huge body was trembling with eagerness as if he were about to learn something that was of the utmost importance to him.

Now and then she could catch snatches of their conversation. Dr. Bulfinch was talking, as he continued to peer into the eye-piece.

"The cell structure in this specimen is more compact, but still distinctly normal."

Thorkel's expression of satisfaction echoed around the compound.

"Ah!" he breathed deeply. Hastily he shoved a third slide into position. "Now we will take specimen C . . ." His excitement was growing.

Bulfinch grunted as he examined the new specimen. It was evident that the slide showed a considerable change over the previous one. He was reluctant to announce his discovery, but finally said:

"This shows progressive deterioration, even disintegration—of the structure."

If Dr. Bulfinch felt that this discovery would be disappointing to Thorkel, he was in for a surprise. Instead, the hermit scientist said:

"Good! Very good." His next action was hard to interpret. He almost jerked Bulfinch away from the microscope, then called: "Mr. Stockton—quick!"

The crisis had come, and Mary did not know what to do about it.

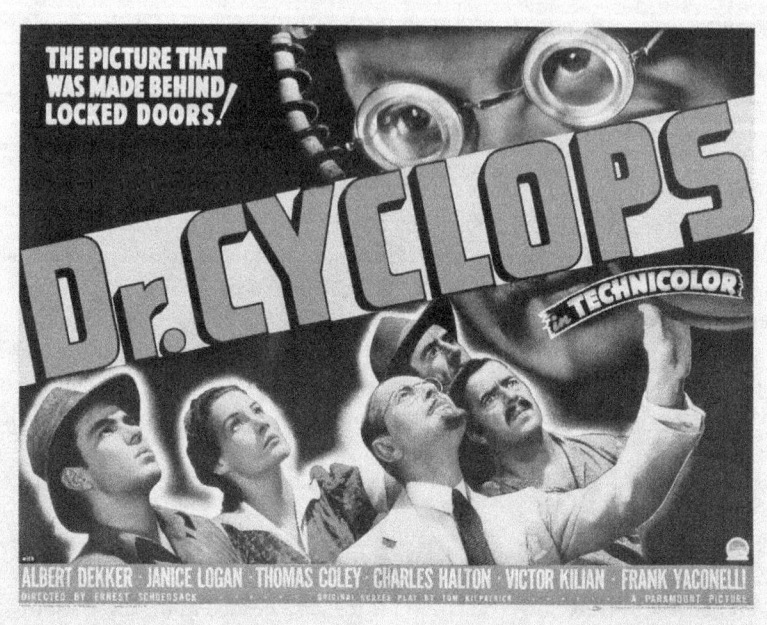

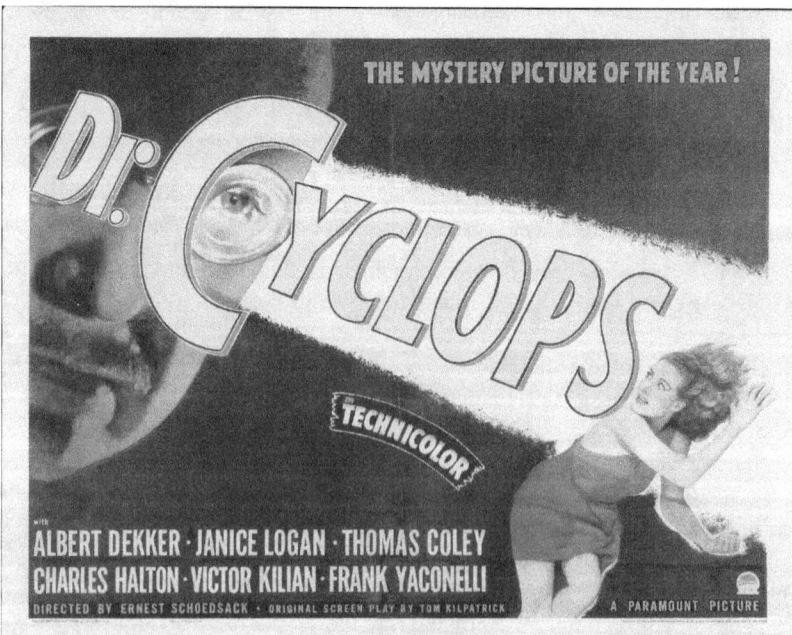

CHAPTER SEVEN

Only Bill Stockton knew that all during the time they had been in Dr. Thorkel's camp, he had been playing Mary Phillips as a cat plays a mouse. He was getting a real lick out of her fear and trembling, and when the husky, excitement-filled voice of the hermit scientist came to him, he said:

"He seems excited." The very calmness of Bill's response was enough to fill Mary with panic. She looked at him, but he didn't move out of his chair. Finally she lowered her voice to a pleading whisper and said:

"Please—you can't refuse . . . ."

Bill seemed to have suddenly made up his mind, and said:

"I would—if I had to walk any further than I do now." He rose to his feet lazily, and started toward the camp table. Mary, with the typical contrariness of a woman, was more angry than if Bill had actually refused to cooperate with Dr. Thorkel.

Dr. Thorkel watched the approach of Bill and the girl, his whole body quivering with anticipation. Bill settled down on the camp stool before the microscope. Mary and Dr. Bulfinch stood behind Thorkel with some misgivings. They wondered whether Fred Harper's confidence in Bill Stockton would be upheld. They sincerely hoped that it would for more reasons than one. Their excitement was increasing sympathetically with Thorkel's, and now everything depended upon Bill Stockton, the drunken sot whom they had dragged out of his jungle habitat only a short time before.

But the mining engineer seemed oblivious to the mental turmoil that he was causing in the minds of at least two of his collaborators. He peered into the microscope and said:

"Odd-looking cells—"

Dr. Thorkel interrupted him brusquely with:

"I don't need your opinion on cell structure." Then his voice took on a new intensity as he went on: "Tell me if you see anything you *do* know about."

Bill looked up at the hermit scientist calmly and replied: "Certainly I do. Iron crystals. Say, they must be pretty small to show up no bigger—"

Before he could go any further, he was startled into silence. Dr. Thorkel's huge body dropped into the chair beside him. The scientist was panting as though he had just finished a long race. When the first fever of excitement had subsided somewhat, he turned to Dr. Bulfinch and Mary and said:

"Forgive me if I seem overwrought. But what you have just told me proves the theory upon which my work has been based for the last two years." He paused and turned his attention to Bill. "And your eyes, young man, have given me the clue to my only error."

Dr. Thorkel removed his thick glasses and rubbed his eyes. He suddenly looked very tired. For his own part, Bill Stockton seemed to catch something of the enthusiasm that possessed the three scientists, and a new feeling of importance engulfed him like a wave of warmth.

Bill rose to his feet slowly, looked at Thorkel, then said:

"Glad I happened to drop in." He grinned at Mary, and then, when it seemed as though Thorkel had dismissed him, walked toward the girl. Again Mary Phillips did not know just how to accept Bill's actions. She found herself torn between gratitude and anger. Finally she found her tongue and asked:

"Did you intend to do it all the time?"

Thorkel seemed to return to his present surroundings with a snap. He addressed Dr. Bulfinch.

"These eyes—what a handicap—How they have held me back these many months . . . And what a journey they have caused you, my good friends."

Bill was anxious to get back to his chair, and Mary turned from him to Dr. Thorkel and said:

"Better say, Dr. Thorkel—what a privilege."

Steve Baker shoved past Bill with little more than a nod, and burst in on the scientific discussion with more practical considerations. He addressed Dr. Bulfinch emphatically.

"We can't keep these mules here in the yard—they'll eat up all our feed." Dr. Bulfinch had no immediate solution, but Steve ran on, this time addressing Thorkel: "Your man here says there's some pasture down by the river. I'm gonna move the mules down there."

As Steve's words dissipated his scientific musings, Thorkel rose and replaced his glasses. Then, with a finality that could not be mistaken, and which came as something of a surprise and a shock, he said:

"That won't be necessary, Mr. Baker. Your party will be leaving in the morning."

As the significance of the words impressed itself upon Mary, Rupert and Bill, they looked at the doctor. None of them seemed to know how to accept Thorkel's statement, nor what to say. Thorkel, on the other hand, self-assured, and with his plans already forming in his active mind, turned and started to withdraw from the group. As he went, he remarked:

"You will pardon my returning to my laboratory. I have some processes under way that require constant attention." He bowed low and took a few steps toward the house. Just before opening the door he again turned to the stunned quartette and said: "I shall hope, tomorrow morning, to find a minute to bid you farewell. But if not, please accept now every expression of my esteem and gratitude. Goodbye."

Dr. Rupert Bulfinch was the first one to shake off the chain of silence that bound him. He took a quick step in the wake of Dr. Thorkel and, before the other had closed the door, asked:

"Are you attempting to intimate that you summoned me—Dr. Rupert Bulfinch—ten thousand miles—just for *this!?*" He gestured dramatically toward the microscope on the camp table.

Thorkel was still master of the situation, however, and retorted stiffly"

"I am not intimating, Dr. Bulfinch, I am stating a fact." Then he turned his attention to Mary and Bill, bowed courteously, and went on: "At a most critical period of my work, you have been able to give me the benefit of your trained sight.

I do not, however, require further assistance. Now you must permit me to return to my work. It is most absorbing. Goodbye."

This time there was no holding the hermit doctor. The door opened and closed behind him. Dr. Bulfinch looked at Mary, the pair of them were thunderstruck. Bill nudged the girl, then with mock humor said:

"We go home now, eh?"

Mary's face flamed, and her hand came up as though she wanted to smash Bill across the mouth. But suddenly she realized the humor of the situation and her fury relaxed into a grin. She gripped Bill's fingers in her own and squeezed, then said:

"Maybe I had it coming to me. But you've been a brick so far, Bill. We'll have to keep it up, I'm thinking."

Dr. Bulfinch said nothing. It was all too much for him.

The tropical night, usually so swift in coming, seemed to crawl upon the jungle camp of Dr. Alexander Thorkel with all the slow-moving patience of a web-spinning spider. The doctor himself did not appear outside the mud walls of his house, nor did his form show through the wooden shuttered confines of his window.

The visiting scientist, Bill Stockton, and Steve Baker the mule owner anticipated a waning of Thorkel's anger, but no such thing occurred. Meanwhile, they had not been wasting their time. The bulky cases and the canvas-wrapped loads that had been tied upon the backs of the willing mules had been unlashed and piled on the ground about the compound. Three tents had gone up. One sheltered Dr. Mary Phillips. Another was for the use of Dr. Bulfinch and his equipment, while the third was shared by Bill and Steve. The baggage and camp boxes were piled around, and a camp table had been set up in front of a cactus patch that rose picturesquely in an angle of the wall. The lower end of the compound was now fading from gray to black and was marked by the undulating backs of the tethered mules.

Dr. Bulfinch was seated at the table, his shoulders dropped. He have a convincing picture of complete discouragement, both scientific and personal. Bill was at one end of the table leaning toward a gasoline lantern that stood in the middle of the oilcloth top. He was laboriously shaving with one hand while holding a portable mirror with the other. It seemed as though, no matter how he stood and how he moved his elbow, he was continually throwing a shadow upon the blueness of his beard.

Mary Phillips was standing beside her more austere scientific colleague, looking very womanly with a wet silk stocking in either hand. She had jus turned around from a camp chair on which there rested a bucket of water. One corner of the chair was serving as a clothes pole, and the line ran from it to the corner of the tent. Already three pairs of stockings were swinging in the early evening breeze, lending the severe masculinity of the Andean camp a novel feminine touch.

It was evident that Dr. Bulfinch was now nearing the end of a jerky, if not disjointed series of emphatic statements. He pounded his fist upon the quivering table with determination and said:

"I tell you, I will *not* be treated this way! What will people in New York and the rest of the country say? I will not be treated like an errand boy."

Mary Phillips immediately assumed a familiar role. Ever since she had joined Dr. Bulfinch in his work as a laboratory assistant, several years previously, she had been constantly soothing his ruffled feelings. She had to admit that never had she been faced with such a difficult situation as the one that now confronted her. But she was more than equal to the occasion.

If I were in your position, Dr. Bulfinch, I wouldn't stir a step away from here until Dr. Thorkel had given me a full explanation!"

"You're right, my dear—as usual. But I can scarcely descend to the indignity of bickering with him," Dr. Bulfinch replied with acerbity.

Bill Stockton stopped shaving long enough to look around and inject his opinion into the conversation.

"Doc's right. Thorkel doesn't want us, so the thing to do is to be on our way."

Obviously Mary did not feel the same as Bill did. She bundled up the stockings she was holding and threw them into the half filled bucket with a soapy splash. Then she turned on Bill furiously and said:

"Can't you even get mad about it?"

Bill started as though this outburst were entirely unexpected and uncalled for. He shrugged his shoulders. Mary glared at him for an instant, then turned back to the bucket and furiously started to wash out her stockings again.

"What's the use?" Bill broke in. Mary ignored him, and he turned to Dr. Bulfinch. "Maybe his mind's failing from overwork. That often happens when you work to hard—too long—and too much in this climate."

Mary cast a disdainful glance at Bill over her shoulder, wacking the wet stockings indignantly against the side of the pail. Bulfinch appeared to be oblivious to this bit of byplay. He merely said:

"More likely he's afraid my assistance will overshadow his own efforts thus far. Thorkel was always inclined to be jealous of his colleagues. That was the basis of our earlier rivalry. I thought his isolation might have changed him. But apparently it hasn't—except for the worse."

Bill didn't seem to hear Dr. Bulfinch at all, but continued with his own thought.

"Then again maybe Thorkel wanted just the help he got and no more."

He brushed his face with a towel, carefully put away his shaving kit, then stretched and yawned. At this juncture Mary whirled around with an impatient exclamation. She came forward wringing out a stocking vigorously as if she wished it were Bill's neck.

"Do you realize," she said to Bulfinch, "that after coming all this way, we still haven't the faintest idea what Dr. Thorkel is working on?"

Even as she spoke there was a heavy tread, then Steve Baker's form pushed into the tent. He was beaming proudly as he declared:

"Maybe you haven't, but I have."

Dr. Bulfinch and Mary looked up, their startled expressions mirroring their feelings clearly. Baker paused dramatically, and Dr. Bulfinch prompted irritably:

"Well, what is it, a secret?"

"Not any more," Steve continued grandly. "It's a mine. Just like I always figured—"

Rupert Bulfinch's mottled face regained its earlier placidity, and his shoulders again drooped as he rested his elbows on the table.

"Nonsense," he retorted.

"Have it your own way, Doc," Steve insisted, "but somebody's been mining here—off and on—ever since the Incas built that wall." His arms swept around like those of a conqueror delineating his new domain, indicating the ancient wall nearby.

The doctor did not vouchsafe a reply. Mary broke in impatiently:

"You're just dreaming, Steve. Whatever it is that Dr. Thorkel is doing, it certainly is not mining."

She shook out a stocking, returned to her wash pail and showed no more immediate interest in the wrangle. But Steve was not to be denied.

"You two are sure hard to convince," he declared. Then he lifted the flap of the tent behind him and called: "Hey, Pedro!"

Pedro had been lingering on the edge of Bulfinch's camp ever since the foursome had begun setting up the tents. Hoping for a chance to join the group at the fire between the tents, he was all dressed up. He was wearing a red sash, his best shoes, and a wide grin of expectation. He hair was shining like a light. At Steve's call he swung an accordion over his shoulder and came forward carrying an earthen jug. He was smiling broadly in an excess of sociability.

"For a long time there is nobody—" Pedro explained gaily— "but tonight there is many people—We have fiesta, eh?"

Pedro started to seeing the jug up on the table. When it had come to a tottering rest, he brought his accordion around into position.

"Hey, wait a minute," Steve interposed. "First tell these folks about that last guy that worked the mine here.

"He died," Pedro declared. "That was a long time ago."

Steve turned triumphantly to Bulfinch and then to Mary, who had returned to listen to Pedro's report.

"Hear that?" he asked.

"Rubbish!" Bulfinch retorted.

"Are you the only one that's ever worked here with Dr. Thorkel since then? Mary Phillips interposed.

Pedro turned to the girl, his gay mood—submerged for a brief moment: "There is just Pedro—and Mira Santiago."

"Mira Santiago?" Mary was curious. "And what became of her? Did she die too?"

"Some of the peons say she die. Others say she run off into the jungle when Dr. Thorkel beat her and burn her. The people in Iquitos, very superstitious, they say Dr. Thorkel sell her to the devil." He lifted his hands, palms out, their pinkness shining in the light, then shrugged and said: "Mira ess gone."

Steve was not to be denied, however. He broke in upon Pedro's harangue with an emphatic:

"Mira may be gone. But the mine's right here—" he pointed over his shoulder— "back of that fence."

His fear of Mira's fate apparently sidetracked by Steve's insistence, Pedro's interest return to his proposed fiesta. He swung the jug upon the table and bowed hopefully to Mary.

"*Senorita*—I will play to you the music. It has come down to me from my fathers, the descendants of the powerful Inca."

Bill, apparently attracted by the sound of gurgling liquid in the stone jug, and aching for a taste of something that would make him forget the loss of his private stock in the river that morning, leaned in front of Mary. He removed the cork and applied his eye to the neck of the jug as though it were a microscope.

"Ah!" he cried. "Corn crystals!"

Mary was so depressed by the recent collapse of all her hopes for scientific recognition of herself and Dr. Bulfinch that she was equally uninterested in Bill's jug, Pedro's accordion and Steve's mine.

All of this conjecture appeared to do nothing more than confuse Dr. Bulfinch. He shook his head wearily and declared:

"Of all the violations of scientific thinking that have occurred this dreadful day, none could be less intelligent than to imagine Dr. Thorkel's secret activities concerning themselves with a mine!"

This argument among the newcomers apparently meant little to Pedro. He began gently tooting sad little notes on his accordion. He was anxious to have this discussion finished so everyone could start having a good time. Since Dr. Bulfinch seemed to have had the last word in the matter, Pedro remarked:

"Good—now we drink—and sing."

Dr. Bulfinch snorted with disgust and rose from the table. As he started to stalk toward his tent, Pedro called after him:

"*Señor*—come back! I will play music for you!"

The worthy scientist ignored the native servant. Pedro was not to be put off this easily, however. He looked after Bulfinch in surprise, then turned to Mary.

"Maybe if I play for you—very small—?"

Bill Stockton was enjoying the situation. Up until today Mary and Bulfinch, between them, had seemed to be masters of almost any situation that had developed. Bill followed Pedro's lead. He whispered to Mary:

"Maybe if we drink very small—"

Mary grimaced, then said sarcastically:

"To the success of the expedition—of course!"

Before Bill Stockton could wipe the smile from his face, Mary, too, had left the fire and the camp table, and was going toward her tent. When Steve Baker also started to leave, Pedro looked around. The aimless little tune the Peruvian was starting to play on his accordion began to die away as he gradually came to realize that his fiesta project was a bust.

At this juncture, however, Bill began to hum the tune that Pedro was playing. Instantly Pedro's face lighted up, and with his accordion he picked up the tune with spirit. Bill poured two cupfuls from the jug. He passed one of these to Pedro. The

Peruvian managed to get a drink without interrupting his playing.

"Tell me more about Mira," Bill Stockton urged, after putting down his cup and wiping his mouth with the back of his hand.

"Mira, she housekeeper for Dr. Thorkel. Come from Cajamarca. Have cousin at Iquitos. Dr. Thorkel say she run away. Pedro not know. But why do we worry about Mira? Women they always make the so great trouble."

"Maybe you're right," laughed Bill Stockton. He poured another drink, picked up the tune that Pedro was playing, and leaned back against the canvas back of the camp chair.

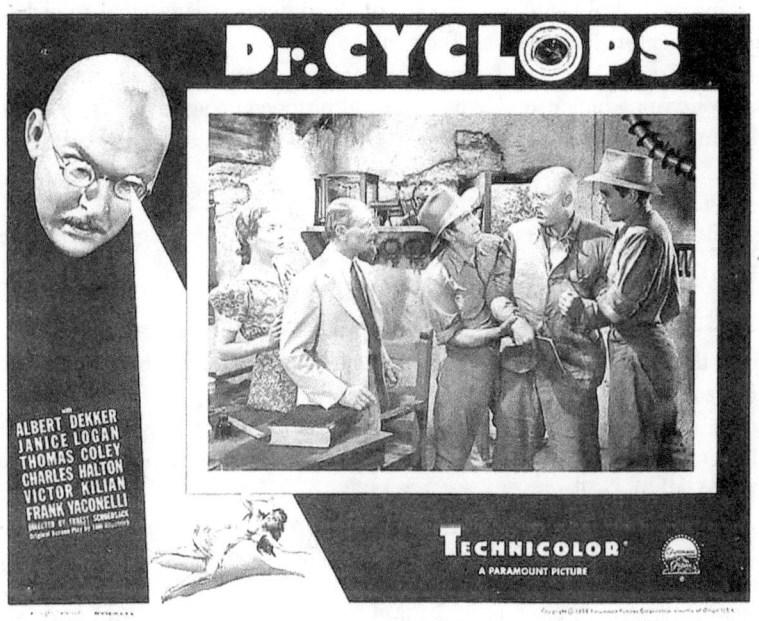

CHAPTER EIGHT

In her tent, Mary Phillips was lying on her cot, staring sleeplessly up at the tent roof over her head. She had counted so much on the results of this trip. She knew that she could depend upon Dr. Bulfinch for her scientific future, but at the same time, the failure to accomplish anything after journeying ten thousand miles down the Atlantic Coast, through the Caribbean and the Canal and down the Coast of South America would be constantly coming between them like a grim spectre.

In the interior of the house loomed the figure of Dr. Alexander Thorkel. The heavy darkness of the jungle night that closed about his clearing in the Andes worried him not at all. He did not need the illumination of the stars overhead in the black-blue dome of the sky. The moon that was rising and topping the jungle giants with its silvery beams was an unimportant natural phenomena.

He was making his own lights. His huge figure was hunched over his work table. His whole body was again clothed in the leaden armor, making him look like some mediaeval figure stepping out of the pages of King Arthur to pick up a pointed lance for a joust or a tournament.

For his part, Dr. Thorkel's rival of other years, Rupert Bulfinch, was sitting up in his cot writing on a pad. He held the pad propped up against his raised knees, and framed the words in a neat, clear-cut hand.

"Dr. Thorkel—
This is to serve notice upon you that I cannot tolerate your ignominious treatment . . . ."

His eyes ran over the words he had written. They did not seem adequately to express the thoughts that were racing through his mind, making his usually orderly mental equipment a chaos of unhappiness and displeasure. He tore the sheet off the pad, ripped it into bits and started writing anew. The cot was already littered with former efforts, and some of the crumpled sheets had dropped off on the dirt floor beneath the pallet.

Of all the individuals in the group that had arrived so proudly that morning, Steve Baker was the only one who seemed to know what he wanted to do. What was more, he was in the process of doing it. He had retired dutifully to his tent, in case any prying eyes were following him. Then, after moving around for a while, his lamp had gone out. With it, he had lifted the side of the tent farthest from the campfire, the table and the house, and had moved, fully dressed, into the darkness under the mud wall.

He was very alert as he edged toward the bamboo gate in the wall surrounding the mine yard. He opened the gate carefully, and a moment later was inside the preserve that held the mine in its center. Baker waited for a moment to determine whether he had been observed, then crept stealthily toward the mine shaft.

For a moment the vista before him was lighted by a strange green light. Steve Baker ducked back into the shadows and scanned the side of Thorkel's house. The window on this side of the house was not completely closed, and through it Steve could see the gleams from the machine at which Dr. Thorkel was working.

Immediately a wave of panic swept over him. Perhaps some of the stories told by the natives about Dr. Thorkel were true. Perhaps Mira Santiago had not escaped into the jungle. Perhaps Dr. Thorkel's torture of the native girl had taken a more definite shape than mere horse-whipping.

In spite of the thoughts that possessed him, Steve's avarice and curiosity were still his most compelling emotions, and he was determined to find out what he could about the mine.

He finally found himself alongside the shaft of the mine, and immediately began examining the windlass. It was of primitive native workmanship. Attached to it now was a new rope which extended from the windlass to the pulley above, and then ran down the shaft. The handle of the windlass was tied with another piece of rope, indicating that the main rope was supporting some weight down the shaft.

This in itself might not have been curious, but the thing that did arouse Steve Baker was the sight of a metallic, corrugated tube. This extended from the corner of the house like a great snake, and disappeared down into the mine shaft. As far as Steve could see, this was the only thing in sight that could be connected with Dr. Thorkel's operations. Everything else in the mine yard represented merely the crude fixtures left when the last native miner had abandoned the digging.

Now that he was this close to the mine, Steve Baker found himself reacting to the sounds inside the house. Usually when the hum of the dynamos increased in tone, the fluctuation was accompanied by an increased sheet of green light. Even though several of these flashes had occurred since Steve had passed through the bamboo gate, he started with each new gleam.

Finally he managed to control his shivering form, and peered down the mine shaft. It was so dark that he could see nothing. Finally he picked up a pebble and dropped it. He cocked his ear over the opening and listened. It was some time before he heard the faintest sound drifting back to him from far below.

Steve muttered:

"Plenty deep, all right."

Suddenly an electric light above the windlass, which Steve had not noticed before, flashed on. It flooded the entire area with daylight brilliance. Steve jumped straight up into the air in panicky surprise. Then he darted behind a broken barrel which formed the nearest place of concealment.

A moment after Steve had taken up his precarious position the back door of the house opened and Dr. Thorkel came out. He was wearing the grotesque helmet with its exaggerated eyeholes. Almost at once, Steve felt that the fearsome glance of the scientist was trained directly upon him. Frightened, he crouched lower.

If the doctor saw Steve hiding there, his next action did not indicate this. He removed the helmet, set it down on a backless chair, and began to operate the windlass. He started to raise from the shaft whatever was attached to the rope.

Steve managed to subdue his fears long enough to watch the activities with a fascinated gleam in his eye. Finally Thorkel brought his cached secret into view. It was pretty much like an enlargement of the tube, that extended across the yard. To it was attached the piping that ran into the house.

Steve was torn between fear that prompted a hasty retreat, and curiosity that demanded more information concerning Thorkel's activities. The hermit scientist made some minor adjustments on the tube, then began to lower the contraption back down the shaft.

In his desire for a close-up, Steve Baker leaned forward. One of the rotten slats in the barrel gave with a sharp crack. Steve quivered with fright. Dr. Thorkel looked around quickly, but apparently his heavily glassed eyes, behind the thick bifocals, saw nothing suspicious. His quick ear failed to hear anything more that was abnormal. Satisfied, Thorkel tied the windlass handle and started toward the back door of the house.

Steve Baker was afraid to move from behind the barrel. The entire area about him was still lighted by the overhead floodlight. Finally the floodlight went out again. Steve did not move immediately for fear that Dr. Thorkel might be watching from the window. However, when he saw the doctor's figure moving around inside, he lost no time in scurrying toward the gate. He laughed at his own needless panic and, again in full possession of his nerves, turned and crawled back to the ore dump beside the mine shaft.

Casting a glance over his shoulder, he knelt and began to pick up pieces of the ore. These Steve Baker thrust into his pocket.

Inside the house, unaware that his excursion to the mine shaft had been observed, Dr. Thorkel had again donned his lead helmet. Although he had not lain down on his cot for something like thirty hours, nevertheless his zeal kept him working with fiendish fury. His hands moved up and down over the switch panel board, and as he moved the controls his manipulations brought fixed changes in the humming sound of the dynamo and the flashing of the green light.

At the camp table, Pedro Caroz and Bill Stockton were busying themselves with their own kind of a celebration. Bill had indeed fallen from grace, and had Mary seen him, she might have despaired of ever salvaging him.

Pedro and Bill had been doing very well with the bottle. However, they were both past-masters at drinking, and neither could properly be called drunk. They had merely reached the point of mellowness that made them both amiable and sociable.

In between their drinks, Pedro managed to draw changing rhythms out of his music box. He finished his latest effort with a "boop" or two. Bill shook his head, then said:

"No Pedro. It goes like this." He started to hum some odd sounds which might have been almost any song.

Steve Baker had no ear for music, and in view of the discoveries that he had made, he cared little about Pedro's efforts at this time. He came into the light of the fire and settled down beside the camp table, containing his excitement with difficulty. Before either Bill or Pedro could stop him, he began emptying his pockets of the bits of ore and refuse he had picked up at the mine. He dumped the samples on the table beside Bill.

The words that flowed from his stammering lips were shot through with excitement.

"What'd I tell you, Bill—an' it's heavy."

Bill Stockton vouchsafed one look in Steve's direction, then went right on humming to Pedro. The Peruvian paid no attention to Steve's interruption. A puzzled frown crossed his brown face. Maybe it's 'Yira-Yira'?"

But the mining engineer shook his head seriously and replied:

"No—no. That goes up where this goes down. Listen—"

He began to hum again, and then showed with one finger that his song did go up at a certain spot—even though he couldn't make his voice do it.

Steve Baker could not stand this lack of interest. One heavy hand fell on Bill's should, and the mule owner shook the mining engineer. His voice was hoarse with the significance of his discovery.

"We'll test this ore; then we'll know just where we're at."

Bill Stockton went right on humming, holding Pedro's undivided attention. But Steve Baker was not to be rebuffed. He left the table and ran over to the tent he shared with Bill. Inside the tent, Steve snatched up the field locker containing a mineralogical kit and, with this under his arm, ran back to the camp table.

In his impatience he began to open it almost before he put it down. With it safely resting on the table, Steve's hands were all thumbs as he began to remove the electroscope, bunsen burner and other articles used in mineral testing from the kit box.

Then he broke in on the musical memory test.

"It don't look like any ore I ever saw before."

Pedro hit a few notes on his accordion, a smile crossed Bill's face, and, thus encouraged, the Peruvian went into a full-throated song on his music box.

"That's it!" Bill declared enthusiastically. "You've got it!"

Pedro began playing this new tune with renewed vigor. Bill was delighted. But Steve Baker was at the end of his patience. He jerked Bill Stockton around.

"Hey," he half pleaded, "everything's all set."

"Last time I heard that tune was in Paramaribo," Bill declared enthusiastically, ignoring the mineral paraphernalia. "Like it?"

"No," Steve retorted emphatically, "Now listen, Bill, get going on this ore, will you?"

Steve Baker had a vision of Dr. Thorkel, with or without his weird mask, erupting out of the door of his house and discovering the raid that had been made on his secret mine.

Bill Stockton practically ignored Steve as he turned to Pedro and said:

"Steve doesn't like our music. Let's try it on Brother Bulfinch!"

Pedro was willing, and a moment later, still playing and singing, they crossed the few yards separating them from Dr. Bulfinch's tent. Steve went along with them, plucking helplessly at Bill's sleeve. When the trio was at the flap of Rupert's tent, Bill said:

"Now smack it, Pedro!"

Pedro gave the accordion everything it would take. Inside the tent, Dr. Bulfinch was visible, a blanket wrapped around his nether body. He was still sitting up on his cot drafting notes to Dr. Thorkel. He looked up, a frown of annoyance on his face, and cried:

"Go on away, will you? Instantly!"

Bill permitted a mock frown to cross his placid face. He turned to Pedro. "He doesn't like it either." His glance ran toward Mary's tent; then he hesitated momentarily. Pedro sensed his attitude and came to the rescue eagerly.

"To women, music is—magnificent."

Steve was fit to be tied. He looked from the group around Bulfinch's tent to the equipment and samples on the camp table beside the lamp. Then he said:

"Come on back and test this ore. We gotta know about it before Thorkel throws us out in the morning."

But Bill Stockton had other things more pleasing on his mind as he approached Mary's tent. Pedro halted the wailing of his accordion temporarily. Outside the tent he got set.

"Smack it?" he asked expectantly.

"No," Bill replied. "Give it some oomph this time."

"*Si*," turned the beaming Pedro.

Pedro started to play again. Mary appeared in the doorway. She had already had more than she could bear for one night, and this exasperation showed in her face. But Bill failed to realize this. He approached her with two or three dance steps, calling:

"Put on your spurs, girlie—we're going to tango."

"*Stop it!*" Mary screamed.

The gay Peruvian was stunned. The music stopped. Mary's self-control gave way, and she broke into violent sobs. She turned swiftly and ran into her tent. Bill looked after her, abruptly sobered. Then he pushed back the tent flap and stepped inside.

Mary had thrown herself down on her cot and was sobbing wildly.

Bill coughed. Mary looked up and saw him. For a moment she was speechless. Her eyes were deep, limpid, haunting. Her words were hoarse as she said:

"Go away—please . . ."

Apparently expecting that Bill would go without delay, she hid her face again and sobbed a few more times. Then, aware that Bill was still there, she turned around, hunched herself up on her elbows, and, like a small girl pleading with her father, said:

"I—I did want to stay here—and work. And now—it's all gone to pieces."

As Mary dissolved into a new wave of tears, her small bit of linen handkerchief became entirely inadequate. Bill pulled a clean, new handkerchief that was first cousin to a bedsheet from his pocket. But unaccustomed to weeping women as he was, he did know quite how to offer it to the girl.

The feminine doctor was still stammering between her tears:

"Everything I've ever wanted—and hoped for—is ruined. *Everything!*"

Bill Stockton had a lurking feeling that he might be included in the word "everything," but there was no way of determining this at the moment. The very feminine quality of Mary's outburst did things to him, however. She was no longer the formidable biologist accustomed to commanding less humans and having them obey her.

She was just a woman; and a weak woman at that!

The discovery was a startling one to Bill.

He knelt down alongside the cot, reached one hand toward Mary and said huskily.

"Listen, kid. You're being a cry baby. Big scientists don't cry."

Mary tried to control herself, and succeeded with some difficulty. Then she said:

"They do too! And why shouldn't I! Steve is digging around after a mine, and maybe causing us more trouble than we already have. The two doctors are *hating* each other . . . and you're glad!!"

The flash of anger that marked the last three words was enough to give Bill pause. The bundled handkerchief in his hand came up as though to fend off a physical assault. He said:

"Here . . . ."

He tossed her the handkerchief as he straightened up. Mary took it and got to her feet to confront the mining engineer.

"You don't care!" she cried half hysterically. "And you're gloating because we've got to go back!"

Bill Stockton sensed the approach of the point of hysteria. He touched her shoulder lightly.

"Take it easy . . ." he soothed.

"I won't!" roared Mary furiously.

But almost immediately she was sorry for her outburst. She promptly subsided. They stood facing each other in silence for several moments. Then Mary gained control of herself. Her warm vibrant body crushed closer to Bill. Her fingers gripped the flap of his jacket pocket. Then she said in a more normal voice:

"On top of everything that's happened, you go around screaming that we *must* start back tomorrow!"

"We've got to go somewhere," declared Bill practically.

Mary had another thought in mind. Now that she had viewed this new side of Bill Stockton, she was willing to consult him. "If we could wait—even another day—maybe the doctors could settle their quarrel—maybe things might work out after all." Again her sterner streak took possession of her. She tugged at the pocket and the button snapped off. Bill laughed, but the laughter only piqued Mary further. "No! You've got to get back—to your Indian girl I suppose—this very minute!"

At this point Mary discovered that the handkerchief with which she was wiping her eyes was not her own. She thrust it at Bill gingerly, and said:

"Here."

Bill fumbled for the bit of cloth, took it, and stood holding it in the uneasy manner of a punished child. Finally he mustered enough courage to reply:

"Now listen, if you won't cry any more, I won't talk about going back any more."

Dr. Mary Phillips looked at her companion with surprise mirrored in her brimming eyes.

"All right. I won't," she agreed readily.

"Then I won't either," Bill declared emphatically. "Now stop sniffling."

Before Mary could say anything Bill turned on his heel and went out. Mary's face was wreathed with a smile. Her heart was at ease, and gracious satisfaction encompassed her.

Pedro and Steve stood watching Bill thoughtfully as he came out of the tent.

The Peruvian came forward slowly, his accordion dangling from one wrist. He was almost whispering as be breathed:

"Is she angry to us—?"

The mule-owning prospector was still thinking of the possible importance of the discovery he had made inside the bamboo fence, and he looked at Bill Stockton curiously as he asked:

"How about it? Now?"

A knowing smile began to spread over Baker's face as he started to edge toward the camp table and the mining instruments, and he permitted himself a chuckle of pleasure as Bill began to follow him. With this smattering of encouragement, Steve went around the table and reached one hand for the ore.

But it was soon obvious that Bill Stockton had no immediate intention of examining the results of Steve's night prowling expedition. He brushed past the table, almost jostling Steve's finds, and went on toward the tent the pair was sharing.

Steve was still glancing at Bill's broad back when Pedro came to a halt beside the table. The mule owner shrugged his shoulders, gripped the Peruvian by the arm and asked:

"Pedro, is there anything left in that jug?"

Bill strolled past the tent, his hands thrust deeply in his pockets. When he came to the gate in the bamboo fence surrounding the mine yard, he did not hesitate, but brushed it open with new determination. From the window at the rear of the house he was aware of a deeper hum and Dr. Thorkel's apparatus rose to a higher pitch. With sudden decision Bill Stockton started in the direction of the house.

He ignored the mine shaft entirely, strolled toward the heavy back door, and knocked loudly upon its panels. There was a stirring inside as Dr. Alexander Thorkel heard the knock. He shut off the switches jerked off the lead helmet and whirled toward the door.

"Who is there?"

"Me—Bill Stockton," Bill managed.

"I'd hate to have to knock all night," insisted the mineralogist.

Finally Bill drew back as he heard the heavy tread of the mad scientist on the puncheon floors of the house. Then there was a rattle as Thorkel unbarred the door. As the portal swung back, Bill took a step up to enter the house. But instead of letting Bill in, Dr. Thorkel came out on the step, brushed Bill's burly figure back, and closed the door firmly behind him. He fairly bristled as he asked:

"Why are you disturbing me?"

Someone less determined than Bill Stockton might have been frowned down immediately, but the mining engineer was resolved to have his say:

"Dr. Thorkel," he began, "how about letting us stay around for a while—until everybody feels better about things?"

Dr. Thorkel moved with all the grace of an irate elephant as his bulky shoulders shivered, then replied:

"No! No! That is impossible."

"A few days won't make any difference one way or the other," insisted Bill determinedly.

Suddenly Dr. Thorkel's tone took the shape of a determined parent:

"My dear friend, I repeat—that is impossible."

Bill managed a brief node in the direction of the still lighted tents in the encampment, then went on: "They're sore enough to stay—whether you like it or not."

This declaration had a marked effect upon the doctor, and it was easily apparent to Bill that Dr. Thorkel was greatly perturbed. He eyed the mining engineer shrewdly, fought to collect himself, then said:

"In that case, my good friend, there is something you should know. I have been trying to conceal it for your own good, but now that you have persisted in your desire to remain here, I will tell you."

"A sense of foreboding transmitted itself to Bill Stockton, and he peered up at the doctor, striving to penetrate the thickness of the glasses that served as shields to his glittering eyes.

"I don't think I understand you," Bill declared.

"It is simple," Dr. Thorkel continued. "My work here has been with tropical diseases—" He put his hands up before him as though to push Bill away, then after pausing dramatically, he said: "While you and your friends were on the way here, I contracted one of the most malignant types."

Bill started at this information, but he was not to be turned aside by any trick that the scientist might try. He was still skeptical as he said:

"But why be so mysterious about it? Why not tell us?"

The scientist sat down on the top step. He looked up at Bill and reasoned gently:

"Dr. Bulfinch and Dr. Phillips are scientists. If they knew about it, they would not leave me—they would want to help. But they cannot stay here—especially that beautiful girl. They must leave me."

Bill looked at Dr. Thorkel with mixed feelings. The scientist could see that the mineralogist was only partly impressed. He plunged ahead doggedly:

"Will you strike a match, Mr. Stockton?"

Bill fumbled in his pocket and brought out a wooden match stick. He whipped it across the cloth of his trousers. As the little light started to gleam, Thorkel pulled up the sleeve of his linen coat. Bill Stockton started back as the flickering flame of the match delineated a ghastly sight. Dr. Thorkel's entire forearm was covered with an angry blotch of scarlet scar-tissue. As the match went out, the usually hard-boiled mining engineer felt a wave of revulsion gripping him.

"That's terrible," he stammered. The full weirdness of his jungle surroundings closed in upon him. Dr. Thorkel took a backward step as though to retreat to the protection of his laboratory.

"Good night, Mr. Stockton," Dr. Thorkel said finally. Bill mumbled unintelligible words, then turned and started toward the camp.

Behind him the door opened and closed, and Dr. Thorkel was gone. Suddenly the sounds of the dynamos increased in their fury. The green light burgeoned forth from the slats over the window. Bill's eyes glimpsed a flash of Mary's figure through the flap of her tent, but he turned his attention to Dr. Bulfinch's shelter.

At the flap of Bulfinch's tent, Stockton halted.

"I'm going to get our things together," he said emphatically.

Bulfinch peered past the lamp that had been lighting his letter-writing efforts, then said:

"You may as well save your breath, young man. I have decided to stay."

Before Bill had a chance to say anything further, Bulfinch threw the blanket off his legs, knocked the crumpled papers on the floor, and came toward the mineralogist.

"I'm afraid you don't realize what you're doing," Bill insisted.

"You can't subject Mary—Dr. Phillips—to the dangers that one finds—in the jungle."

Even as they were talking, Mary, fully dressed, was fixing her hair at a mirror outside her tent. She could not help hearing the sounds of their angry voices. Her agitation was evident as she whirled around and headed toward Bill and the doctor.

The heavy blackness of the tropical night was rapidly giving way to the grey of morning. The once opaque blackness of the surrounding jungle was now replaced by the increased sharpness of trees and vines, the steady line of the adobe wall. Dr. Bulfinch was glaring at Bill as he said:

"After a sleepless night, I have decided that my position in science makes it impossible for me to go until I have had an adequate explanation of his actions from Dr. Thorkel."

"I have my reasons for asking you to go without further argument."

"Name one," insisted Dr. Bulfinch.

Conscious of Mary's approach, Bill returned weakly:

"Well, we're not wanted here."

Dr. Bulfinch snorted in disgust, then turned and walked away. Bill turned to face Mary where she stood in the doorway of her tent. As he approached her, the girl showed her own displeasure.

"Your promises are rather short-lived, aren't they?" she inquired.

Immediately on the defensive, Bill bristled. He knew that he was at a disadvantage.

"There's no sense in sticking around here. What difference does it really make?"

"Does anything ever make any difference to you?"

"Not usually," Bill admitted dully, "but don't give up. You'll understand later . . ." Dr. Bulfinch's voice came to him peremptorily:

"Mr. Stockton!"

Bill whirled around. Mary, tucking her hair in, turned to follow Stockton's gaze.

The elderly biologist was standing beside the camp table fingering one or two pieces of debris from the mine dump which Steve Baker had left on the table. Bill and Mary moved toward the table, their own dispute forgotten on account of Bulfinch's evident excitement.

"Where did these come from?" demanded Bulfinch. His eyes sparkled with eagerness and anticipation.

"From the ore dump behind Thorkel's house," Bill stammered.

Bulfinch bent over the collection. His capable fingers sorted out the materials, then he peered at them carefully.

"This is not mineral," Rupert Bulfinch declared emphatically. "These are bits of bone."

At this revelation both Bill and Mary pushed up close to the doctor's elbow. He went on, declaring:

"Dicotylinae!"

Dr. Bulfinch looked up at his colleagues as though he had just announced that Gabriel's horn was blowing.

"What's that?" Bill wanted to know.

The middle-aged scientist was examining two small pieces of the bone. He handed them as though they were a couple of diamonds. Mary's breath was sobbing in her throat as she explained to Bill:

"Dicotylinae—a species of native wild pig."

It was obvious that Dr. Bulfinch was trying to minimize the importance of his discovery. He turned to Mary slowly, offered the bones.

"Dr. Phillips," he said, trying to subdue his excitement, "I will ask you to attest that the specimens are of recent origin."

The scientist turned to Bill Stockton with a tolerant smile and replied:

"On the contrary, it was fully grown—observe the molar surfaces."

"For my dough, it was a rat," Bill declared emphatically.

The scientist glared at Bill, then turned to Mary.

"Dr. Phillips," he said, "you are to be congratulated. You have been present at the identification of a species of midget pig hitherto unknown to science." His voice trembled with excitement as he paused. "This animal was exactly four inches long at maturity!"

The good doctor fondled the bones, seemed to be breathing the sacred lines of a prayer, then concluded: "I shall call it dicotylinae Bulfinch."

Suddenly they were startled by an unexpected interruption.

"You are quick to take credit, Dr. Bulfinch." The voice was that of Alexander Thorkel. The three whirled around to face the hermit doctor. They had been so absorbed in the dicotylinae that they had not noticed his approach. He was smiling slightly with inscrutable amiability. As Dr. Thorkel came forward to join the group,

Bill quickly pulled Mary away from Thorkel's infected arm so that she would not be contaminated.

"May I see the evidence?" Dr. Thorkel asked pleasantly.

Grudgingly Rupert Bulfinch held out the two bits of bones. His eyes gleaming behind his thick glasses, Dr. Thorkel glanced at them with interest.

"Undeniably a very small pig," he finally agreed.

"Absolutely a new species," Dr. Bulfinch defended.

Mary Phillips, apparently pleased with the manner in which Dr. Thorkel had accepted their discovery, entered the conversation rather aggressively.

"Shall I prepare them for mounting, Dr. Bulfinch?"

"Thank you," Dr. Bulfinch agreed.

Mary looked toward Thorkel challengingly. He showed no sign of objection. Mary took the bones and started away toward her tent. After one worried glance at Dr. Thorkel, Bill followed her. The two scientist were left alone.

CHAPTER TEN

While they were busying themselves with a further examination of the bones in Mary's tent, Bill and the woman biologist were able to observe the dialogue taking place at the camp table. It was obvious that Dr. Bulfinch was all ready to fight, but Dr. Thorkel was disarmingly polite, and inclined to continue inscrutably pleasant.

The hermit scientist gripped his hands behind his back, looked up at he widening panel of morning light, and said thoughtfully:

"Strange how absorbed man has always been in the size of things."

Dr. Bulfinch was inclined to be dogmatic. "As a biologist, you should remember that size represents the chief difference among mammals. In all essentials a mouse and a whale are identical.

It was obvious that Dr. Thorkel had hardly heard him. There was a faraway look in the latter's eyes as he continued with his philosophizing on the subject that had been brought to his attention.

"We really know so little of this Amazon jungle below us—the greatest rain forest on earth. We know it possesses no great animals such as the elephant and the rhinoceros of Africa and Asia. But who knows how many other midget species there are such as the one you have discovered?"

"Mere speculation is always idle," Bulfinch insisted.

"Not always," Dr. Thorkel declared philosophically. "It may often point the way. For example: has it ever occurred to you that, while thousands of savage natives have practised head-hunting, only the Jivaro Indians of the Amazon shrink captured heads to the size of an orange, and sometimes to the size of a walnut? Might this not suggest a racial memory of some earlier times when their enemies were a very little people?"

Dr. Bulfinch sniffed at this suggestion. But he tried to maintain his calm in the face of this new Dr. Thorkel.

"If I may say so, Doctor," he declared, "that is not even speculation. It is sheer whimsy."

Mary and Bill had paused in their own work to listen to the two scientists. Now Dr. Bulfinch was gripping Dr. Thorkel's arm, and they were strolling toward the opening in the compound wall that led to the green of the jungle.

Dr. Phillips turned back to her own chore. The walls of the tent were rolled up by a dutiful Bill Stockton, and the entrance was pinned back to catch any breeze that might blow from the winding river beyond. Mary had her kit box open on her cot, and with the alcohol and a camel's hair brush was cleaning the dicotylinae bones. Bill was lounging uneasily in the tent doorway.

"I wouldn't handle those things if I were you," he finally declared.

"I'm sure you wouldn't if anyone wanted you to," Mary replied sarcastically.

Bill, ignoring this, protested: "Honestly, I don't care where I am—just so it isn't here.

Mary stopped work and glanced at Bill. Her lip curled.

"Why can't you be like anybody else?" she asked him plaintively.

"But listen," Bill went on, confident of the righteousness of his own cause, "Thorkel's nobody to pal around with. He's nuts."

"Why?" Mary demanded.

"He's too—" Bill began weakly, then finished lamely— "he's too moody."

Disgust washed over Mary's face, as she went back to her job. Bill, glancing uneasily across the compound, watched the two scientists. He crossed over to the table, picking up some more of the bones and handled them gingerly. Returning with these to Mary, he asked:

"Where's Steve?"

"I haven't seen him this morning," she replied. "Maybe he's rounding up something to eat. I'm getting hungry."

"Ha!" Bill declared lightly. "A human being after all. Science can wait while the stomach is satisfied." He fumbled the bones in his hand. "Maybe we can have a small-sized ham sandwich if we can find one of the dwarf pigs. Four inches— hum—that would make a nice mouthful, on a frankfurter roll."

Mary was on the verge of boiling over. She snatched the bones out of Bill's hand. Then her mouth dropped open.

Her eyes went past Bill toward the activity in the compound. The missing Steve Baker was down near the gateway, coming in from the jungle trail. Under his direction the muleteers were untying the mules and starting to lead them toward the gateway.

Dr. Thorkel and Dr. Bulfinch again came within the hearing of the couple.

"Our discussion has been very interesting," Dr. Thorkel said. "We don't seem to agree any more than we did when we were back in New York. But I don't blame you, Dr. Bulfinch, your research has been along such different lines. In any event, I am delighted that you were slow in getting started this morning. It has given me the opportunity to pay my respects once more—" he bowed politely—"before you depart."

Dr. Mary Phillips was restraining the excitement and horror of her most recent discovery. Bill sensed her unrest.

"We are not departing!" Dr. Bulfinch declared emphatically. He thrust his hands deeply into the pickets of his jacket and looked up at Dr. Thorkel in a challenging manner.

"But I do not want you here." Dr. Thorkel was equally emphatic.

It was obvious that Dr. Bulfinch had been saving up all night for this particular moment. Mary and Bill watched him go into action with baited breath. Bulfinch inhaled deeply, much relieved at this final opportunity to express his views.

He chose his words with great care.

"The discourtesy, Dr. Thorkel, not to mention the outright deceit, with which you have treated me, relieves me completely of any obligation to consider your wishes in the matter"

A rising anger made the nearsighted scientist a victim of his own fury.

"I will not permit you to stay," he insisted. "You must leave at once—"

Dr. Thorkel raised his hamlike fist as though he would plant it on Rupert Bulfinch's nose. Bill was to far away to intervene. Mary was about to give voice to a very unscientific scream when succor came from an unexpected source.

Steve Baker elbowed into the fray, caught Dr. Thorkel's arm, and laughed gaily as he said:

"Don't fight, boys, don't fight." He grinned genially. "Nobody can leave until the mules have some rest." His arm encompassed the moving grey backs of the patient pack animals. As though momentarily hypnotized, four pair of eyes followed Steve's motion.

At the gateway several Indian mule drivers were driving the mules off into the jungle.

"They need a couple of days down on that river pasture."

The "couple of days" had a decided effect upon Thorkel.

"You can't do that!" roared the hermit scientist. "Call them back at once!"

"I can't do it, boss." Steve was thinking of the mine behind the bamboo fence, the shaft and the ore pile. Bill shoved in between them before Dr. Thorkel's fury took any toll of the smiling Steve.

"Yes, you can, Steve. Thorkel's right. We've got to get out of here this morning. You think we should go, don't you Mary?"

"Certainly not," Mary declared emphatically.

Bill shrugged, then resignedly declared: "Listen, all of you. I've tried hard to be a hero, but it hasn't worked." He whirled on Thorkel, pointed at him accusingly, and said: "He's got a malignant disease, and is only trying to keep you fools from getting it."

At this startling news both Steve Baker and Rupert Bulfinch stared suspiciously at the hermit scientist. Dr. Thorkel didn't change expression by one iota.

"If it's a gag, it's a good one," Steve Baker vouchsafed.

"Mr. Baker has expressed my thought precisely," Dr. Bulfinch clipped.

Bill Stockton hesitated for the merest fraction of a moment. Then he replied: "If you think it's a gag, take a look."

Before Thorkel could prevent it, Bill jerked up the loose sleeve of the scientist's linen jacket, exposing the glaring red scar.

"How do you like that?" Bill demanded triumphantly.

Steve Baker was nearest to the doctor. He jumped back in horror. Mary took one look but did not seem to be particularly disturbed. Dr. Bulfinch took the suspense out of the situation when he said calmly:

"A radium burn. Calm yourself, Mr. Baker. Dr. Thorkel's trouble is quite harmless—to us—" With a leer of sardonic condemnation, Dr. Bulfinch turned to Thorkel and continued: "You must have been extremely awkward to subject yourself to such and accident.

Bill Stockton, up until a moment ago the master of the situation, at least in his own mind, now realized that he had been made to seem a fool. He glanced instinctively toward Mary, and the feminine scientist gave him a faintly derisive smile.

The change that had come over Dr. Thorkel was the most significant factor in the whole exchange. His placidity had completely vanished. The discovery of the wound which had impressed Bill had definitely influenced his attitude toward the visiting scientist. His face was screwed up into a menacing leer, his eyes seemed to flash through the thick lenses of his spectacles and his voice was icy cold as he roared:

"I have only one comment to make. If you remain here another hour, you do so at your own peril."

After the ultimatum had been pronounced there was a short, tense silence as Thorkel glazed from one to the other of his tormenters, as though challenging them to resist his will. This silence was broken by a startling sound coming from the direction of the house.

It was the faint, shrill neigh of a horse!

CHAPTER ELEVEN

The sound had varied effects on the several auditors. Dr. Thorkel was particularly impressed by it. He whirled toward the house with excitement mirrored on his ruddy countenance, looking toward the open door.

Steve Baker's attention was turned toward the gate, as though the sound might have come from one of his mules. He dismissed this idea almost immediately. Thorkel's lips moved almost reverently. His words were no more than a whisper, but a whisper filled with scientific fevor and far-reaching possibilities.

"He lives!"

Perhaps the most significant contribution to the scene, however, came from an altogether different direction. Pedro, more or less worn out with his libations and his musical efforts, was sleeping in the thatch-roofed hut at one corner of the compound. Nobody had noticed him particularly since daybreak.

Now, however, the placid Peruvian came erupting from his hut like a lively ball of lava from the throat of a volcano. Even a person unused to analyzing human emotions could see that the sound had excited him.

"Pinto!" he called. "That's my horse Pinto. He has come back."

Pedro started to run past the group at the camp table. He was close to the house when Thorkel yelled at him sternly:

"Pedro!"

Accustomed to cower before the hermit doctor, Pedro paused fearfully, and turn on his bare feet.

"But that is Pinto," he pleaded.

Thorkel strode past his native servant, and said:

"Nonsense. Remain here."

While the others watched this exchange between master and servant, Thorkel walked toward the door of the house. Pedro took a step or two after him. There was a slight clattering sound inside the house. Dr. Thorkel quickened his step. There was no doubt now that the clattering sound was that of shod hoofs. Pedro's anxiety about his faithful animal overcame his fear of the doctor. The presence of the visiting scientist lent him courage.

Making up his mind with delay, Pedro ran toward the house. Dr. Thorkel turned around at the top step to observe the reactions of his servant and his unwanted guests. His tone was stern as he addressed the Peruvian:

"Pedro!"

The native shrank back. Thorkel slammed the door in his face.

The entire dialogue and action had taken place so suddenly and so unexpectedly that Bill, Mary, Steve and Dr. Bulfinch were more or less flabbergasted. They all stared wonderingly after Dr. Thorkel. Steve Baker found his tongue first.

"That sure sounded like a horse to me," he said.

Dr. Bulfinch's practical mind would not accept this at once.

"I doubt that even Dr. Thorkel would keep a horse in the house," he insisted.

But Steve Baker was not to be put off this easily. The back door of Dr. Thorkel's house opened and closed with a loud slam. The mule owner, curious as ever, moved toward the bamboo fence. The other three followed after him. They were faintly amused at the manner in which Steve tiptoed to a position where he could peek through the breaks in the bamboo.

Instantly Steve began waving to the others to join him. Bill took Mary by the arm, and they stood thus, aware all to well of their proximity as they peered through the fence.

Beyond the mine shaft, along the back wall, they saw a patch of grass about two feet high. Apparently there was something too small to appear above the grass. From Dr. Thorkel's actions, the object, whatever it was, was running through the grass.

The hermit scientist had come out of the back door, and was now running frantically in pursuit of the thing. He was carrying a specimen case by a strap over his shoulder. In his right hand he held a butterfly net. After looking through the tall grass and took up a position as though cornering something in an angle of the mud wall. The high grass made it impossible for Bill and Mary to see what this might be.

Finally Dr. Thorkel's voice came to them. He was speaking soothingly.

"Who, boy. Whoa."

Bill looked at Mary. Dr. Bulfinch shook his head sadly. Steve alone put their thoughts into words as he whispered huskily.

"Damned dope. Thinks he's chasing a horse with a butterfly net."

The hermit scientist was obviously entirely oblivious to his audience. Now he was crouching and edging forward nearer the angle of the wall. Suddenly he lunged forward with the butterfly net. He came down on his knees and his hands closed over the mesh of the net as though he had captured something in the grass.

He swung the specimen case forward to the ground. Then he lifted the net and its strange contents over the top of the case and transferred his capture to the metal container. Closing the box, he rose, brushed his sloppy suit, then, with the box hanging from his shoulder, started toward the back door. He was definitely proud and pleased of his exploit. He patted the box and addressed it softly.

"Whoa, Pinto—steady boy."

Mary turned to bury her face on Bill's shoulder. Her whole body was quivering with the shock of what she had just seen.

"And he was such a great scientist," she mumbled. "And now—this."

Dr. Bulfinch was equally moved by the spectacle. It was obvious that he was struggling for some mental guidance that would dictate his next step. Steve Baker and Bill Stockton expressed their feelings in an entirely different manner. Baker cursed gruffly. Bill spun a mocking finger alongside his forehead.

Fully expecting Dr. Thorkel to appear at the front door at any moment, the quartette, with Pedro in tow, walked quickly to the center of camp. They looked at each other as if to make sure that they had all witnessed the same thing. Each one appeared to be a bit ashamed.

Pedro was the one most agitated by the scene. He turned to Bill Stockton anxiously and asked:

"You think maybe—it is the ghost of Pinto—that the Mister doctor catch?"

"That seems like it might be the answer," Bill replied laconically.

Dr. Bulfinch felt that the trusting native merited a better response. He looked at Bill with some misgivings, then addressed Pedro:

"No, Pedro. I very much fear that Dr. Thorkel only *imagines* he has something in that box."

Pedro was puzzled.

Steve Baker tried to clarify the situation, priding himself on his understanding of native wit.

"What Doc means is your boss is cutting up paper dolls."

Mary gripped Bill's coat and asked fearfully:

"What can he be doing in that house? What is it that none of us may see—not even Pedro?"

The mule train owner shivered as he said: "Maybe the things he's got in there nobody can see but him."

But Bill Stockton, realizing that for once Mary Phillips was depending upon him, approached the matter from a more practical angle. He turned to Pedro curiously.

"How long you been here?" he asked

"Five—six months," Pedro replied. "Ever since I come down here with the rats."

Mention of the rodents did not improve Steve's feelings.

"What rats?" he demanded nervously.

The dusky Peruvian began counting on his fingers. His mathematical potpourri was diverting to say the least.

"Four dozen rat, three dozen chicken, fourteen dog—not counting Paco." He indicated his dog playing about his feet. "Seven cat, beside Santanas—" his pointing finger went in the direction of a large black cat busy at the rubbish pile.

As though she were conscious of the attention thus focused in her direction, Santanas looked up, then leaped to the top of the mud wall and proceeded to sun herself. A red tongue darted out and began to lap the glossy fur of her coat.

Pedro continued counting on his fingers.

"Four pig—"

Bill had heard enough. "What happened to all this zoo? he interrupted.

"I don't know." Pedro shrugged. "Except for five chicken—" he gestured around him—"they all go in the house with the Mister doctor."

Mary interrupted, frankly trying to reassure herself:

"I see nothing so very unusual in a biologist using animals in his experiments." Even as she spoke, her fingers went into her jacket pocket and closed over a handful of bones. They were the bones that Bill had given her while she was working with the pig bones. Her heart leaped up into her mouth. With the intrusion of Dr. Thorkel, she had been unable to call these other bones to the attention of Rupert Bulfinch and the others.

Steve was addressing his curiosity to Dr. Bulfinch:

"What kind of tricks do you s'pose Thorkel plays with them animals, Doc?"

Bulfinch either did not have the answer, or was hesitant about giving it. Whatever the reason, Pedro supplied his version of the hermit scientist's experiments.

"I don't know. But Santanas there on the wall—every day she get more fat."

Steve Baker shivered as though he had suddenly been bathed with the blast of an Arctic wind, instead of sweating under the climbing tropical sun. He declared decisively:

"Let's get packed and get out of here."

The matter was one that rested with the two scientists. Rupert Bulfinch looked at Mary, as though inviting her reaction.

"I can't feel guilty about going," Mary finally declared.

"Dr. Thorkel would certainly reject any offer of aid," Dr. Bulfinch remarked judicially.

The two scientists turned to the others. They directed their attention to Steve Baker. Dr. Bulfinch put the decision into words.

"Dr. Phillips and I agree that it is useless to stay. You may get your mules, Mr. Baker."

Bill was amused by the seriousness of the doctor's statement. He turned to Steve and laughed gaily.

"I don't even have to change *my* mind. How about you, Pedro?"

It was obvious that the native was still doubtful.

"If I only find Pinto—" he hesitated.

"Speaking of Pinto," broke in Steve, "I'm going out and find my animals." He hurried out of the compound in the direction that had been taken some time before by the Indian muleteers and the pack animals.

As though by common consent, Bill, Mary and Dr. Bulfinch retired to their tents to prepare for their departure. A few moments later Dr. Bulfinch was out in the compound again. This time he walked toward the camp table. He picked up the dicotylinae bones. As he did so, he noticed the electroscope that was a part of Bill's mining equipment.

Absently he looked at the device, and saw that its leaves were reacting to some force within its scope. Immediately Dr. Bulfinch's mind was curious about the problem thus presented. He looked over the other objects on the table, and finally picked up a piece of the ore that Steve had brought back from the dump. As he moved this closer to the electroscope the reaction increased in force.

His mouth dropping open at the importance of his discovery, Dr. Bulfinch looked around him hastily to see whether he had been observed. Then he stuck the piece of ore in his pocket and ducked back into his own tent. Bill approached the table a few minutes later to put away the apparatus that Steve had removed from its case when endeavoring to persuade Bill to assay the or samples. As Bill picked up the electroscope he suddenly stopped. He set it down and examined it carefully. Then he straightened up with sudden interest.

Immediately he turned to look around the compound. Then he called excitedly:

"Steve! Hey, Steve! Where are you?"

Steve was already out on the jungle trail, but at the sound of Bill's shout he came back to the gateway in the compound. Bill spotted him and called:

"Come back here."

Steve Baker hastened toward the table. Bill was holding up a piece of the ore and moving it to and fro farther and nearer to the electroscope. Steve strolled up.

"What's up?" Baker demanded.

"Like I told you last night—from the dump in back of the fence."

Bill Stockton nodded soberly. He offered Steve one of the ore lumps.

"Here, take this."

There was a puzzled expression on the mule owner's face as he took the piece of ore.

But the mining engineer seemed to know what he was doing.

"Now back up," he commanded. He was watching the electroscope as Steve obeyed.

"Farther. Farther," Bill instructed, as the sensitive instrument on the camp table reacted favorably.

"What do you think it might be?" Steve asked.

"I know what it is," Bill declared emphatically. "It's pitch-blende."

Steve Baker's eyes popped open. He looked at the bit of mineral in his hand. "The stuff radium comes from? he stammered.

"Uranium ore," confirmed Bill Stockton, "and a baby could tell it's a hundred times richer than any deposit ever heard of before . . ."

Immediately Steve approached, grabbed his arm and waved a finger empirically.

"Shh! Somebody'll hear you."

They both looked around like a pair of conspirators. Finally Bill said: "We don't have to worry about them. They're both packing."

Steve Baker wasn't taking any chances. He hastily put the remainder of the ore back in his pocket . . .

But the pair at the camp table might have been amazed at what was taking place in Mary's tent. The two scientists were moving about with semi-furtive air, looking much like a couple of conspirators themselves. Mary was working with a changing bag developing tray. Bulfinch was looking at a dripping wet photographic plate which was evidently on that Mary had previously developed.

As he examined the photographic slide he said:

"Extraordinary! I wouldn't have believed it."

Mary removed the second plate she had been developing from under the black cloth and held it up. She examined this carefully, as she remarked:

"This is the one you exposed at ten feet."

Bulfinch turned his attention to the negative in Mary's hand, looked at it carefully, then said:

"Completely fogged. Dr. Phillips, this ore contains an unprecedented proportion of radium."

The feminine scientist appeared to be more than pleased with the find. She wiped her hands with an air of determination.

"We'd better hurry," she suggested. They started out of the tent.

In the meantime Bill's field kit had been stowed away, and the camp table had been cleared of everything except a piece of bologna and a knife which had evidently come from the camp larder.

Bill and Steve were standing with their backs toward the scientist's tent as they examined a piece of the ore Steve was holding in his hand. They instantly stopped their whispering as they heard the approach of Mary and Rupert Bulfinch. Steve fumbled with his pocket for a moment as he hastily put away the piece of ore. He snatched up the knife, and began to cut a slice of the bologna on the table. His action was arrested in mid-air as Dr. Bulfinch opened the conversation.

"Dr. Phillips and I have reconsidered the situation here. We have decided to remain here to care for Dr. Thorkel."

Seeing all of his own plans falling about his ears, Steve Baker replied too quickly: "But you folks are real important. You're needed other places. Bill and me are used to this place. We ought to stay and help the doc."

Dr. Bulfinch shrugged his shoulders, stretched his palms out before him as though dismissing the matter, then said: "We are better equipped for the task. And after all, he *is* a fellow scientist."

Bill Stockton was enjoying the situation that had come up so unexpectedly. He looked from the biologist to the mule owner and then sat down. A faint smile crossed his face. Finally he broke in with:

"Why don't we quit trying to double cross each other? After all, we all came up here together. Let's play ball."

Steve was a much taken aback as Bulfinch and Mary.

Dr. Bulfinch whirled on the mining engineer and said:

"What a pity you recognized the ore . . ."

"The same to you . . ." Steve was grinning. "But I guess a few million bucks split four ways ain't too bad."

"It isn't just money to us," Mary interposed. "We're thinking of how important it is going to be to clinical and research laboratories."

Steve nudged the doctor peremptorily "Quiet," he said. "Here comes Pedro."

Just what the native had been doing while the ostensible preparations for departure were being made, no one knew. Now there was a beaming smile of Pedro's usually passive face, and as he pushed into the group he said:

"Pinto, he may come back. I think I stay here."

The mule owner laughed.

"I think we all stay here."

Dr. Rupert Bulfinch tried to regain control of the party and the situation. He glanced at Steve reprovingly and said:

"I fail to see why we should conduct ourselves like a lot of gangsters. We have nothing to keep secret. We must merely decide whether we should permit a madman to retain in his keeping something that is of such consequence to humanity."

Bill was cynical about the scientific attitude that Bulfinch and Mary insisted upon taking.

"He won't be permitted to retain it if we can get it into our keeping," Bill insisted.

Apparently Bulfinch was accustomed to interruptions of this kind by now. He ignored Bill as he went on:

"We must remember that Thorkel has certain interests that should be protected. However, it seems to me that it is incumbent upon us to take charge of his affairs at once."

While this discussion had been going on, Mary had plunged her hands deep into her pockets. The fingers closed over the bones she had been trying to call to the attention of the others. Finally she brought them out and said:

"This may have something to do with our actions, too."

"More dicotylinae?" asked Bill.

Bulfinch cast a pitying glance in Bill's direction, then his eyes popped open. Mary's face was white. She knew what the doctor was going to say, even before he said it.

"These are human bones!"

CHAPTER TWELVE

"Has anyone been here with the doctor while you have been here, Pedro?" Dr. Bulfinch asked soberly.

"Only Mira Santiago," Pedro replied. "She have come to take care of the housekeep. But she is gone—out there." Pedro gestured in the general direction of the jungle.

"This couldn't be Mira," Mary Phillips insisted. "These must be pygmy bones."

Dr. Bulfinch settled into a camp stool. He laid the bones on the table then said:

"So far as we know, there are no pygmies in South America. They are native to central Africa." He pounded his fist emphatically. "We've just got to get inside of that house and find what's going on."

Even as he spoke a creaking sound broke in upon their reverie.

To Steve Baker this was a familiar note, and he turned to the others quickly.

"He's out there fiddling with the windlass. Now's the time to get in."

As though motivated by a single giant brain, the five people in the yard started for the front door. They walked ahead like a close-order phalanx, determination showing in each face. Passing one corner of the bamboo fence, they were able to see Dr. Thorkel raising his contraption to the surface and adjusting it.

When they had mounted the steps to the front door, Steve Baker whipped out his clasp-knife and inserted it between the door and the jamb. It was only a moment before he was able to raise the bar inside. The mule owner pushed open the door, and the quintette entered furtively. Pedro's dog, who was following him as usual, sniffed once, then dropped his tail between his legs and refused to enter. He scampered back into the yard, whining sadly.

If they had expected Thorkel's house to present a complete and up-to-date laboratory appearance, they were destined to disappointment. Their first impression of the interior of the abode was disappointingly meager, scarcely enough to sate their active curiosity. The place consisted of a single small room. The walls were of plaster over mud. There was a back window which was not shuttered like the front one, and through this there swept the square of sunlight that illuminated the interior.

Mary pointed to a door at the side of the house, and said:

"That must be the kitchen."

"The other one is the door into the mine yard," Steve explained.

Dr. Bulfinch and Bill Stockton were probing around the room with some interest. The furniture in the room was bare and simple. There were Thorkel's cot, and a plain wooden table which he obviously used as a desk, three heavy wooden chairs, and a work bench along one wall.

On the table were his microscope and notebooks. The bench held several square wicker baskets. Littered about the room, chiefly on the floor, were some of Thorkel's effects, wherever he had happened to drop them in the midst of his hard work. These included a rack of test-tubes, a number of books, a glass beaker, some dirty dishes, several articles of wearing apparel, a pair of boots, a duffle bag, two or three small boxes and other impediments.

Steve Baker immediately called Bill's attention to the corrugated tube that ran to the instrument hanging over the mine shaft. This tube came through a hole in the wall from the direction of the mine shaft and was attached to a plate of heavy electric switches. The switchboard was fixed to the wall beside the kitchen door. In the door itself there was a small mica window.

Pedro was the first one to make a startling discovery. Suddenly the native pointed to the floor and said:

"Pinto—he was here!"

The others followed Pedro's pointing finger, and in the dust of the floor saw hoof prints. There was no mistaking them. Dr. Bulfinch and Mary Phillips did not appear to be particularly interested in the discovery. Bill Stockton shrugged. But Steve Baker voiced the opinion of all as he glanced behind him.

"No horses in here now."

Outside the mine yard, Dr. Thorkel had adjusted his contraption to his complete satisfaction, and then lowered it down the shaft again by means of the windlass.

After their first group invasion of the hermit scientist's privacy, each of the invaders followed the bent of his own curiosity. Pedro was kneeling on the floor examining the hoof prints. Mary was inspecting Thorkel's microscope. Bulfinch was turning over and identifying such books as were on the table. Steve Baker was frankly opening drawers and prying into anything else that occurred to him.

Only Bill seemed to be oblivious to his surroundings. He had his hands in his pockets, and was sauntering about giving everything a casual inspection.

Mary turned to Bill and said:

"He certainly hasn't used this microscope for months."

"He told you that," Bill reminded her. "That's why he asked us to come up here."

Dr. Bulfinch closed his fingers over a loose-leaf book with satisfaction.

"Here are his notes," the scientist declared. He picked it up and examined it carefully, turning each page over reverently after he had digested it contents.

By this time Steve's inspection tour had taken him to Thorkel's trunk. He removed a tray on which there were a number of extra pairs of glasses. As he examined several of these, he remarked:

"The old boy sure brought plenty of spare specs."

From a distance there came the faint sound of a horse's neigh. This repetition of the sound that had stirred them all in the compound immediately gave them pause. Pedro stiffened.

"That is Pinto," he insisted.

"He's not here, Pedro," Bill declared. "That sound came from outside."

Bulfinch seemed to agree with Bill's statement, and his eyes went back to the notebook with evident interest.

"Ah!" the biologist breathed.

Mary Phillips turned to her colleague. Bill and Steve came over to see what

Rupert Bulfinch had discovered.

"My diagnosis of the burn was correct. He has been using radium."

Before they had a chance to go into the matter further, the door slammed open with a bang. The heavy tread of Dr. Thorkel sounded behind them, and his voice rose in furious anger:

"Bandits! Thieves!" he raged.

The quartette whirled to face him. Pedro had left the group to go in search of his horse. Thorkel tottered back and forth on his heels and surveyed the group about him, his face livid and his jaws working.

"So you would steal my discoveries?" he roared more calmly. He advanced toward them menacingly. Bill Stockton balled his fists and stepped in front of his companions.

"Take it easy," he declared, "Nobody's stealing anything."

"Then what are you doing in my house?" Thorkel demanded. "You have no right to be even in my camp. You are merely my employees, whom I have discharged and instructed to leave. Now you have the nerve to break into my laboratory. Get out! Get out instantly!" His rage reached new proportions, and his fist swung back and forth before him like giant walking beams.

This time it was Steve Baker who took the initiative. He looked toward Bill, then said soothingly:

"We're your friends, Doc. We only want to help you."

Alexander Thorkel snorted.

"Friends! I know what kind of friends you are. I know what you want. You have broken in here to learn what I am doing so that you can share in the importance of my work. But I will not permit it. No one can share. And I do not need help. Everything here is mine. *Mine*—do you understand?"

Dr. Bulfinch felt that this was certainly no time for temporizing. He assumed a stern mien and broke in:

"There are more things than your discovery of the radium mine."

"And what are they?"

"On your rubbish pile there was more than the bones of the dicotylinae. We found the bones of a human being. How do you account for that?"

Thorkel choked, then said:

"I did not *discover* the mine. It was worked originally by the natives. They knew nothing of the properties of radium, no of the protective measures necessary to offset its effects. Perhaps one of them was killed by the burns, and his skeleton was destroyed by the heat and rot of the jungle. How do I know?"

"Perhaps," agreed Dr. Bulfinch. But it was obvious that he was not impressed. "What became of our housekeeper, Mira?" was the biologist's next question.

Thorkel was evidently master of himself again. He laughed loudly at this query, then turned to Bill and said:

"You know how these native women are. They aren't satisfied merely to be housekeeper. They have other ideas. She became obnoxious to me, and I had to ask her to go, just as I am asking you to go."

There was a momentary pause. Bill's face was suffused with color. Mary felt sorry for him. But Thorkel's attention was diverted to Dr. Rupert Bulfinch. He was becoming more and more agitated. At this instant he caught sight of his notebook in Bulfinch's hands.

"My notes!" he screamed

He leaped upon Bulfinch like a madman and tried to wrest the book from him by main force. Steve and Bill were only a step behind the hermit scientist and they seized Thorkel and held him back. He struggled against them, but Steve was tough and Bill was a mountain of strength in spite of his earlier dissipations

Presuming that Thorkel's actions had justified their belief in his insanity, Steve Baker looked toward Bulfinch and Mary Phillips and asked.

"Can't we lock him up somewhere?

This question made a marked impression on Thorkel. He ceased to struggle. For a moment he glared from one to the other of his enemies. Then he sighed and suddenly relaxed. Bill and Steve released him, but continued to stand close, ready to grab him if he made another move.

Instead Thorkel removed his thick-lensed glasses and rubbed his eyes with a gesture of fatigue and resignation. In a low voice, he confessed:

"I realize I have been hasty. I'm not surprised that you have doubted me." He replaced his glasses. His harsh face softened somewhat, and he scanned the group with a conciliatory expression. "I have been working so hard in the last two years that perhaps I have lost sight of true scientific values. What difference does it make in science who helps or who shares in some great new discovery? None. It is the discovery itself that counts. Will you forgive me, my friends, if, as a penance, I explain to you what I've been trying to achieve?"

This sudden about-face on the part of the doctor left Bill and Steve somewhat flat-footed. They exchanged glances, wondering whether to relax their watchfulness. Mary Phillips decided them as she broke in sympathetically:

"Perhaps we have all been hasty, too

Dr. Bulfinch added his assurance to the conciliation.

"I give you my word, I, for one, will take no dishonorable advantage of your confidence."

Dr. Alexander Thorkel drew himself up to his full height, then said:

"Thank you."

They gathered about the hermit scientist like neophytes about a master. Thorkel began his explanation.

"I mentioned the possibility of native miners dying here, because this radium mine was undoubtedly an Inca gold mine before I came here. All of those who in the past dug here for gold died without knowing they had uncovered something of far greater value—a deposit of the richest radium-bearing ore known to man."

This conformation of their own analyses of the morning caused varied expressions to appear on the faces of the four. Thorkel nodded knowingly.

"I see you are already aware of that fact," he concluded.

"How much have you mined so far?" Steve Baker inquired.

"So far I have extracted nothing from the mine but the usefulness of the radium." He pointed toward the tube that ran from the corner of the kitchen door though the wall to the mine shaft outside. "This," he explained, "is my conducting channel." They all followed him to the window, clustered about him and peered out.

"My contractor hangs down that shaft in proximity to the main deposit," continued Dr. Thorkel. "With it I gather and conduct under my control the immense radioactive force of nature itself."

Dr. Bulfinch listened to this explanation with obvious skepticism. He muttered: "Impossible."

The quick ears of Dr. Alexander Thorkel caught the comment, and he turned gently to his fellow-scientist.

"Impossible?" he asked. "Once Benjamin Franklin drew lightening out of the sky with a kite in an electrical storm. I my crude way I am likewise drawing cosmic force out of the bosom of the earth"

Mary Phillips seemed to reflect Dr. Bulfinch's doubt, but Steve Baker was evidently enthralled by Thorkel's recital. He pushed forward eagerly and demanded:

"Then what do you do with it?"

"Come, I will show you," invited Thorkel. He led them toward the door with the mica window.

For the first time Bill and Mary noted Pedro. He was paying no attention whatsoever to the scientific discussion. His attention was centered entirely in the task of finding Pinto. His center of activity was the several boxes on the work bench in an alcove partly shut off from the main room.

Now Dr. Thorkel and Steve Baker were approaching the door that Mary believed led to the kitchen. Thorkel threw open the door for inspection. It did not lead to any kitchen, but merely a small closet. The inner surface of the closet was lined with lead plating. Hanging from the ceiling was a large projector of the type used in hospitals to handle radium in the treatment of cancer.

"This is my condenser." Dr. Thorkel waxed enthusiastic about his apparatus. "You will note that it is similar in design to the instrument used in hospitals to attack cancer tissue. Though immeasurably more powerful, I am able to employ it with such delicacy as to treat the wing of a butterfly with injury. If you will examine it closely you will note the simplicity of construction."

Now that they could actually see something that struck a note related to their past scientific life, Mary Phillips and Dr. Bulfinch hustled forward with scientific interest prodding them. They stepped into the closet and examined the condenser carefully. Bill and Steve started to follow.

Over in his corner of the room, Pedro was making a discovery of his own. He bent down and opened one of the boxes on the bench. For a moment he was transfixed with astonishment as he discovered his albino horse, Pinto. But Pinto was no more than eight inches high.

"Pinto!" gasped Pedro.

Dr. Thorkel whirled around. The others were too interested in the apparatus before them to notice Pedro's excitement. Alexander Thorkel looked at his servant, and called peremptorily:

"Pedro, come here!"

The native servant jumped as though he had been stung. The other four were already inside the closet, fingering and examining the huge condenser hanging from the ceiling. Pedro came toward Thorkel, stumbling in a daze. The hermit scientist addressed him curtly:

"You come in too, Pedro. I want you to see this as well as the others."

Pedro shuffled in obediently. Thorkel gave him a shove and then slammed and locked the door. Quickly he grabbed one of the switches beside the door. Instantly there was a hum rising to a sibilant crackling buzz. The intense green light flashed on back of the mica window. Thorkel grabbed his lead helmet from the shelf, pulled it on quickly and leaned over to look through the mica window. In this position he turned on a second and a third switch, increasing the sound and the intensity of the light.

The scene inside the closet reflected a strange mixture of human emotions.

Bill Stockton's arm dropped around Mary's waist as she let out a very feminine scream. Dr. Bulfinch continued staring at the giant condenser, now roaring into life, until the weird green light caused him to blink and turn away his eyes to prevent blindness.

Mary forgot all about her scientific training, and let out one more scream before she collapsed in a faint, hanging from Bill's arm.

Steve was pounding on the locked door, as though he expected it to give way to his futile assault. Bill Stockton appeared to be the only one keeping his head at the moment. He looked at Bulfinch for an instant, then said:

"What do we do now?"

"I'm afraid this is beyond me," admitted the biologist drowsily. Then they looked toward Pedro. The Peruvian was kneeling in one corner of the cramped space, intoning fervent prayers to his God. "Looks like Pedro's the only one with the right idea. I guess Thorkel's secret is going to stay with him. I don't believe we'll be able to do anything about relieving it."

The curtain of green light turned to a deep black as far as Bill could see, then engulfed them in a sea of darkness.

CHAPTER THIRTEEN

Bill Stockton, the last to succumb in the lead-lined closet, was the first one to awaken from the strange nightmare that had closed in upon him and his companions. He was in total darkness, and his back rested upon a damp dirt floor. From the ceiling above him there hung an infra-red lamp which reflected a rich warm glow downward. This glow dimmed and brightened in a slow, regular rhythm.

The mineralogist felt about his body. He did not seem to have been injured by his ordeal under the condenser. But he was no longer garbed in his tropical suit. What felt like a bed sheet was draped over his form. As he surveyed his prison, Bill noticed a glass dish in the center of the floor. This contained a colorless liquid which boiled gently as it was warmed by an electrode hanging over the edge. From this boiling liquid there rose a thick vapor. Flowing over the edge of the dish like a small cloud, it rose slowly and clung to the floor with rootlike tendrils.

There were rock walls in the dim corners beyond the gleam of the infra-red light, but the vapor was so thick and opaque below as to shroud anything that might be on the floor.

Close by Bill saw, lying flat on the floor, the dim outlines of a human figure which, like himself, was swathed in a silken wrapping. This form stirred and began to breathe gaspingly. Then it started to struggle under the silken shroud like a sleeper

fighting to awaken from a nightmare. The silken wrappings were loose and failed to impede greatly those first attempts a movement.

Bill Stockton climbed to his feet and moved over to help his companion. The latter opened his mouth and gasped loudly. The wrapping fell away from his face, and Bill saw that it was Pedro. The Peruvian servant coughed as if fighting for air, then staggered to his feet.

Bill supported the native with one hand. When they had both risen to the clearer light above the low bank of thick vapor which was about knee deep, Pedro gasped and opened his mouth widely as if struggling to breathe. Beads of sweat stood out on the faces of both men. Pedro, with the superstition of an untutored native, was frantic with the elemental fear of suffocation. However, with each effort he seemed to breathe more easily. Bill Stockton had snapped back to normal much more rapidly. Fear did not seem to be a part of his makeup.

Breathing deeply, Pedro finally started looking around him. He forced a smile as he glimpsed Bill beside him.

"Take it easy, Pedro," the mining engineer told him. Together they turned their attention toward where another person was gasping and choking. They moved in the direction of the sound, and Pedro asked:

"Who ess it?"

Out of the vapor at their feet there rose another shrouded figure gasping and choking with that initial spasmodic effort to breathe. Pedro started back fearfully from this apparition. But again the individual clawed loose its silken wrappings. The face and head of Steve Baker appeared.

"Pedro," Steve managed asthmatically. "And Bull!"

"I think so," Pedro replied fearfully.

Steve took two or three very deep breaths. "Air is sure better up here," he managed, gaining new control of his faculties. "Where are the others?"

"We'll have to find them," Bill replied, his own thoughts racing to determine the fate of Mary Phillips.

"Let's dig around and look," Steve suggested.

Suiting the action to the words, Bill, Steve and Pedro began groping around in the mist on the cellar floor searching for the companions. Finally Bill's fingers closed over a familiar form, and he breathed a sigh of relief.

"Here is one," he said. As he pulled the shrouded form up out of the vapor he hoped against hope that his original feeling was accurate. He hastily uncovered the face. It was Mary Phillips.

He shook her vigorously, then hollered:

"Hey! Are you all right?

Pedro broke in with:

"Here is the old one!" Steve hastened to help the native with Dr. Bulfinch. Bill Stockton tightened his grip on Mary, and, as the woman scientist opened her eyes and looked up at him, he said tenderly:

"I thought I'd lost you then. I thought we were all goners."

"I'll bet I made a fool of myself," Mary breathed. "Didn't I?"

"Under the circumstances, I wouldn't blame any woman for screaming and fainting. I almost fainted myself. But there wasn't room enough in the closet to fall down."

Dr. Bulfinch was being steered toward the romantic pair by his two discoverers. Even as he approached, Mary asked:

"Where are we?"

"Down in Thorkel's cellar, I guess," Bill decided. "But we'll have to get more light before we can do very much."

They all stiffened at the sound of a chair moving about above them. Then there was the heavy tread of feet, which they recognized as Dr. Thorkel's stumping walk.

Upstairs things were quite different from the way they had been preceding the closing of the switches on the panel. It was broad daylight now, and the windows and doors were wide open. The previously mysterious room now had a peaceful, sunny appearance. Dr. Alexander Thorkel was at the table with his notes. He seemed very fatigued, as though he had gone without sleep for a long time. Finally he dropped his head on his arms.

Santanas, the big black cat, was sniffing at the trap door. The cat snarled. Thorkel glanced at the feline and grunted reprovingly. Then he consulted his watch. His eyes brightened, their expression magnified by the heavy glasses.

"Maybe you are right," he remarked. "It is nearly time."

Unhurriedly he began to assemble his notes and stow them away in the corner of his trunk.

Downstairs in the cellar the five objects of Thorkel's attention were now standing and breathing successfully. Each was engaged in twisting and folding his sheetlike wrapping into the semblance of a garment. Mary was the only one self-conscious about her appearance.

"Judging from these Roman togas, Thorkel must lean toward the Classical era," she observed.

Bill Stockton was watching the curtain of vapor that still swirled about their knees. He chuckled at Mary's comment, then said:

"Maybe so. But let's break out of here before we *are* asphyxiated."

Pedro seemed to think this was an extremely good idea, and at once he began feeling his way stumblingly through the vapor and along the cellar wall. Even in his present predicament, however, Rupert Bulfinch was still the investigating scientist.

"You may calm yourself on that score," he declared. "We are not in any danger of asphyxiation." He sniffed the vapor and then glanced at the light hanging overhead. "Ozone—ammonia—humidity—temperature—the heart-beat rhythm of the lamp—all these factors were intended not to suppress consciousness, but to revive it."

Mary Phillips gripped Bills's arm, apparently feeling that a weird form of adversity had united them. She turned to her colleague and asked:

"Then what has he done to us?"

"However criminal his design," Dr. Bulfinch mused, "it has so far stopped short of murder."

Steve, following Bill's mood, tried to lighten the situation. "Sure," he declared, "the doc's just been giving us a new kind of a Turkish bath.

In spite of everything, Bill Stockton was still inclined to feel that they would be much better off outside. He glanced around him, then called:

"Hey, Pedro. You know this place better than we do. How do we get out of here?"

Pedro was not immediately visible, and Bill moved away from the others in search of the Peruvian. Finally he overtook the native in one corner of the earthen pit.

"Where are we?" the mining engineer asked.

Pedro turned slowly through the eddying vapor to face Bill. He ignored the question entirely, either because he did not know the answer, or was afraid to give in. He had just remembered something. His words held horror as he said:

"Pinto—he has made Pinto little."

Bill did not immediately hear Pedro's remark. Instead, his fingers groped ahead of him, touched his own question. "I know now. He's got us down in the mine."

Steve Baker had followed Bill, and now came up to the mining engineer. They were both standing beside Pedro when the little Peruvian shivered with fright.

"I know what's happened," Pedro cried. "He has made me little, too."

Steve Baker shook the half hysterical native and said:

"This is no time to go balmy on us. We've all got to stick together until we get out of here."

Now that he had made up his mind as to his location, Bill returned to Mary's side. Dr. Bulfinch joined the others, and his ears pricked up as he heard Pedro's voice rising with certain horror.

"He has made me little like my albino horse."

Again Steve Baker sought to quell Pedro's panic.

"Sure. But he's also made you big like me. See—you're just as big as Doc or any of us."

He stood with his back to the Peruvian and measured heights solemnly. Something of Pedro's panic had subsided, soothed by Steve's statement. The five were now slinging to each other's wrists and hands as they started to move slowly, feeling their way along the nearest wall.

"Watch which was you step in this fog," Bill cautioned. "We don't want to fall into any deeper hole."

As they proceeded farther from the light, the fog became less evident. Then there was a noise on the stairs outside. Pedro heard it first, and whispered hoarsely:

"Somebody is come."

It was true. Upstairs, Dr. Thorkel had meticulously put away his notes. He turned to open the trap door in the center of the floor. As he started down the cellar stairs, the cat darted down ahead of him.

As Thorkel reached the bottom, he turned on a switch near the cellar door. The fluctuating overhead lamp began to dim rapidly. Bill Stockton looked up at it. Mary quivered against him. The others reacted similarly to the phenomenon. Then they all turned toward the noise at the door again. The door at the bottom of the stairs had been sealed around the edges with paper tape, evidently to assist Thorkel in maintaining within the cellar the humidity and temperature and other factors he desired. Dr. Thorkel began ripping off this paper preparatory to opening the door.

The red glow from the lamp had now almost entirely disappeared, so that Bill, Mary and the others were merely the faintest of silhouettes in the darkness. They shivered and cold chills ran up and down their spines as they heard the sound of the paper being ripped away.

Dr. Bulfinch, because of his age and experience, offered to take charge of the situation.

"If that is Dr. Thorkel," he declared, "I will appeal to what reason he has left."

Expecting some lively action when the person beyond the door finally entered, Bill pushed Mary behind him, and took a step forward with Steve. Finally Thorkel had the last bit of paper ripped off, and started to open the door. As he did so, a broad shaft of light fell across the huddled group of prisoners. They turned to face the door, and then they found themselves looking up.

They were astounded by this first sight of anything which could permit them to realize their own size.

Bill Stockton whistled. Mary was amazed. Dr. Bulfinch's mouth dropped open, and Steve and Pedro just looked.

The cellar door was a high as a two-story house, the cat was as big as a saber-toothed tiger, and their enemy, Dr. Thorkel, appeared to be a thirty-foot giant.

As Mary and Bill and the others looked from the cat and Thorkel's feet up his full length to his face, he peered down at them. It was obvious that this encounter brought him great gratification. His feeling of lassitude and fatigue appeared to drop from his like a tattered cloth. His face brightened with excited interest. His fingers opened and closed.

"So—my little chicks break out for themselves," he commented. "That is excellent."

Santanas the cat spat, and the little people jumped away. Suddenly Bill began to realize the great handicap which their size, or lack of it, gave them. From now on everything in their normal lives would represent a menace to them.

Thorkel laughed aloud at the apparent discomfiture of his new human guinea pigs. He bent to pick up the cat. Now the five miniature people were grouped in a semicircle for common defense. They watched Thorkel's every movement. The hermit scientist stroked the big black car, and seemed to be purring to it as he said:

"No, no Santanas, we must not let you frighten them."

Then the scientist stepped down into the cellar and bent over to inspect the little people better. They shrank back from him, and clung to each other. Their only emotion was one of incredulous horror. Thorkel, holding the cat, dropped down on one knee, in order to look at them more closely.

"Come, come, my friends," he requested softly. "There is nothing here to alarm you."

The tension was too much for Mary. Bill felt her fingers closing over the flesh of his arm and her nails biting into his biceps. Then the girl screamed and his her face of Steve's shoulder.

Thorkel's heavy glasses came toward Mary with renewed interest. It was obvious that he was very pleased.

"Vocal chords quite unimpaired," he said. "A very good sign."

He leaned closer and peered at all of them.

"You have no temperature?" The question was addressed to all five of them, and then Dr. Thorkel turned his attention to Rupert Bulfinch. "Dr. Bulfinch," he went on, "would you be good enough to take the pulse of your companions?"

Now his breath was coming in deep rhythm, and the gusts from his excited lungs were like the wind in the tropical trees during the first flush of the rainy season. In speechless horror the five small folk pressed away from him and glanced in the direction of the stairway as though instinctively contemplating escape.

Dr. Thorkel was obviously amused by their fearfulness. He shook his head in mock sadness. Bill Stockton spotted the flight of steps leading up to the open trap door. But Thorkel was again talking in a jesting fashion.

"As with all little people, all small creatures, the first instinct is to escape when a giant comes along." His fingers came up and pointed toward the stairway. "Well, there is the stairway. Run for it, if you like."

Bill was uncertain for a second. The others seemed to be looking toward him for leadership. They all glanced at Thorkel fearfully, then started to run toward the stairway in a chain that resembled a whip of some ice skating pond.

When they approached the lowest step, Bill Stockton began to realize something of the problems that were going to confront them continually. The first step was high enough to reach to his chest. Finally it became obvious that the task of mounting the stairs was going to require complete cooperation.

Bill Stockton gripped Mary Phillips under her armpits and boosted her up to the first step. Then he clasped his hand in a fireman's lift and hoisted Dr. Bulfinch and Steve Baker to the step beside her. They knelt down, turned and gave him a hand up.

Pulling and pushing each other in this manner, they managed to swarm up over the first step or two with remarkable agility. Then they were aware of Dr. Thorkel's giant form looming over them He was watching them with growing delight.

"Strong," he muttered. "Active." He shook his head as he marveled at the sight. There was real enthusiasm in his tones as he concluded: "This is really wonderful."

Concentrating all of their efforts in the difficult task of mounting the stairs, the quintette did not have any chance for sensible and reasonable reaction to their new environment, They merely seemed hunted and frantic like so many little animals.

Thorkel crossed to the foot of the stairs and dropped the cat in the cellar before closing the cellar door. Santanas tried to brush past his leg, but he thrust it back and said:

"No—no, these mice are not for you—at least not yet."

For the first time since he had observed the results of this newest experiment his eyes were bloodshot, and a drool came to the corners of his mouth as though he savored the memories of previous encounters between Santanas and his earlier victims.

With the cat disposed of, Dr. Thorkel turned again and started to climb the stairs, watching the five little people ahead of him admiringly.

"Muscular coordination—perfect. Reflex actions—perfect. Physical structure—perfect."

As they neared the top, the stairs began to quiver beneath them. Bill, Mary and the others realized that Thorkel was mounting the steps behind them.

CHAPTER FOURTEEN

The little people scrambled into the room through the trap door. Thorkel's head and shoulders appeared behind them. Finally he emerged from the stairway and turned to close the trap door. As he straightened up, he looked around the room with some surprise. The miniature humans had disappeared while he was closing the door.

Dr. Alexander Thorkel was more amused than dismayed, for he knew that his quarry was somewhere in the room. He looked around him slowly, taking in all of the appointments of the place. Not one of the little people was in sight.

Finally he spoke.

"There is no need to hide," he announced. "I am not going to hurt you, and I have shut out the cat."

He crossed the room to one of the chairs and sat down. While Thorkel didn't seem to know where they were, each member of the quintette was aware of the location of his fellows. Bulfinch and Mary were hiding behind a pair of Thorkel's boots. Bill and Steve had taken refuge behind a pile of books in once corner of the floor. Pedro was almost literally glued to the back of a chair leg.

Dr. Thorkel's first remarks did not prompt the little people to reveal themselves. They remained hidden. Thorkel looked around slowly, willing to wait for them to gain enough courage to emerge.

"See—I am sitting down," he went on. "I threaten nothing. Come on out where I can see you. I like to look at you."

His quiet suavity was becoming a bit pointed. Still there was no slightest sign of the five people concealed about the room. Thorkel chuckled as he resumed his monologue.

"How fearful you are. You have changed in nothing but size. Have you forgotten breaking in to steal my discoveries? Have you so soon lost all interest, now that you know what I have been doing? Where is your scientific spirit? Ah!"

The ejaculation was drawn from him by his first glimpse of Rupert Bulfinch as the scientist stalked out into the open and across the floor to confront Thorkel. The biologist halted just out of reach of Thorkel's grip.

The hermit scientist beamed, then said:

"Come closer. Have no fear."

Bulfinch moved slowly closer. His eyes were examining Thorkel from head to foot, as though the small man were master of the situation rather than the large one. His glance at the experimenter seemed to confuse Thorkel. With sudden alarm he asked:

"What is the matter, Bulfinch? Can you not speak?"

"Yes, I can speak," Bulfinch replied gravely.

A sigh of relief gushed from Thorkel's throat. "And a fine, natural voice, too," he declared. "But come—are you not curious? Have you no questions to ask?"

"Only one," stated Bulfinch with deliberateness and gravity. "Why does Providence permit the existence of such a monstrosity as yourself? I have no illusions about the fate of Mira and the others who have undergone your experiments. I do not doubt but what we will merit a similar fate: to become a meal for your paunchy black cat. It is a cruel destiny for one so young and clever as Dr. Phillips. For myself, I had expected something better, but one never knows."

Dr. Thorkel laughed in pure delight. Then he replied:

"Marvelous. Exactly in character." He sobered a bit as he went on: "Nervous system and brain have come through undamaged. As for your other accusations— Mira was a martyr to science. I did not expect her to die, but something went wrong. That is why I sent for you."

"Your animals died, didn't they?" demanded Bulfinch emphatically.

"Yes," admitted Thorkel. His face screwed up into a mask of cruelty.

"Then why did you think that the fate of your human victims would be any different?"

Thorkel shrugged. Obviously there was no answer to this logic. Dr. Thorkel had made himself a cold-blooded murderer in the name of investigative science. Were these five to be added to his list of victims?

The other little people had timidly come forward, emboldened by Bulfinch's courage. Now they were grouped just a little behind the biologist. They quivered for a moment at his exchange with Dr. Thorkel, then apparently resigned themselves to circumstances. Bill, for his part, decided that he wasn't going to be cat meat without putting up a struggle.

Alexander Thorkel peered at the others and motioned for them to come closer. They shrank back. Even Bulfinch retreated a step or two as Thorkel leaned down and reached toward them.

"I'm not going to eat you, I only wish to weigh and measure you," Thorkel explained.

Now the hermit scientist was leaning forward out of his chair until his knees were almost on the floor. He was making amiable bearlike gestures for them to come near enough for him to touch. However, they were afraid and backed out of his reach.

"I'm not going to let the maniac get his claws on me," Bill Stockton told Mary in a whisper. Mary nodded, and clung to his arms.

"But what are we going to do?" she stammered. I never realized until now how an ant must feel when you're about to step on it."

But Thorkel was talking again.

"Perhaps your hearing has been affected," he suggested. No one answered him. Suddenly he twisted up his mouth and roared:

"Boo!"

At the exclamation all five miniatures mites turned and ran, panic-stricken. Thorkel slid back in his chair, roaring with laughter. Finally, when they heard no sound of Thorkel's heavy footsteps behind them, the quintette paused in the middle of the floor. Bill and Mary turned to look back at Dr. Thorkel. They were all just a little ashamed of their fright, but this situation was no joke to them.

Finally Thorkel's laughter diminished to a series of chuckles. He removed his glasses and wiped his eyes. The excitement of the discovery that his experiment was a perfect success was climaxed in the laughter. He now seemed to be suffering from the reaction of sleepless hours, and his shoulders hunched forward. He was very tired again.

Bill Stockton sensed the change in the doctor, and felt that it might give them an opportunity to work for their release from the house, unhampered by the constant scrutiny of the jailer. It was soon obvious, however, that Dr. Thorkel was not going to rebuild his energy by such a natural process as sleep.

"Now, my little friends," the doctor began, "it will be necessary to check again your various weights and sizes." He rose and stretched. Then he started walking toward a shelf near his bed.

Just as though they were engaging in conversation with him, instead of mutely watching his every move, Thorkel went on:

"But first you will forgive me if I am so rude as to resort to a stimulant. During

the period of your transition, I have not had an hour—not one moment's sleep.

He began measuring and pouring into the graduate from several bottles on the shelf. "Caffeine citrate and—" he poured from another bottle— "tincture of ferric chloride. As a mineralogist, Mr. Stockton, you will recognize that as iron compound . . . and now!" a third bottle came into his grasp, and he poured some of its compounds into the solution he was making— "benzedrine sulphate. Under your microscope, Dr. Phillips, you would find it rather a cloudy globule, but—" he chuckled—"I'm taking it so that I won't be cloudy."

"That's going to put him away for quite a while. Don't worry dear."

The use of the word "dear" moved Mary. She sobbed, then tightened her grip on herself. Thorkel was beaming and smiling around for some recognition of his pun. No one was amused by it. The hermit scientist merely shook his head. "I hope your sense of humor has not be impaired," he offered.

With the graduate in his hand, he felt for the cot behind him, then sat down. Then he sipped the drink as one would a highball.

"You should be very proud, Dr. Bulfinch," Dr. Thorkel declared. "In the past two years I have been able to alter the size of many organisms, but you are the first specimens to survive the ordeal for more than a few hours."

With this pronouncement, which was received by the quintette with sudden confusion, Dr. Thorkel gradually appeared to lose interest in the proceedings about him. He removed his glasses, rubbed his eyes and relaxed against the pillow and wall at the head of the cot. He tried to continue his oration, but his voice became thicker. In spite of the stimulant, it was obvious that fatigue was overcoming him.

"You should be proud—" he drowsed—"I repeat—because it was your assistance—you gave me the clue—to my only error—" His words became more incoherent as sleep overwhelmed him.

The little people moved closer to the cot, and watched Thorkel with the fixed attention of little animals. His words did not sound across the room now, but were merely confused mumbles with here and there an audible phrase.

"It was the iron crystals—identifying the iron crystals—Now I can control life—absolutely—I can shape the very substance of life—"

His voice trailed off, and he began to breathe deeply. The little people remained silent and immobile for perhaps ten minutes until Dr. Thorkel gave way to heavy snoring.

Relaxed for the first time since their rude awakening in the cellar, the five little people began to consider their plight. Watchful of thorkel, they began tiptoeing away, their only thought to escape the room.

With the door looming up above them, and the knob 'way above their heads, it looked like a monumental task. The window was even further out of reach, and dropping to the ground outside would mean a broken leg, or may even a broken neck.

Their group gathered together and held its first council of war.

CHAPTER FIFTEEN

The first thing they did was to tiptoe quickly under a chair; then, after one swift inspection of the avenues of escape, they headed for the front door. Bill Stockton and Dr. Bulfinch were talking rapidly to each other. With the others grouped about them, they looked up at the latch so far above their reach.

They had not yet become used to the fact that a door knob was as far above them as Mount Everest. Finally Rupert Bulfinch pointed across the room, and said:

"Those books are the solution."

On the floor, beside the table, were about a dozen books of varying thickness. With all the eagerness of Egyptian slaves anxious to complete their chore on a growing pyramid, the quintette hastened over to the books. Each one of the five picked up a book and carried it to the door.

Bill Stockton kept an eye on Dr. Thorkel, but the tired hermit was sleeping soundly on the cot. At the door the books were piled up, with the corners turned to form a flight of stairs. The chore of moving the heavy books was a burdensome one, and Mary soon found it necessary to stop and rest. But the four men went on with the job, and as the pile of books became higher, their task became more difficult. It was necessary now for them to pass the books up from the floor to the top of the pile. Bill Stockton, on top, was carefully to keep the pile from toppling over.

Suddenly Dr. Thorkel moved restlessly in his sleep and turned over. The little people at the door froze with anxiety, then resumed their work as Dr. Thorkel subsided again. Bill was the tallest of the group, and finally he was able barely to reach the latch, but could not quite turn it. The supply of books had been exhausted.

"Bring me that pencil." Bill pointed. Steve Baker hastened to carry out this suggestion. When the pencil had been passed up to him he tried it again, but still the latch would not budge.

Finally Bill called to Mary:

"Come up here. Maybe you can get at it.

Mary climbed up obediently, and after she regained her breath on the top book, Bill lifted her to his shoulders, handed her the pencil and she went to work. Using the pencil as a lever, she managed to move the latch. Down on the floor, Pedro, Dr. Bulfinch and Steve took hold of the door and managed to work it open an inch or two, although it was comparable to opening huge airplane hangar doors by hand.

The first three members of the group slipped through the opening, while Mary and Bill clambered down the book stairway and joined them. Just as they were slipping out into the compound they again heard Dr. Thorkel moving restlessly in his sleep and mumbling something. By this time, however, they had darted out of the crack in the doorway and were scuttling down the steps.

Finally Bill and Mary, still holding to each other, hesitated in one corner of the compound wall. Dr. Bulfinch, Pedro and Steve Baker were close beside them. Now they began to believe and realized that the outside world was an immense place. In the house there were some confines, but here, beyond the compound wall, there were none.

The area before them contained the piles of crates, camp chairs and table, various pieces of camp equipment and paraphernalia. Beyond the camp table, against the compound wall, there was a small cactus patch. In and about this camp area there were many opportunities for the little people to keep near or under cover.

Each time they moved forward, they took refuge behind some barrier that would cut them off from the house. Their posture here, sticking close to the nearest wall, was like that of a line of skirmishers entering a village which they suspect may still contain enemy snipers. Up until now they had had no concerted plan of action. They did not want to make any, either, because the exigencies of their life were changing with each fleeting second.

Tropical insects that buzzed around about them sounded like miniature airplanes. For the time being their chief interest was in remaining hidden. They moved out under the camp table, and stopped, altogether overwhelmed by their first complete sight of the outer world.

After the first shock of realization their instinct was to hide. Each one of the five faces mirrored bewilderment; in spite of their scientific and general knowledge they felt that they were still unequipped to cope with this new state of thing.

Bill finally screwed up his courage and turned to address the group.

"This business of being afraid of everything we see, and worrying about things we haven't even seen, is foolish. We're going to have to get hold of ourselves, and really make a stand. This running isn't going to get us anywhere. We're liable to run away from one thing and bump into something ten times worse."

As if to give his words particular emphasis, the quintette edged their way along the side of a box. As they reached the space between two of the cases, they were confronted by several chickens. The chickens were equally surprised at the encounter and clucked their feelings in no uncertain terms. Their chief reason was the natural curiosity of barnyard dwellers over strangers in the confines of the place. The little people, however, were so keyed up with nervousness that they recoiled and jumped back around the corner as if they had faced a pack of tigers.

Almost as soon as they had retreated, Bill sniffed and said:

"Fine way for us to act." The others shuffled and dry-washed their hands as an indication of their own discomfiture at their timidity.

Their courage renewed, they retraced their steps to the corner of the box. The chickens were still there, pecking away at the inhospitable ground. One of them looked up curiously, but made no hostile move. Emboldened by this lack of interest, Pedro took a step nearer to them and snapped his fingers. One of the hens eyed him and then clucked loudly. Pedro jumped back.

Bill Stockton laughed, and held tight to Mary Phillips as she turned to run. Steve Baker pointed off to one corner and said:

"I think we can get by over there."

The group followed his suggestion, and very cautiously they began to edge forward again.

Even as they were striving to escape the menace of the chickens, something a good deal more dangerous was goading itself into action. Through a small hole at ground level, Santanas the cat, whom Dr. Thorkel had shut in the cellar, had worked her way out into the compound. The cat looked around the yard but did not immediately spot the little people.

With their entire attention concentrated on the chickens, the miniature men and woman continued to move slowly away. Finally it became obvious that Santanas was on their trail. She began to stalk them, belly close to the ground, front paws moving forward one by one, hind quarters coming up carefully to make no sound.

In spite of Bill's efforts, the little people were still very much alarmed. Bill Stockton said:

"Just take it easy. If we hurry we're likely to excite them."

This sounded like good advice, and the others followed it.

Then Pedro cast a careful look ahead and saw the cat off in the distance. Immediately he sensed the feline's design, since it had clearly indicated its intention in the cellar, and Pedro had every reason to believe that Santanas had already devoured the remains of the miniature animals.

"Look out!" the Peruvian shouted.

The four others sensed the danger and its source at almost the same moment, and they all dashed for the shelter of the cactus. Even as they came to a panting halt in the shelter of the thick-spined plants, they knew that this haven was only temporary. They were panic-stricken.

"What do we do now?" Mary asked, and the question was almost a whimper.

"Take it easy," Bill cautioned. "Everything will come out all right. We're going to have to get some kind of weapons, so that we'll be ready for emergencies of this kind."

Succor came to them from an unexpected source when Paco, Pedro's dog, appeared lazily around a corner of one of the crates. The animal sensed that something was wrong, but for the moment could not decide what it was. Then he stiffened at the sight of the cat. He barked and dashed forward.

Santanas fled into the tangle of boxes and crates that littered the camp site. The dog followed her into this hideaway, and finally Santanas leaped to the top of the mud wall and disappeared into the jungle. Paco barked helplessly at the foot of the mud wall, then rushed along to the gateway, and out into the green-walled verdure that surrounded Thorkel's retreat.

As soon as the menace had been definitely removed Bill Stockton led the exodus out of the shelter of the cactus. Pedro had become something of a hero in a moment. He thumbed his arms proudly and said:

"Paco, he is my dog."

"He's sure a fine dog," Steve agreed.

"Paco is mag-ni-fi-cent!" Pedro insisted.

"Paco! *Vente* !

He whistled.

Finally Paco stopped barking out on the edge of the jungle, turned, came back through the gateway and hurried toward Pedro with eager feet. Suddenly he saw the Peruvian, and slid to a surprised halt. Pedro began to realize the dog's difficulty.

His voice adopted a pleading tone, and he walked toward the dog.

"Paco—" he said— "I am *me*—Pedro."

Paco looked more and more unhappy as Pedro approached. The native was cajoling the animal, and puckering his lips in a familiar whistle.

"Don't you remember when we hunt, Paco?" He gestured with an imaginary gun, then went: "Boom!"

Instead of remembering, Paco began to howl mournfully. Pedro was forced to admit his defeat. The others had been watching him sympathetically, and when he turned to them there was moisture in several small eyes.

"*He* is my dog," declared Pedro, "but *who* is Pedro?"

The five little people finally established their base under a water bucket a short distance from the friendly cactus patch. Here Bulfinch summarized the situation.

We've got to be careful of all the animals and birds around here that are bigger than we are. But at the same time, our greatest enemy is still Dr. Thorkel. I think it would be a good idea if one of us kept an eye on him all the time. We'll take turns at it."

Bill and Steve nodded in agreement. Hours had passed since they had managed to open the door and make their escape. A man of Thorkel's habits would probably be refreshed and ready to go ahead with his experiments now.

"I'll take the first shift," Bill Stockton offered.

Mary Phillips did not seem to be pleased with this arrangement. But it was necessary, and she said nothing against it.

"All right," agreed Dr. Bulfinch. "The rest of us will have other things to do. Let's get at them.

Bill Stockton headed toward the house, scrambling up the front steps, and took up his position on the door jamb just beyond the still open door. Dr. Thorkel was awake. He was sitting on the edge of his cot, blinking his eyes sleepily and polishing his glasses. For the moment Bill was prompted to hasten back and sound the alarm, but then he realized that Dr. Thorkel would be no menace inside the house, unless he picked up some weapon. He determined to stay there and do a real job of scouting.

Alexander Thorkel put on his glasses and looked at his watch. Suddenly he realized that he had been sleeping several hours, and he looked around for his specimen little people. He started talking in a fatherly tone.

"You have been very quiet. That is good. Now come out. I want to look at you again."

Naturally there was no answer. Dr. Thorkel rose to his feet, looked around him, and immediately discovered the books at the door. Bill Stockton darted back so that the doctor's glance would not include him. Instead of coming toward the door, Thorkel headed for the front window. He raised the shutters and peered out.

For a moment there was an expression of fear on his face, then this look was replaced by a smile, and his stiffened shoulders relaxed.

Outside, secure in the safety of their own numbers, and with Bill Stockton as their scout, the little people had been relieved of immediate pressing fear. All of them were busily engaged. They had adjusted their clothing in a more serviceable fashion and were now interested in food, weapons and other practical measures.

Bill Stockton followed the doctor's glance to learn what was prompting his amusement.

Pedro Caroz was on the top of the camp table cutting slices of cheese with a knife that was bigger than he was. Mary was seated in the shade of a camp stool which effectively shielded her from the tropic sun. She was holding a needle in her capable fingers and fashioning a pair of sandals.

Steve Baker was aiding Pedro in the commissary department and was making a brave effort to open a can of beans with an unwielding can-opener.

Bulfinch was sprawled face down at one corner of the table, consulting one of his scientific books which he had presumably extracted from his baggage. Looking up from his book, Bulfinch remarked:

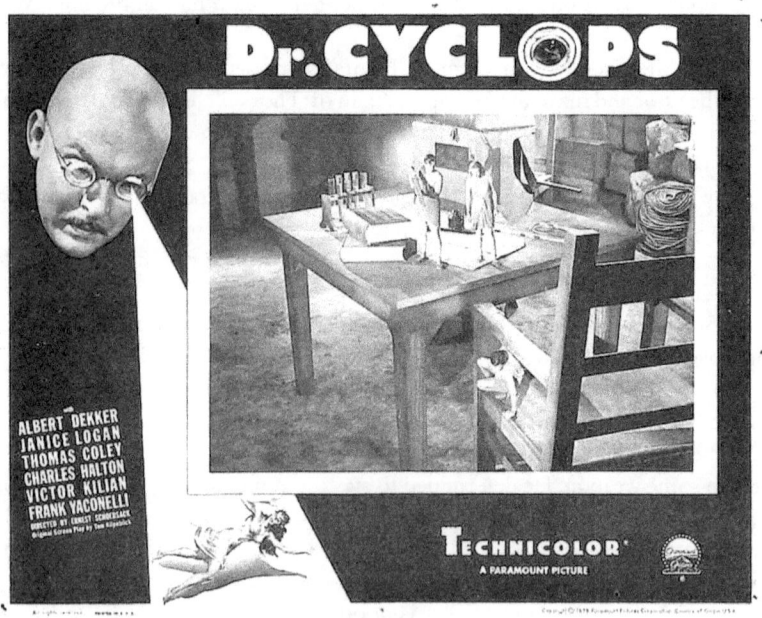

"I will grant that it is theoretically possible to break down organic tissue by subjecting it to radio activity. But Dr. Thorkel is wrong about everything else. You cannot channelize a radioactive field. He is absolutely wrong."

"Maybe you're right, Doc," Steve replied with a laugh. "Maybe he hasn't made us small after all. Maybe he's just made everything else big."

Bill Stockton chuckled at this remark, which came clearly to him across the width of the compound. Dr. Thorkel was now leaning out the window. Apparently he was very much amused at the homemaking activities of the little people.

At this point Bill dropped down off the steps, darted behind a pile of boxes and made his way back to the camp.

"Thorkel is at the window," he reported.

After passing the warning, Bill watched the others turn to look at their tormenter. Then Bill returned to a pair of scissors that he had been working on before Bulfinch had sent him to scout. He was taking the screw out of the scissors, and planned to use one of the blades as a sword. Finally he succeeded in his mammoth attempt, and whirled the single blade into the air experimentally. It was about the right size for a sword for him.

Dr. Bulfinch, Steve and Mary began a strategic withdraw to the cactus patch. Pedro was more vociferous in his reaction. He looked up from his supply of cheese and saw Dr. Thorkel peering at him. Pedro immediately leaped from the table top into a canvas chair, and bounced from there to the ground like a circus performer coming down from the high wire.

Dr. Thorkel laughed jovially at these antics. He leaned his chin on his hands and peered out at them through the window, calling:

"My little friends, I am proud of you. You are most resourceful. Now come back. We must resume the examinations."

There was a hurried conference among the group of miniature folks. They were all grouped at the edge of the cactus. They were afraid to obey Thorkel, but yet did not know how to refuse him.

Again Dr. Bulfinch assumed the responsibility. He gestured toward Bill Stockton, with his scissor sword. "All of you remain here. Bill, you take charge. I'll try to reason with him."

"Don't go," Mary Phillips pleaded. "Let's see what he plans to do next. There's no sense in our putting ourselves back in his hands."

"Think nothing of it," Bulfinch replied. "I think we can talk to him intelligently."

The elderly doctor started forward. Bill Stockton took two steps after him. A grim foreboding of evil gripping him. This would be the first showdown with Thorkel, and Bill, somehow, was not very sanguine of their success.

CHAPTER SIXTEEN

The four onlookers were aware of the fact that Dr. Thorkel was extremely interested in Dr. Bulfinch's approach. At the window the scientist watched until the little professor reached a position on the ground below him.

The hermit scientist's gigantic hands were dangling out of the window, and with one of them he gestured toward the door.

"Come right in, Dr. Bulfinch," he invited. "I shall be glad to take you first."

Bulfinch drew himself up to all the majesty of his fourteen inches of height and said firmly:

"I most certainly shall not come in."

Dr. Thorkel was amused rather than perturbed:

"What?" he roared. "You don't mean to say that I have a mutiny already."

The elderly biologist was sober and demanding.

"I insist that you send for the mules and have us transported back to civilization."

This picture in his own mind seemed to add to Dr. Thorkel's hilarity, and he asked:

"In a saddle bag? What an undignified position for the great. Dr. Bulfinch." Then he finished casually: "In any event, the mules have already returned."

"You don't dare keep us here, or do us any harm," Dr. Bulfinch pointed out. "People will wonder what has happened to us, and will institute a search. You cannot expect to get away with this forever."

"Maybe," agreed Thorkel. "But not for some time. Your world fully expected you to remain here with me for months, and even years. It will not be disillusioned."

This frank statement on the part of the hermit scientist seemed to give Dr. Bulfinch the clue that he had been seeking.

"Then you mean we are to consider ourselves your prisoners?"

"Suppose we consider you—as—er—well self-invited guests in my laboratory.

Bulfinch again drew himself up to his full, though meagre, height, put a hand across his breast in the best Hamlet manner and said theatrically:

"Prisoners—prisoners in Cyclop's cave."

"Cyclops, eh?" Thorkel was smiling. "Is that a reflection on my poor vision?" He took off his glasses and wiped them as he squinted down at the visiting scientist.

"Not at all," Dr. Bulfinch returned with acerbity, "on your intellect. Cyclops, too, thought size and strength were sufficient. He was a very ignorant fellow."

Apparently Dr. Thorkel was willing to follow Bulfinch's mood. He replied ironically: "While Ulysses possessed a very superior mind, is that it? Well, look out Ulysses Bulfinch. There's a hen about to peck you."

Even as he spoke, Dr. Thorkel could not contain his laughter. Dr. Bulfinch cast a quick glance over his shoulder upon hearing Thorkel's warning. Sure enough, one of the chickens was eyeing him hungrily. Seeing that the effect he had been striving so carefully to achieve had been shattered by the untimely arrival of the hen, Dr. Bulfinch shouted in exasperation:

"Go away, you ridiculous fowl."

Instead of retreating, the hen clucked and advanced a step or two. Bill Stockton and the others were watching the little drama and when the hen became aggressive, Bill hurried forward with his scissor-sword. But before he could get into action Bulfinch had turned to flee.

Thorkel seemed to be enjoying the little marionette drama on the worldly stage before him, and he laughed immoderately as Dr. Bulfinch too refuge in the nearest hiding place, and over turned, broken basket.

The sight of the pointed weapon in Bill Stockton's hand was enough to discourage the chicken, and she flapped off to join her sisters at the other end of the compound.

The hermit scientist stopped laughing then, and called:

"We have had enough of this foolishness, Dr. Bulfinch. Come here now."

At a nod from Bulfinch, Bill Stockton returned to the others. Mary was quivering with a mixture of fear and curiosity.

"What do you think he's really going to do?"

Bill Stockton tried to soothe her. "I'm afraid we can't tell. It's obvious that Dr. Thorkel has never had any specimens quite like us to play with. He'll probably be reasonable for some time to come. I'm sure we have nothing to fear."

Even as he spoke, Bill knew that he was whistling in the dark, for in his knocking about on all the coasts and beaches of the world, and in the rugged bowels of the mountains where his engineering and mining work had taken him, he had found that there was nothing so unpredictable as a half crazed scientist riding his favorite hobby.

But now the four members of the party were again watching the little drama that was unfolding between Dr. Thorkel and Dr. Bulfinch—the new South American jungle version of David and Goliath.

Dr. Bulfinch emerged partly from under the basket and made sure that the chicken was not threatening him. Then he straightened up and addressed Thorkel firmly:

"Under the circumstances, Dr. Thorkel, I will not cooperate with you in any manner whatsoever."

Instead of adding to the humor of the situation, this definite riposte on the part of the elderly, though now diminutive scientist, turned Dr. Thorkel's amusement to irritation.

"Come here at once!" Thorkel ordered sternly. "This is a command! I am not inviting any more."

"I will not," retorted Bulfinch with equal sternness, although his size put the words on the piping side.

A flush of color suffused Thorkel's face as he pushed back through the window and rose to his feet. Then he disappeared from the window.

Bill Stockton put one arm around Mary's shoulders as he spoke.

"Boy, the fat's in the fire now."

Mary Phillips shared Bill's interpretation of the aftermath of the exchange, and called:

"Come back here, Dr. Bulfinch. Our maniac is going to have another one of his spells."

For answer Dr. Bulfinch looked around again for the hen, then faced toward the house.

"I'll never come to you, Dr. Thorkel, never!" he roared, even though the hermit scientist was now nowhere in sight.

Bill Stockton commanded the others to seek shelter in the cactus, and went forward to take up his scouting position near the front steps of the house. Dr. Bulfinch watched him, standing stiffly at the point where he had challenged Dr. Thorkel. Suddenly the elderly biologist started with a new fear. Bill whirled around to see Dr. Thorkel come charging out of the house with a butterfly net in his hand.

The raging scientist ignored Bill entirely, concentrating his attention on the tiny scientist who had defied him. Bulfinch felt definitely that discretion was the better part of valor, and with a single long leap jumped from the basket and ran into a crack between two camp boxes resting on the group nearby.

Thorkel began rummaging among the boxes for Bulfinch. He was holding the net ready to fling it down over the small figure of the elderly biologist. In his frantic efforts the blundering giant turned things over roughly in his search. By this time Pedro, Steve and Mary were peering fearfully out from the shelter of the cactus. Bill was behind the first step of the stairs leading into the hermit's house.

Occasionally they got a glimpse of Dr. Bulfinch as he ducked from one hiding place to another, like Theseus in the Cretan labyrinth. Thorkel's failing eyes were definitely a handicap to him in the search, and he seemed to be squinting almost constantly through the heavy lenses that were over his orbs. Finally he spotted the nimble miniature biologist and started forward.

Bulfinch was winded by the efforts he had made to elude his tormenter. His area of vision was limited by two boxes. Thorkel was straddling these boxes, and therefore the triangle between his legs gave the impression of a complete lack of menace. But the towering bulk of the mad scientist was looming over Bulfinch even before he realized it.

Bill Stockton, aware of this situation, tried to voice a warning, but the horror of the impending crisis seemed to freeze the words in his throat.

Dr. Bulfinch crouched against one of the boxes and cautiously peered through the space between them as Thorkel's head and shoulders appeared above him. The net came down with a swish before Bulfinch's face, and its mesh fold engulfed him like a dry cloud mass.

The elderly scientist wriggled inside the net, and his sharp fingers strove in vain to dig an exit under the corner of one of the boxes. Thorkel let out his breath in a gust of satisfaction, and said:

"Now you will not be so obstinate, my friend."

Realizing that his struggles would be in vain, and that his strength might be needed for another ordeal a bit later on, Dr. Rupert Bulfinch subsided and settled down in the bottom of the net.

"That is much better," approved Thorkel. "Now you are beginning to show some of your famous common sense."

Dr. Thorkel got to his feet, holding the net gingerly. He caught Bulfinch in his searching fingers, then strode back into the house.

Bill Stockton crouched down alongside the stoop, then cast an inquiring glance toward the cactus patch and the others.

Finally the group in the cactus patch summoned up enough courage to come and meet Bill Stockton. Instinctively, now that Dr. Bulfinch was gone, all seemed to turn to Bill.

"What are we going to do?" he asked.

They were now standing in the shelter of the camp table and gazing toward the house fearfully. It was obvious that they were all terribly worried about Bulfinch and his fate, but it soon became apparent that there was very little they could do.

"We might set the house on fire," volunteered Steve.

"That wouldn't do much good," Bill declared. "Thorkel could get out as soon as he smelled the smoke or saw the flames, but he might leave Bulfinch in there to burn to death."

Mary Phillips rang her hands in despair as she said: "I never felt so helpless in my life before."

Suddenly a new thought struck Bill Stockton and he turned to Pedro.

"Are there any of your people near here? If we can't fight Thorkel ourselves, maybe we can get some full-sized men to do our fighting for us."

Pedro shook his head sadly.

"Natives fear Dr. Thorkel. They run away. Government send policeman. He talk to Dr. Thorkel, nod his head, then salute grandly and go away. People in jungle can do nothing, they go down to Iquitos."

"If that's the case," Bill remarked, disappointed, "all we can do for the time being is watch and wait. I'll go ahead and take up my post on the stoop. He's left the door ajar!"

"Maybe it's a trap to lure us into the house," suggested Steve Baker.

"I don't think so," Bill insisted. "If the coast is clear, you can all come up. That hole in the wall the cat made will give us a good hiding place if we have to duck quickly."

The others nodded, and Bill Stockton hastened forward fearful of what he might see from his observation post.

CHAPTER SEVENTEEN

Bill Stockton reached his destination in time to see Dr. Thorkel cross to the table and unceremoniously dumb Dr. Bulfinch out. Then the hermit scientist dropped his net to the floor and bent over the table.

Dr. Bulfinch appeared to be stunned by the fall, and remained inert for several moments. Thorkel pulled his chair up to the table as Bulfinch regained control of his muscles and scrambled indignantly to his feet. He had lost none of his determination during the ignominious journey to the house in Thorkel's big paw.

"I warn you, I will not tolerate this outrage, Dr. Thorkel," snapped the elderly biologist.

"Calm yourself, Professor," Thorkel replied. "I'm surprised that a figure of your scientific attainments should be guilty of such emotional outbursts."

Ignoring Bulfinch for the moment, Dr. Thorkel turned to his trunk, groped about for a while in the tray of yellow paper, and began arranging his notes.

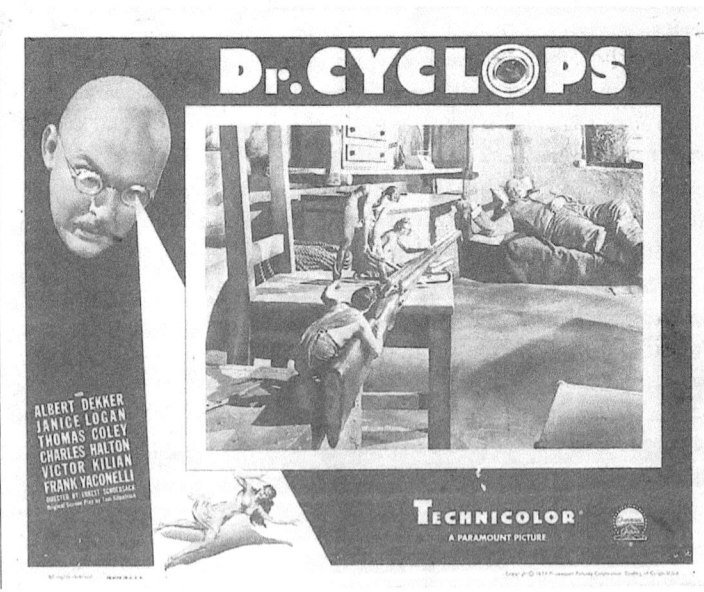

Since Dr. Thorkel had returned to his cajoling mood, Bill Stockton decided that it would be safe for the little people to come closer to the house to observe the happenings inside. He rested one arm on the round end of the scissor blade, and motioned toward the others with his other hand. Expecting them to come up immediately, he turned his attention back to the action inside the house.

It was obvious now that Dr. Thorkel was chiding Dr. Bulfinch on his earlier determination, prior to the diminution of his size.

"So you will be the one to tell the world of my work, Dr. Bulfinch?"

"Of your crimes!" stated Bulfinch emphatically.

Thorkel shook his head solemnly and replied: "You will find the world far away for legs as short as yours." Before Bulfinch realized what the scientist was doing, Thorkel stood up a ruler beside him.

"A little straighter, please," commanded the experimenter.

Bulfinch bristled indignantly, as Thorkel had expected him to do. The hermit scientist patted Bulfinch's shoulder and said:

"Ah, very good. Thank you, Doctor."

With a stubby pencil, Dr. Thorkel entered the measurement in his notebook. Bulfinch jumped up on the pan of a set of scales, so as to bring himself slightly nearer to Thorkel's face.

"Dr. Thorkel," he roared, "I demand your attention."

"Exactly fourteen and five-eighths inches," Dr. Thorkel mused. Then, without observing Bulfinch's latest action, he went on: "Now Doctor, hop on the scales."

He looked up from his notebook and realized where Dr. Bulfinch was. "Ah, thank you. I see you have anticipated my wishes."

"It certainly was not my intention," Dr. Bulfinch replied heatedly.

Dr. Thorkel was peering nearsightedly at the indicator on the scales. Even as the hermit scientist was marking down the figures and grunting with satisfaction, Dr. Bulfinch jumped off the scales again. He noticed now that Dr. Thorkel seemed greatly concerned about the weight reading. A stirring of understanding swept through him. Dr. Bulfinch could not contain himself any longer.

"So—something has gone wrong," he gloated. "You are surprised."

Thorkel shrugged, then snarled:

"Be quiet."

At the same time the hermit experimenter was consulting something in the earlier pages of his notebook, and comparing his calculations again with the reading on the scale.

Seeing that his taunts were having a marked effect on Thorkel, and overlooking the possible consequences, Bulfinch went on:

"The great mind is not infallible after all, is it?"

Dr. Thorkel picked up his pen, and indicated a point closer to himself.

"Stand here," he ordered Bulfinch.

Instead of advancing, Bulfinch backed away, shaking his head. Thorkel threw down the open and reached for the little biologist. Almost as soon as the pen left Thorkel's hand, Bulfinch snatched it up and struck Thorkel with it. The half-mad scientist jerked back his hand quickly and picked up a ruler.

He brought the ruler back in a menacing gesture, and growled threateningly: "Stand here!"

Dr. Bulfinch, now fully aroused, and determined to make a last-ditch stand, held up the pen to ward off the threat of the ruler. He realized, only too well, that this was after all a puny weapon. Still belligerent, he backed up slowly. What he did not realize was that he was backing directly into the clutches of Thorkel's left hand.

When he was finally within a few inches of the closing fingers. Dr. Thorkel grabbed him. Dr. Bulfinch wriggled for a few moments, then subsided.

The disturbed investigator, holding Dr. Bulfinch in spite of his struggles, picked up a pair of calipers and began to measure Dr. Bulfinch with great care. Bulfinch gasped and panted and struggled against Thorkel's gigantic hand, but to no avail. Even the sharp pricks of the pen no longer gave him even momentary surease.

After the calipers had supplied their own particular brand of information, Dr. Thorkel consulted his notes again, then looked at Bulfinch.

"I suppose you know what is wrong," Thorkel gritted.

He released his hold on the struggling professor long enough for him to get his breath and find his tongue.

"Of course," replied Bulfinch belligerently.

"Most unfortunate," Thorkel declared gravely.

"So you've made a mistake," Bulfinch chided.

"It is nature who is making the mistake," Dr. Thorkel replied.

Dr. Thorkel subsided. Bulfinch was glaring at him with all the fury that he could inject into his almost pin-like eyes.

"I am surprised that even you will admit that nature has a habit of undoing things that you have done."

"But you can't know what is wrong," Thorkel declared emphatically.

"I do!" Bulfinch insisted eagerly. "And later there will come a reckoning."

"I am well aware of that," Dr. Thorkel remarked. "And it is that which is most unfortunate.

The change in Thorkel's tone gave Bulfinch pause, and for a moment a wave of panic ran through him. Bill Stockton, in the doorway, also sensed the subtle difference in the mad scientist's tone. He tightened his grip on the scissor-sword. With his free hand, Dr. Thorkel drew nearer a jar of chloroform. Then he removed the cover.

"What are you going to do?" Dr. Bulfinch inquired, panic creeping into his words for the first time since the beginning of this weird adventure.

Thorkel shrugged his shoulders.

"I cannot take the chance of you and your friends interfering with my work here. That is something I can never permit."

With a pair of tweezers, Dr. Thorkel dipped a wad of cotton in the chloroform and suddenly forced Bulfinch down flat on the table.

A muffled ejaculation slipped from Bill Stockton's lips. He was afraid, for a moment, that Thorkel might have heard it, but the scientist was much too immersed in his own particular problem to worry about outside elements.

Then Bill was aware of the fact that Mary, Steve and Pedro were mounting the steps behind him. They cowered at the side of the partly opened door. It was obvious that they were still fearful of consequences, but nevertheless were driven by the necessity of discovering what was being done to Bulfinch.

"Go back," Bill Stockton called softly. "We've got to get out of here."

Mary Phillips paused uncertainly on the step below Bill. The mineralogist looked through the crack in the door. Dr. Thorkel was pressing the wad of chloroformed cotton down upon Dr. Bulfinch. A shrill yell of fear came to the ears of the four on the steps, then the cry died away in a smothered gasp.

Dr. Thorkel tightened his hold on the cotton. Bulfinch struggled and wriggled ineffectually, then suddenly ceased to struggle.

Bill Stockton shuddered. Mary was putting up her hand to pull herself onto the top step. Bill watched the scientist's facial expression. He did not doubt that Dr. Thorkel had deliberately murdered the inoffensive Bulfinch. Thorkel's face was a study on sombreness. It did not suggest any particular emotion. He was as calm about the job he had just completed as though he had been anesthetizing any other animal object of his biological experiments.

Mary was kneeling beside Bill Stockton, and she asked softly:

"What's happened to Rupert?"

Bill tightened his grip on her arm, and said slowly:

"He's dead—murdered. Thorkel's killed him."

"Oh, no!" the girl shrieked, her nerves giving way. "Oh, my God, no! What's going to become of the rest of us?"

The sound carried to Dr. Thorkel with all the directness of a thrown lance. He whirled around and glanced toward them. By this time, Pedro and Steve Baker, impelled by curiosity, had joined Mary and Bill on the top step. They had ventured enough around the corner of the door to be able to witness the last death throes of the murdered scientist. They were petrified with terror.

Thorkel cursed fluently.

"So you would spy on me?" he screamed in rage.

Then he reached for the butterfly net and started to get up. But the quartette in the doorway did not stand on the order of their going. They jumped and scrambled down the steps, and scampered across the yard.

Inside the house, Thorkel rushed around the table, pulled a chair out of the way, snatched up the specimen box which had contained Pinto, the albino horse, then lunged toward the door. Dr. Bulfinch's body lay inert under the wad of cotton. He had become perhaps one of the strangest martyrs that science would ever know.

When the first panic of their hasty retreat had worn off and they had put several yards between the door and themselves, the little people slowed their flight. Bill Stockton, now more conscious than ever of his increased responsibility, loitered behind the others as sort of a rear guard. He turned a round wooden water bucket on its side and rolled it toward the foot of the steps.

Thorkel dashed out of the house in a rage. He hesitated on the top of the steps, peering around him, but the little people were nowhere in sight. He hurried down the steps, and as he reached the bottom the wooden water bucket rolled between his legs and sent him sprawling.

Chuckles of midget laughter came to him from various parts of the compound, adding to his fury. He regained his feet, straightening the bent frame of the butterfly net, then began kicking over boxes and stirring things up in his angry search for his quarry. Presently he put down the specimen case and intensified his rough search, starting at one corner of the camp equipment and putting aside each piece carefully.

But the little people were not in that particular area. They had long since left the protection of the boxes and crates, and were now crawling under a section of tent wall. Out of the corner of his eye, Dr. Thorkel, in spite of his nearsightedness, noted the movement of the canvas, and rushed in and started to pull up the tent flap.

"General!" Bill Stockton decided that their current strategy would not assist them for long, and a brief and hasty council of was determined that the tent wall was an insufficient hiding place. They scrambled out from under it, and headed swiftly as they could toward the cactus patch.

His examination of the tent convincing him that his victims had fled, Dr. Thorkel lunged out into the broad daylight again, and glanced across the compound, squinting sharply. Finally he spotted Pedro, just ducking into the cactus.

Thorkel was only a few moments behind the miniature men and woman when they took shelter. He dashed into the cactus patch, trampling down the spiny plants with his heavy shoes. But he could not be certain that his small specimens were not under the growth he had already trampled down

He knelt in the little grove, heedless of the sharp prickly spines that tore his knees. His butterfly net was cast aside for the moment, and he rooted in the green pulp with his thorny hands. Soon they were a mass of prickles that resembled the hide of a young porcupine.

The net result of the search was nil. Bill Stockton, still "fighting" a rear-guard action, kept close watch on every step and action of the ponderous scientist. The other three had long since gone to safety.

When the cactus spines had irritated him to the full, Dr. Thorkel stamped out of the patch, snatched up a shovel and started cutting down the cactus.

Sweat popped out over his face, the boiling tropical sun was streaming down upon him. In the shadows at the corner of the wall, Bill Stockton leaned upon his scissor-sword and chuckled.

The sound was lost in the noise of Thorkel's activity.

Finally Thorkel ceased and rested his weight on the handle of the shovel. He had broken down all the major cactus stalks, and cleared and area large enough to realize that the little people were no longer there.

At one corner of the wall, behind the cactus growths, Dr. Thorkel discovered the means of their escape. It was the end of a tile drain pipe which extended under the wall. After one glance at this he realized that the little people had defeated him, for the moment at least, by scampering through the opening and into the jungle.

He straightened up and looked over the wall into the curtain of green that marched almost up to the other side of the mud boundary marker.

Bill Stockton still crouched in the darkness at the mouth of the drain pipe and watched the infuriated scientist. Thorkel raised his voice and called after the little people:

"You'd better come back. You will never live half an hour in the jungle."

He cocked his head to one side, as though awaiting an answer, but none came. There was new determination in his walk as he turned and started toward the house.

Bill Stockton gave him a head start, then darted along in his wake. They ought to have some idea of the menace that still confronted them. Back on the top step, Bill peered into the now wide-open door and saw Thorkel opening a gun case. From this he took out a shotgun. He broke the gun down, sat down on a chair and began to clean it carefully.

The miniature mineralogist beat a strategic withdrawal, ducked through the scattered camp equipment, found the drain pipe tunnel, and rejoined the balance of the party on the edge of the jungle.

"He's oiling up his shotgun," he announced promptly. "The more distance we put between us, the better it'll be."

Mary Phillips nodded. Then Steve Baker broke in.

"But what about supplies? Food and warmth, and those things? And we're due for a nice cold tropical rainstorm."

Even as he spoke, the semi-darkness of the jungle seemed to be heightened by clouds that closed in above them.

"We'll make out," Bill assured them. "Other people have been lost in the jungle without equipment. We'll have to use some of our God-given brains, and man-made experience."

"Bravo!" gritted Mary, but there was something pathetic about her effort at lightening the situation.

CHAPTER EIGHTEEN

They ran along a jungle trail until they were almost breathless. Finally they realized that they were doing nothing more than tiring themselves out. Bill Stockton brought them to a halt under a fallen log. Then he asked:

Neither Steve Baker nor Mary Phillips seemed to know. Pedro Caroz merely shrugged his shoulders. They were all gripped by the fascination of the strange natural phenomena that were taking place all about them. In the ominous quiet before the approaching storm hardly a leaf was stirring. Distant lightning flickered in the sky, and low rolls of thunder followed this at brief intervals.

From their shelter, Bill and Mary, in front of the other two, were able to glimpse a small section of shrubbery a short distance down the trail. This quivered for a moment, then bowed forward and the form of an ant-bear thrust itself through, long snout carried well down. Its lithe body followed in a burst of gray, and the animal darted across the rut of a trail, and vanished into the jungle below them.

Bill watched it as it topped a slope in the distance, only its undulating back now visible, and finally disappeared in the undergrowth.

"Whew!" whistled Mary. "I'm glad *that* didn't come our way. He might have mistaken us for a bunch of ants."

Bill laughed, then tightened his grip on Mary's sleeve, and said:

"I know we're small, but I didn't realize we were that small."

Their attention was immediately taken up by more distant lightning and thunder. Then a brighter lightning flash gleamed above them and they strained their necks out from under the fallen log. In a tree crotch above them, against a backdrop of shaking leaves, they saw a mother monkey scramble up. She was clutching the form of her baby close against her breast. The thunder boomed over the entire area like heavy field guns.

"I guess we're not the only ones getting panicky," Bill soothed his quivering companion.

Mary pointed to another object in the tree. It was a large bird flying into its nest. Bill nodded. The wind was whipping up now, and seemed to carry his words away from him almost before he had the chance to string them into sentences.

A deer bounded through the growth in back of the log, leaped the log itself, and cast a strange shadow over the four little people cowering beneath. The roar of the approaching storm increased in fury, and the wind began to whip through the trees with renewed vigor.

The mother monkey tightened her clutch on the baby, and there was a rustle in the branches above her as another monkey dropped down on the limb beside the matron.

The whole panorama in this little section of storm-tossed verdure was delineated by a bright lightning flash. A screaming parrot added its note to the abrupt symphony of sound that accompanied the wind. The trees and foliage were lashed by the driving gale. Suddenly another lightning flash brightened everything, and with a louder roar the rain arrived, driving across the jungle trail, and whipping against the trees and undergrowth with all the furor of a solid sheet.

The monkeys huddled disconsolately on the limb, their grey backs turning black and sodden in a moment. The tree tops waved and bent under the assault of the elements. The storm mounted in force and terror for the little people. Another brilliant lightning flash struck, almost cleaving the log beneath which the miniature men and woman had taken shelter.

Mary cowered closer to Bill Stockton. The young mineralogist realized that they were in imminent danger of drowning. The water was forming in puddles about them, and the rushing tide that swept along the depressed jungle trail was running close to their knees now.

Even as Bill was watching and trying to decide upon his next course of action, there was a rending crash, and the top of one of the trees above them was torn away. A stray gust of wind caught it and toppled it down before the fear-stricken eyes of the little folk.

"We've got to get out of here," Bill decided without delay.

The others did not question Bill's judgement, and a short time later they were ducking under the outflung branches of the fallen tree top, and scampering through the water on the jungle trail.

Bill halted in his headlong flight, his fingers tightening on the handle of the scissor-sword as two green orbs loomed up ahead of him on the low-growing trunk of a jungle giant. The owner of the eyes was a quivering, eight-foot jaguar that had taken shelter from the storm on the leeward side of the tree.

But the jungle denizen appeared to be an anxious to keep out of the rain as the little people were desirous of gaining some refuge, and Bill and his companions were able to detour without interruption. They were on the edge of a waterfall now, and Bill was able to orient himself. This would be the little cataract above the point where they had forded the river on their arrival at Thorkel's camp. All of that seemed so long ago. Could it be that it was only two days before?

"There's an opening in the bottom of that tree," Mary declared.

All eyes followed her pointing finger, and then the eight little feet were turned in that direction. They climbed over the sprawling roots of the tree and headed for the shelter that was offered them. Even as they were about to dart into it, however, Bill, ever cautious moved ahead. He was wet and uncomfortable, the single garment that Dr. Thorkel had left him in the dark cellar plastered to his small, yet vigorous frame like a bit of wet paper.

Finally he raised his hand and the trio behind him slid to a muddy halt. The long, curved snout of the ant-bear greeted them, and the darting tongue of the animal whipped forward as though challenging their right to his refuge.

Frightened by this second natural interruption in almost as many minutes, they fled on. Then Bill turned to Pedro and asked:

"Isn't there a cave just under the river bank, about a quarter of a mile from the ford?"

"Yes, Mr. Bill," Pedro replied emphatically, glad to be of service in this emergency.

"Then that's where we'll go," Bill decided. The others nodded in agreement, then settled themselves to battle the full power of the storm that was now closing in about them.

After almost half an hour of fighting the elements, they came to the bank above the Dave. Bill lay down on his stomach and peered over. So far as he could determine the cave was still unoccupied. He climbed down the slippery band and reconnoitered. Then he gestured for the others to follow him. Steve helped Mary down until Bill could catch her. Then he and Pedro followed.

When they were together again, they ducked back into the depths of the cave, and settled down in the darkness. It was cold there, even though the biting wetness of the storm was kept out. They took off their wringing garments and squeezed them as dry as possible. Then they busied themselves with gathering accumulated driftwood in the cave.

Bill Stockton knew more than a little about primitive forms of fire making, and not many minutes later he added the first ray of warmth to their new home when a spark lighted up in rotten tinder and a curl of smoke soon grew into burgeoning strength. Dried grasses in the back of the cave formed both beds and blankets, and the tired, worn-out miniature men and woman settled down to sleep.

The next day dawned bright and clear. Mary Phillips was the first one to awaken, and she looked down along the beam of light that entered the cave and saw the men huddled in their make-shift beds, she suddenly became conscious of her own nudity. The four toga-like garments, soaked by the storm, were hanging over the fire's still warm embers to dry.

Viewed now, they were nothing more than four of Thorkel's large handkerchiefs. She took down her garment, draped it about her, and walked toward the front of the cave. She looked out through the opening to see a brilliant morning sky. Birds were singing. The songs cheered Mary. Everything appeared to be right with the world. Inside the cave, behind her, the rest of the little people were awakening.

It was not long before they spotted Mary, and with Bill in the lead they came to join her. The bank which had been so low that the mules could easily scramble up over it when they had passed this way on the journey to Thorkel's camp was now a cliff, and the little, barely perceptible niche in it was now the cave that was sufficiently large to give them their shelter. The little people came out of the mouth of the cave and looked about them.

Still aware of the difficulties that confronted them, the Americans found it hard to accept immediately the beauty of the sunny morning, and the lush perfume that came from the jungle around them. They could not forget Thorkel and his shotgun, and the jungle beasts that had haunted their passage to this point. Pedro, however, brought up in this neighborhood, and inclined to worship the sun after rain, became articulate.

"Nice morning, eh?" he asked cheerfully.

Steve took the initiative for the other trio.

"Sure," he replied grudgingly, "but what for?"

For almost the first time since they had left Thorkel's house and the sight of the cold-blooded murder of Dr. Bulfinch, they were moved by an emotion other than fear. Bill caught Mary's arm.

"Look, Mary." He pointed. "This is that same jungle cover—remember—where we talked."

Mary nodded.

"That was a long time ago," she declared.

"Some things haven't changed," Bill insisted warmly.

"Maybe they never will," Mary replied, looking at him steadily. Instinctively they drew closer to each other and, seemingly oblivious to both Pedro and Steve, kissed each other boldly. The thrill that ran through their small bodies was nonetheless significant, and Bill tightened his grip on the miniature girl.

Finally Bill released the girl and drew away.

"It does seem rather fantastic, doesn't it? Maybe if we did decide to get married, we could pick up a nice doll's house cheap."

Mary laughed. Pedro was scanning the banks of the river above and below the cave, and finally he pointed.

"There's a canoe," he remarked.

Steve broke in on the reverie that had encompassed Bill and Mary and said:

"By George, it is. There's the dugout Pedro was talking about. Come on. She'll ride us clean out of this country."

They all started down toward the canoe, ran eagerly up to it, then recoiled in astonishment. Although it was a small canoe, its sides extended well above their heads.

Steve was the first one to put their disappointment into words.

"Kind of big, ain't she?" he averred doubtfully.

They all stared hopelessly up at the prow of the canoe towering above them. Pedro reared back, and spoke philosophically, and with a memory of what seemed to be a dim distant past.

"She was very small canoe—I paddle him—like that!"

He snapped his fingers to indicate the ease with which he had once been able to manage the craft.

"Well, now what do we do?" Bill shrugged.

Steve was equally discouraged. Mary was beyond hoping for further miracles. Her very miniature size was the kind of a modern miracle that was enough to amaze her for a long time to come.

"Anything you say is okay with me, Bill," Steve remarked. "Just so long's we stay away from that screwball doctor."

On the opposite bank there was a movement in the underbrush and all four pairs of eyes suddenly whirled in that direction. A small albino horse was coming down to drink at the stream. Pedro whirled to look toward it with the rest. His mouth dropped open in surprise.

"That's my Pinto," he cried.

Bill watched the drinking beast, then patted Pedro on the shoulder and said:

"Maybe it *looks* like Pinto, but it isn't."

"How can you say so?" Pedro demanded.

"Well," Bill pointed out, "it's a cinch that Dr. Thorkel never got that thing into his butterfly net."

The Peruvian looked at the horse again, nodded his head in agreement, then remarked:

"You are very right, Mr. Bill. It could not be Pinto."

Mary Phillips was standing alongside Bill, her hands on her hips. She was still looking at the broad side of the canoe, and one of her little feet kicked out in exasperation. She bit her lip as her unshod toes struck the wood.

"We can't go on like this—" she insisted—being afraid of everything. This canoe's our only chance to get away from here. We've got to do something about it."

Bill and Steve looked at her with the patronizing superiority common to men when confronted by a practical suggestion from a woman. But Pedro's Latin soul too fire at once.

"I will push it off at once, by myself," he told Mary enthusiastically. He leaped to the prow of the canoe and began shoving valiantly against it. It was exactly like the old-time chore of trying to move a mountain.

Finally the courageous native relaxed sadly, moaned bitterly:

"She is very big."

"It may be big," Mary admitted, "but men have launched big liners without any difficulty." She turned on Bill and resumed: "You're supposed to be an engineer. There must be some way to get the boat into the water."

"You're supposed to be a scientist," Bill retorted. "What do you suggest?"

Mary went on impatiently: "People move houses—lots of heavy things . . . Don't you use levers—and windlesses?"

A beam of pleasure crossed Bill's face. He reared back and broke into peals of laughter, then patted Steve on the shoulder and said:

"I hate to have to admit it, but she's on the right track."

After this momentous decision the entire group immediately dissolved into furious, yet directed action. It was decided that Mary would go back to camp and start to round up something in the way of breakfast. While they were searching for firewood the miniature pioneers discovered a number of edible roots and herbs that made a very filling broth when heated with the pure water of a nearby spring.

Then Bill, Pedro and Steve scattered along the edge of the jungle and tore great strips of plant fiber from the giant trees and plants. Lianas were uprooted or cut off with the scissor-sword and carried to the gathering place. When they decided they had enough raw material, the three men squatted down on the haunches like fairy tailors, and began weaving the plant fiber into ropes.

This process took most of the morning. But finally, when the sun was reaching the meridian, they were ready for the task they had assigned themselves. They proceeded to the prow of the canoe and Bill Stockton clambered up the side of the dugout after a boost from the combined hands of Steve and Pedro.

A heavy piece of driftwood had been sharpened and set in a hollowed stone for use as a windlass. At the very prow of the canoe Bill was working with a long piece of bamboo as a lever. Straining hard, they were able to move the dugout, and let out a yell of triumph.

Bill called to Mary, where she was busy at the fire:

"Hey, Mary, look!"

Mary was cooking over a camp fire which was built on the ledge immediately in front of the cave.

"Wonderful," she replied. "How far?"

"Moved nearly an inch," Steve supplied, after examining the gain with practiced eye.

"When you've made another inch, you can have your dinner."

Back at the canoe, the three miniature mariners went to work with a will. They made another big effort. This time the dugout began to quiver a bit, then moved downward slowly.

Out on the surface of the water they were suddenly menaced by a new threat, but for the moment they were ignorant of its presence. A crocodile rose to the surface of the river, apparently disturbed by the rolling of the water and the sounds of voices. Only its eyes and snout were visible as it moved slowly forward in the water of the river near the beach.

Again the three men exerted their full strength on their lever and windlass outfit. The canoe budged again. Pedro suddenly felt in a boastful mood, and called to Mary:

"We'll make two inch or never eat."

His words were freighted with truth, even though he did not know it. For the gliding approach of the crocodile definitely indicated that two inches or no inches, the three at the dugout would never eat again. The crocodile's head, still only a tip of snout and rounded eyes, slowly approached the three men. Their very freedom of action gave evidence of the fact that they were unaware of their danger.

Mary stopped her cooking long enough to glance down at them. She sniffed once, then said:

"Why, I can see it move from here."

Now the crocodile was able to move its short legs on the sandy bottom of the river. Its scaly sides and back thrust above the surface of the water. Still the three men went on working, unaware of the approaching danger. This time the canoe made considerable headway. Bill whistled gaily, Steve laughed aloud, and Pedro thanked the Peruvian gods.

"We've got her on the run now," Steve declared.

Even as he spoke, there was a rush of water as the crocodile swished through the shallows and reached the edge of the river bank.

Mary heard the sound first. She looked up and saw the saurian. Immediately she roared a piercing scream.

"Crocodile!" she shouted.

Distracted by the shout, the crocodile turned toward her and its mouth opened lazily, exhibiting all its cruel, tearing teeth. This interruption gave the three men a chance for their lives. They fled up the ledge to the cave just in time.

Robbed of its prey by Mary's shout, the crocodile turned toward her and its mouth opened lazily, exhibiting all its cruel, tearing teeth. This interruption gave the three men a chance for their lives. They fled up the ledge to the cave just in time.

Robbed of its prey by Mary's shout, the crocodile followed the three men to the foot of the cliff just under the cave. Bill Stockton turned and looked down into the red, beady eyes of the animal. They had come to a ludicrous impasse. The little people were on the ledge in front of the cave, the crocodile in the foreground just below them.

"Fine company to have—" snorted Steve— "just when everything was rolling nicely."

Realizing that they would have to get rid of their unwelcome intruder before they could hope to head down the river, the four little people on the ledge began throwing rocks down on the crocodile. Apparently the saurian was willing to wait for them to exhaust their strength. He remained immovable. Bill angrily snatched up a brand from the dying campfire to drop on the crocodile. Then he got a better idea.

"Wish we had more wood," he remarked.

Steve pointed toward the woodpile they had so laboriously collected. At the moment it was just below them at the foot of the cliff and between the crocodile's hind legs.

"Help yourself," remarked the mule owner. "There's the woodpile."

Bill ignored Steve's sally and turned to Mary.

"Got any bright ideas about this?"

Mary's mind was working rapidly. She carefully surveyed the distance from the woodpile to the crocodile's head. Then she replied: "Do you think you might go after the wood if I keep his attention focussed this way?"

She illustrated her idea by bending down over the crocodile's head and waving her arms at him.

"Sister," Bill declared pleasantly, "I'm beginning to admire that scientific mind of yours."

Steve and Pedro were watching the young couple with bated breath. Mary started to climb down the cliff at a point above the crocodile's head, by clinging onto a trailing vine. With Bill in the lead, the three men started down the ledge which led to the wood pile at the crocodile's hind legs.

"Not too far," Bill called back.

"Get the wood," Mary retorted sharply.

Mary continued sliding down the vine until she was close to the crocodile's head. There she waved her arms and yelled at him to hold his attention. The crocodile opened its mouth and attempted to reach her.

The flanking movement of the male trio was moving along successfully, and, taking advantage of Mary's distraction of the saurian, they made a final dash down to their wood pile which was right beside the crocodile's hind quarters. Once there they grabbed up armfuls of the sticks and scrambled back in the direction of the campfire on the ledge.

With this maneuver successfully carried out, Mary started mounting the vine hand over hand, and a few moments later was beside the others at the fire. The men threw their sticks of wood on the fire, and since they were all rather small, the began burning at once. Bill then hastened to the edge of the ledge to help Mary back over the outcropping of rock that lined their bulwark.

As he pulled her to her feet, he offered his hand.

"Shake," he invited.

"Don't mind if I do," she replied. They shook hands. Then they turned their attention to the fire, now and then casting a glance in the direction of the crocodile which still maintained its dangerous vigil below them. The fire was burning well now, and, using longer sticks as pokers, the little people pushed the burning fire to the very edge of the ledge.

"This has to be just right," Bill cautioned, "because we won't have enough wood to try again."

The others nodded in agreement. The burning embers were confined to a small area at the lip of the bank; then Bill said:

"Righto. Now let him have it."

The four poking midgets shoved the fire over the edge of the bank onto the head of the crocodile. As the fire struck him, the saurian turned and made off. The little people breathed their relief and shouted their victory with a grim yell of triumph. It was echoed by the splash of water as the crocodile took to the water and swam rapidly away.

With this menace removed, their thoughts immediately returned to the dugout, but they did not go back to work until Mary had served piping hot portions of her broth to the workers.

CHAPTER NINETEEN

With the inner man and woman fortified, and emboldened by their victory over something a hundred times their size, it was a vastly different company that set about the chore of providing themselves with a means of escape. For the first time they seemed to see real hoe in the future. Like mankind since the beginning of time, they began talking about the big things they could do.

Steve cast a derisive glance in the direction the crocodile had taken and declared: "That croc wasn't so tough."

"Sure not," agreed Pedro. "He never came back."

Bill leaned on the lever he had been using, and stared up speculatively at the canoe.

"Do you know what I think? he offered. "I think when we get her launched we'd better rig up a sail. With a sail and a rudder we can go anywhere."

Even the usually sardonic Steve was carried away by enthusiasm.

"I'll tell you what I think, he broke in. "These joints of bamboo we're been using for rollers, they're plenty hard. You cover them with clay and bake it, and it would do for a boiler. I'll bet we could make a low-pressure steam engine—and with a paddle-wheel—"

Both Bill and Pedro nodded as though Steve's suggestion were not only a good one, but one that was immediately workable. They were brought up short in their plans by the sudden sound of a barking dog. The wave of enthusiasm that had engulfed them was suddenly swept away by fear.

Bill Stockton dropped his lever and hurried up the jungle trail leading to Thorkel's camp. Steve and Pedro headed for the cave, where Mary joined them, and they prepared for hasty flight.

Finally Bill came upon Dr. Thorkel. He was proceeding through the jungle. He had Pedro's dog, Paco, on a leash. He was carrying the specimen case by a strap over one shoulder. In his other hand he gripped the shotgun. His soothing words to the dog were intended as encouragement to the animal to pick up the scent of its master. He was obviously hunting his little enemies as if they were so many rabbits.

The miniature mining engineer gritted his teeth.

He watched Thorkel, but obviously the scientist did not immediately sense that his quarry was hiding in the cave under the river bank. The mad doctor was waist-deep in the shrubbery, and at such a distance could not possibly have seen or heard them.

But Paco, the dog, was a different proposition. He was straining at the leash and attempting to bring Dr. Thorkel back to the river trail. The doctor was not long in sensing that Paco was near his prey. He leaned down, unleashed the dog, and, as the animal darted away, Thorkel swung his gun around at the ready.

Bill Stockton beat a hasty retreat to join his friends, while Paco began to circle excitedly through the jungle grass, following the trail that the quartette had made through the rain-washed earth. Back on the ledge, Bill soon learned that the little people's first impulse was to hide in the back of the cave. Pedro immediately spotted the weakness in this.

"No, no," he pointed out. "My dog—he follow us."

Bill nodded agreement, took Mary by the hand, and they started to run the other way. Just beyond the prow of the canoe they ran into a patch of grass and small shrubs. Once they were under cover they looked back at their temporary paradise. It had meant so much to them, and now would be a mere figment of a dream.

They scanned the cove, the canoe in position, almost ready to be launched, the semicircular bank, the jungle above the bank, the expanse of sand beach, and the small patch of grass and shrubs in the middle of it.

Thorkel looked on the skyline like a veritable Cyclops of Grecian lore. His gun was held before him, his finer on the trigger ready to shoot. The dog, barking excitedly, came out of the jungle, jumped down the bank to the beach and began sniffing and circling around in the open for a second.

At the sight of Paco, the little people crouched down terrified in their hiding place in the grass; then, gaining a new grip on their courage, and forced by circumstances, they beat a hasty retreat into the tangled roots of the undergrowth.

Thorkel was so close to them that his towering shadow almost shaded them from the afternoon sun. He was alert and ready, waiting for the dog to lead him to his quarry.

Paco soon sensed that Pedro and the others were in the patch of grass, and not knowing that he was betraying his beloved master, he began barking with renewed excitement. Dr. Thorkel understood the meaning of the sustained outburst, and he started forward.

As the gargantuan menace approached them, the little people crawled fearfully away. Paco continued his barking, half afraid, half delighted. He was close to Pedro now, and the four miniature men and woman silently tried to shoo him away.

Pedro whispered:

"*Fuera. Fuera.*"

The faithful hound only wagged its tail and barked more excitedly. Pedro made a momentous decision. He was ready to make the supreme sacrifice for his new-found friends.

"You stay here," he said. "Paco—he will follow me."

Bill Stockton hurried toward the brave little Peruvian and tried to stop him. But before he could reach the fellow, Pedro had gestured to the dog and was hurrying off into the jungle. At the same time, Dr. Thorkel forced his way through the jungle growth toward the beach. He halted for a moment as though to spot the direction of the dog's barking.

The dog hesitated, whined a bit, then started running through the patch of grass and away from the canoe. He was following the diminutive Pedro as the latter darted in and out among the hummocks of green and yellow. Paco followed at a slower pace, but in the same direction.

Thorkel came out of the jungle and stood at the top of the bank, looking after the dog which had run to the edge of the river and was now climbing a slope some distance off. Pedro, still under cover, was leading the way toward a jutting headland above the miniature cataract the little people had skirted on the previous evening.

Finally Paco slid to a halt, sat down, and looked upward as though very pleased. Pedro had taken refuge in a crevice at the top of the high bank. Down in the grass roots, Bill, Mary and Steve were watching the success of Pedro's effort to decoy Dr. Thorkel away from them.

Now the Peruvian was looking back not at the dog, but in the direction of

Thorkel. At the same time the doctor was having some difficulty in negotiating the embankment that had provided shelter for the little people. He sat down and slid down the low bank to the beach, intending to follow the dog. As he did so, something immediately in front of him attracted his attention.

He took one or two slow steps past the prow of the canoe, then his attention fixed on the patch of grass. Some of the blades were trampled down, and the bending tips of these provided a fairly clear trail that led to the hiding place of the trio.

Bill Stockton and his companions were aware of this, and they immediately turned to scuttle deeper into the undergrowth. Pedro was also aware of the danger to his friends, and was horrified to see that, in spite of his strategy, Dr. Thorkel was about to discover his fellow. He stepped out of the crevice in full sight of the mad scientist and yelled:

"Paco! *Fuera.*"

Dr. Thorkel stiffened at the sound. He turned around quickly. With Pedro clearly delineated against the skyline in the crevice at the top of the high point on the cliff, he could not help but see the servant. The Peruvian was directly over the water, as though poised for a high dive. Thorkel raised his shotgun.

Down in the grass Mary covered her eyes with her arm. Bill Stockton rang his hands at his own helplessness. Steve Baker cursed softly. The was a dull roar that beat at the eardrums of the three hidden midgets. Their glances followed the pointing gun in the direction of the courageous native.

Both Pedro's hands went up to his chest, which even though small had been flown to bits by the pattern of shot. He reeled for a moment at the edge of the precipice, then fell backward toward the water. There was a flash as he struck the river's surface, then ruddy spots of widening patches marked the point where Pedro sank to the bottom. Thrashing up and down the river indicated that the crocodiles had smelled the freshly spilled blood, and were coming to take advantage of the feast that had been so recently denied one of their number.

Dr. Thorkel, much pleased with his marksmanship, lowered his gun and began to reload it methodically. Paco was most disturbed by the chain of events. He whined, then jumped into the water and began to swim away after his master.

The remaining three little people cowered in the grass, overwhelmed by the horror of what they had witnessed. Having disposed of one of them, Thorkel began looking around for the survivors. He knew that his voice alone would send panic flooding through them, so he called:

"I know you are here. You might was well come out now and save me the trouble of finding you."

He swung the specimen case off his shoulders, dropped it at the edge of the patch of grass and stepped to the canoe. Contemptuously he kicked it into the water and it started drifting away. The finale to their efforts to launch the dugout left the little people deeply shaken.

Convinced that his quarry was hiding in the patch of grass, Dr. Thorkel began kicking around among the roots looking for them.

"So you are determined to hide from me, are you?" he asked.

There was no response. But Thorkel had his next move all figured out, and it was terrifying enough to shake the hearts of people much more inured to hardship than were Bill, Mary and Steve. Dr. Thorkel was taking a metal container of matches from his jacket pocket. He poured several matches into his hand, then knelt down. He struck one of the matches and set fire to the grass at the opposite side of the patch from where he had left his specimen case. Although the grass could not have been more than twenty yards across, the sound of the fire racing through the sun-dried blades was as menacing to the midgets as a prairie fire in the American Middle West. The embers that rose and danced toward them threatened to burn their quivering flesh. The smoke that hung over everything caught in their nostrils, and Bill, Mary and Steve began coughing.

As Thorkel watched the little grass fire get under way, he raised his gun, ready to shoot the little people when they were smoked out.

Bill held Mary by the hand and started to run through the grass. Steve was hanging on their very heels. Suddenly a huge object loomed above them. It was Thorkel's specimen case.

"We'll put one over on the old boy," he declared with a chuckle. "This is going to be an ideal hiding place."

He jumped up on a stone beside the case, waving for the others to join him. Then Bill pried the lid open with his scissor-blade cutlass and they crawled into it to hide.

There were screenlike ventilators on the sides and ends of the specimen case, and the little people who knelt inside were able to get a gnat's-eye view of their surroundings. Dr. Thorkel looked like a weird devil in the midst of his fiery empire

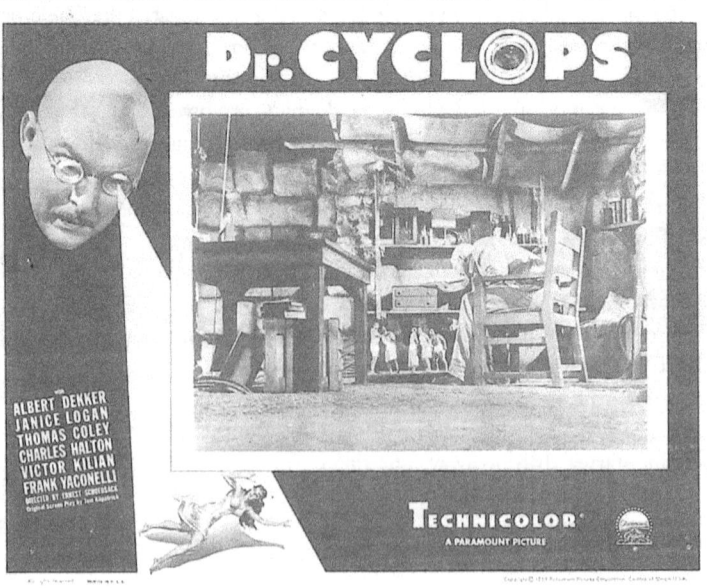

as he crouched behind the smoke and flames that crept through the grass. With the fire consuming practical half of the patch of grass, the crazed scientist, with two recent murders on his conscience, and nothing to prevent his continuing his career of crime, noticed his specimen case and hastened to pick it up.

He then seated himself on the edge of the bank with the case in his lap and watched the burning glade. His gun was ready, as he fully expected the grass fire to drive his prey out into the open. Taunting phrases were dripping from his screwed-up lips, and his squinting eyes were narrowed with savage expectancy.

Bill, Mary and Steve relished the grim humor of the situation. They found it difficult to forestall fits of coughing induced by the smoke that billowed all about them, but somehow managed to conceal their new hiding place.

Now that they were up above the grass and away from the fire, the partial lighting that came to them from the ventilating openings covered with copper wire gave them a broader view of their surroundings. The little people were still tense with terror, since they well realized that in taking refuge in Thorkel's specimen case they had by no means found a place of complete safety.

Finally when the grass had burned down to a hot smoldering mass, Dr. Thorkel cursed savagely and muttered:

"I hope they've been burned to death. It would serve them right. It cheats Santanas out of a meal, but relieves me of a difficult situation. I'll rake for their bones in the morning when the ground is cool.

CHAPTER TWENTY

The tropical night closed in abruptly. The day had indeed been a long one in the lives of the three survivors of the experiment of Dr. Thorkel. As they looked back over the past daylight hours, it did not seem that three small humans could have endured the fear, trembling, and downright sweating effort that had gone into the cooking of their meals, the attempted launching of the dugout, the fight with the crocodile, and the flight from Thorkel's forest fire—not to mention the horrible witnessing of the murder of Pedro Caroz.

Now they had to steel themselves for a renewal of their conflict with Alexander Thorkel, and again they would find themselves in his house, with the problem of escape made doubly difficult.

The three miniature men and woman were jounced about as Dr. Thorkel made his way through the jungle trail, crossed the narrow open stretch outside the compound and then traversed the yard itself. Inside the house he turned on a light, laid the shotgun on a chair and put the specimen case on the table.

The realization that their place of refuge in the specimen case had brought them right back into Thorkel's headquarters was received with mixed feelings. Steve Baker was resigned to anything that might happen to him. He could not decide in his own mind, whether he preferred a chloroform murder such as had been Bulfinch's lot, or a shattering blast of the shotgun such as had killed Pedro.

Mary had sluffed off much of her scientific veneer and was now a woman, even though a little woman, depending upon her man for succor and surcease. Bill Stockton appeared to take on new stature with the assumption of double responsibility and even though less than a foot and a half tall, was undoubtedly the personification of the rugged wild man defending his mate and his household gods.

Momentarily Bill was expecting Dr. Thorkel to open the specimen case, and then they would be helpless against his will. Since there was nothing else in the case, however, the chances of the doctor opening it immediately seemed rather remote. They were all glued to the copper mesh openings, and thus were able to cover most of the room in their inspection. Whispered reports went from one observation point to the other.

Bill Stockton watched while Dr. Thorkel went to the cupboard and took out some food. This he carried to one corner of the table. His refreshment was of the pickup variety and consisted chiefly of some rather hard bread and native vegetables.

As the doctor approached the table, all three of the little people clustered about Bill's loophole, Mary pressing her small form against him and sending electric thrills up and down his scantily clad spine.

Finally Dr. Thorkel laid his food down on the edge of the table, kicked up a chair and settled on it. While still eating with one hand, he pulled a notebook toward him and began to make an entry in it. Undoubtedly it had to do with his observations and his activities of the afternoon, with a presumption as to the fate of his several human specimens.

Bill, Mary and Steve cowered down when they discovered that the specimen case was resting on one corner of the notebook. Dr. Thorkel gave the case a shove, and the three miniature occupants were thrown over backwards inside. They climbed to their knees. Bill lifting his head to the grille and looking out. Thorkel's face was less than sixteen inches away, one heavy-glassed eye shining with all the light and movement of a real Cyclops' orb.

It seemed inevitable that the mad scientist would discover the mineralogist through the mesh. But Thorkel was not expecting to find anything inside the specimen case, so therefore did not look at it very closely. Having made his entry in the notebook, he started to look for something on the table top.

Finally he drew an earthen dish toward him, picked up a bit of meat that rested on it, and began biting at it with all the enthusiasm of a wild animal. With the meat half in and half out of his mouth, Thorkel continued his search for something on the table. Finally he took the unchewed meat from his mouth, laid it down, and then began searching the table with both hands.

Bill Stockton and his comrades felt a wave of defeat when Thorkel lifted the case to look under it. Now, surely, they would be discovered. But no, he slammed the case down hard in a fit of temper, and continued his trip further. Again they scrambled to hands and knees, looked at each other over for bruises or broken bones, then resumed their vigil at the outlet facing the scientist.

Several minutes later the mad scientist gave up his search. Something more important had come up, apparently. Mary was looking out of one end of the case, and at a whispered comment from her, Bill and Steve joined her. They saw Thorkel cross and look at the indicator above the switches beside the radium chamber door. Whatever the dial told him, he seemed rather disturbed, and almost immediately he crossed to the back door, switched on the floodlight and went out, leaving the door ajar.

"Now's our chance," Bill cried. "It takes him about fifteen minutes to get that contraption up out of the mine, to make his adjustments and then lower it again."

Mary and Steve nodded, then pressed against the lid of the case. But with the books on top of them, they were not strong enough to lift it. After a brief rest that consumed valuable seconds of their available time, they made another attempt to raise the lid, but it was soon obvious that their efforts were in vain.

While Mary took up her position at the mesh, watching Thorkel through the open door, Steve and Bill held a council of war. Mary saw the scientist at the top of the shaft. He went to the windlass and began to raise the "concentrator."

After a third and final attempt to dislodge the books, with only slight success, Bill said:

"We'll have to try the ventilators." Steve and Mary nodded emphatically.

Bill picked up the scissor-sword from the bottom of the case and attacked the copper netting vigorously. Mary went back to her scouting loophole while Bill's improvised took hacked and sawed away at the mesh.

"Hurry, hurry Bill," she mumbled.

Bill laughed pleasantly, and then, with a final jab of the scissor point, called: "Come on. We've got it."

Mary turned to see a hole in the mesh big enough for them to get out. She was the first one to wriggle through. Bill and Steve followed her. Outside the creak of the wooden windlass was sufficient to appraise them of the fact that Dr. Thorkel was still occupied with his task.

Moment later the trio was jumping from the table to the seat of Thorkel's chair, and from there to the floor. Then they went to the mine yard door which Thorkel had left ajar.

Steve and Mary evidently planned to make their escape into the compound, but Bill lingered behind. Mary turned toward him and whispered:

"Come on, Bill. Let's get out of here before he comes back."

While Mary was arguing with Bill, Steve was keeping watch in the direction of the mine shaft. He gestured toward Bill, urging him to come on.

"Now's our chance," Steve added to Mary's whispered remarks.

Bill shook his head emphatically. Mary and Steve turned back toward him.

"What's the matter with you?" Steve queried.

"Dr. Bulfinch and Pedro—they stopped running, didn't they? Well—here's where I stop," Bill insisted.

"What are you gonna do?" Steve inquired

Bill looked at the mule owner, then replied stubbornly:

"I don't know yet, but I'm staying right here."

Steve shook his head, turned to Mary, and began pointing to his forehead, convinced that Bill Stockton had gone crazy on account of the series of nerve-wracking incidents through which they had gone. Strangely enough, Mary did not agree with Steve. Instead she was staring admiringly at Bill.

"I'm going to kill him—somehow." Bill shook his fist in the direction of the mine yard. "Anyway, I'm through running." Then he suddenly remembered Mary and the fact that she would be left alone with Steve. Instead of permitting this to dissuade him, he turned to Steve and said: "Take good care of her, Steve."

Instead of thanking him for this attention, Mary Phillips had her own ideas about the matter.

"You can do that yourself Bill," she told him. "Because I'm staying right here with you."

She left Steve Baker's side and came to take up a position at Bill's shoulder. Steve looked from one to the other. Then he shrugged with sold-blooded resignation and said:

"You don't suppose I'm gonna wander away alone, do you? Not at my size."

Even as the last of the trio thus swore fealty to the others, the sound of the windlass outside ceased. Apparently Dr. Thorkel had completed his adjustments to the "concentrator" and was lowering it again.

"What do we do first?" Steve inquired. Mary was looking at Bill as though he were, in truth, "her hero."

Stockton was standing in the center of the room, surveying his surroundings. His hands were poised on his hips, and he was taking in every possibility. Suddenly he whistled softly, turned to the others and declared:

"I think I've got it." He pointed toward the shotgun.

It was resting across the seat of one of the chairs where Dr. Thorkel had dropped it, Its muzzle pointing in the general direction of the mad scientist's cot. Bill Stockton headed for the chair in question, reached up to one of the cross-pieces, scrambled up, and finally clambered onto the seat.

He approached the long, shining metal of the gun barrel, looked at it carefully, then drew his scissor-saber out of an improvised rope belt around his middle. He used the cutlass as a lever to move the gun barrel. Steve and Mary were beside him now.

"Get up on the table, and get me some of those books," Bill commanded hastily.

Steve followed instructions, and as he handed the books to Bill, the latter thrust them under the rifle barrel as a wedge. Mary pushed and tugged at the rifle barrel, and watched it move slowly into line. At a nod from Bill Stockton, Steve came back to the chair seat, and stood by to lend further assistance.

"Now sight it, will you?" Bill asked.

"What at?" Steve wanted to know.

"His pillow," returned the mining engineer.

Steve ran along the shotgun barrel, climbed over the trigger, and then, balancing precariously on the top of the stock, looked along the barrel. Bill and Mary stood on either side of the barrel, both leaning over. The attitude of the three miniature people resembled that of ancient warriors laying a pygmy siege gun on a formidable target.

Steve Baker was signalling with his right hand or left hand while Bill Stockton pried with his lever and Mary, using one of the books as a wedge, kept the gun barrel in each new position.

"Up a little—a little more," Steve Baker called. "Now a hair's-breadth to the right . . . Say, Bill," he finally demanded, "what makes you think he'll go to bed when he comes in?"

Bill was panting with his own strenuous effort with the scissor blade, but he managed: "Remember how tired he looked? Well, he's plenty sleepy. That ought to be enough."

"Hope you're right," Steve responded. "Hold it—there we are. Right on his left ear!"

With the hardest part of their artillery job accomplished, the three plotters again looked through the doorway toward their giant adversary. Dr. Thorkel was tying the handle of the windlass with a small piece of rope. This accomplished, he sighed deeply, then started toward the house.

As Steve watched the plodding advance of the giant, Bill was carefully attaching a piece of thread to the trigger of the shotgun. He tested it carefully, watching the hammer as it rose slowly under the pull from his strong little arms. Then Bill and Mary both took hold of the thread, moved to the edge of the seat and dropped to the floor. Their bare feet had no more than touched the flooring before they were moving into a corner, unwinding the thread behind them.

Steve had taken up his vigil in back of a rack of test tubes. Here he was in excellent position as an observer, being able to watch Thorkel as he entered the house and crossed the room to the cot. When the mad scientist lay down to rest, Steve would signal and Bill and Mary would pull the trigger.

The floor shook with the vibration as Dr. Thorkel counted the back steps, stepped into the room and halted just inside the door. He took off his hat and coat and hung them on a hook beside the door. From their several vantage points the little people watched him intently.

Apparently content with his operations in the mine yard, Dr. Thorkel stalked across the room, sat down on the edge of the bed, then brought one of his beefy hands to his mouth and stifled a yawn. Bill Stockton had properly analyzed the scientist's feelings. He was tired after his day's labors, and obviously not accustomed to threshing about in the jungle.

There was a loud thump as Thorkel too off one boot and dropped it to the floor. A few moments later the second one joined the first. Instinctively Bill and Mary tightened their grip on the improvised lanyard.

Excitement gripped Steve Baker, too, and his hand came up over his head in the first movement of the signal that would see the end of their gigantic enemy. Bill and Mary watched his every movement. Mary was shivering with excitement, and Bill's free hand rested on her arm in an effort to calm her.

The string was taut where it went to the chair, around the bottom of the leg and up to the shotgun trigger. The couple was impatient for the trigger, but with only one charge in the gun they could not afford to waste their bullets.

Dr. Thorkel stirred at the other end of the room. There was no question about his being very sleepy. With a creaking of the springs on the cot, he began to settle himself back for his last nap. Steve's arm came down slowly in the signal as Dr. Thorkel lay back on the pillow.

Their nerves almost snapping with tenseness of the moment, Bill and Mary exerted their full strength on the thread. Then Steve began waving his arms frantically in an abrupt negative. Bill and Mary relaxed.

With his shoulders almost touching the mattress, and his head just above the pillow, Dr. Thorkel suddenly changed his mind. He sat up again, stuck his feet into a pair of straw sandals pointing out from under the cot and rose to his feet.

The trio of miniature folks remained almost breathless as they watched Dr. Thorkel move toward the table-desk. Steve Baker, closest to the prowling scientist, was attempting to pantomime Thorkel's actions to Bill so that the mining engineer would understand what was going on. But the suspense was too much for the young couple on the lanyard. They moved out of concealment so that they, too, could see what was going on.

They made a slight sound, and Thorkel, hearing the noise in the otherwise silent room, looked up from his study of something on the table. Bill, Mary and Steve shrank back cautiously.

Thorkel decided that his overwrought imagination was getting the better of his, and returned his attention to his notebook. Again the demands of sleep wrestled with his will to go on with his experiments, and his bald head began to nod.

Bill hugged Mary at sight of this hopeful sign. Surely the doctor would return to his cot to resume his interrupted nap. Steve beamed on the lovers, echoing their own feelings in the matter.

But Dr. Thorkel seemed to have other ideas. Yielding to his drowsiness, he took off his glasses and slumped down in his chair. It was obvious that he was going to go to sleep right at the table.

When the slow gasps of the mad scientist gave way to regular breathing, then resolved themselves into jerky snores, the little people realized that their first bit of strategy had come to nought. They held a council of was in pantomime, replete with gestures. Their first plan was to shift the shotgun to this new range so that they might attempt a shot at Thorkel.

As they strove to put this plan into effect, it was soon apparent that it would require more strength than they were able to muster. Realizing that they could not hope to swing the gun around in order to shoot Thorkel in his new position, they must need to adopt a new course of action.

"He's blind as a bat without his spectacles," May opined, "that ought to prevent him from seeing us in this room."

"Right," agreed Steve emphatically.

They got behind the tray that held the glasses, and the combined efforts of the three little people were enough to slide it to the edge of the table. Then Mary took up her position on an empty chair, while Steve slid down the chair leg to the floor. With this sort of a human chain. Bill handed the glasses to Mary, and she lowered them to Steve.

Each pair of glasses was then dragged across the floor and thrust out of sight into a hole between two of the rotted boards. When they had successfully disposed of the extra glasses, Bill said:

"He's still got the ones he's been wearing. We've got to get hold of them.

This was much too bold a course of action for Mary, however, and she realized the dangerousness of the mission upon which Bill was About to embark, she grabbed him frenziedly and said:

"No, Bill. You can't do that. I'm not going to let you.

"It's too late for you to stop me now," he said gently.

She held tight to him with clutching fingers, But Bill took hold of her hands, pulled away from her, then started across the table top.

Now Dr. Thorkel had both arms sprawled on the table, his bald head resting on his right forearm. He was sound asleep. The doctor's left hand was dangling over the table, loosely holding the glasses. Bill crawled to the edge of the table, leaned over and reached down to clasp the frames of the heavy spectacles. He soon discovered that he was going to be able to reach them in this way. Next he lowered himself to the chair seat alongside Thorkel's hunched figure. Here it was an easy task to reach out and grip the glasses.

But even as he was about to lunge for the specs, Thorkel stirred fitfully, and drew his hand up onto the table. Bill was about to curse wildly, but restrained himself in time. Then he was clambering back onto the table. On the table top again, Bill moved over to the bulk of the specimen box, cautiously peering around the corner until he was looking into Thorkel's closed eyes.

The scientist's outstretched hand was clutching the glasses. Bill Stockton looked toward Mary and Steve and smiled. Mary's face was drawn, her attitude strained. Bill must succeed now, so much of his future happiness depended upon it. He strutted forward boldly, keeping his eye upon the closed orbs of his giant adversary.

Mary and Steve watched with bated breath. Finally Bill was beside the glasses, and closed both hands gently around the frame of the spectacles. Then with a quick backward lunge he attempted to wrest the glasses from Thorkel's hand without arousing him. The doctor stirred uneasily.

As Thorkel began to awaken, Bill jerked the glasses out of his hand and ran to the edge of the table. Then, suddenly changing his mind, he scampered behind the collecting box. Dr. Alexander Thorkel awoke abruptly. He blinked, brought up his other hand, examined both of them as though he was seeing things. Then, with both hands he began feeling on the table before him for his glasses.

Bill Stockton watched the antics of the half blind scientist from behind the specimen case at the edge of the table. Then he leaned far out toward Mary and Steve and dropped the glasses to the floor. Steve Baker made a frantic effort to catch them as they fell, but was unsuccessful in his attempt.

Dr. Thorkel heard the glasses hit the floor, cut could not immediately locate the sound. He continued his search on the table, half rose and began fumbling toward the box behind which Bill was hiding.

Mary watched these movements with fright and, losing her nerve because of her fear for Bill, shouted:

"Jump, Bill! Jump!"

Bill swung over the edge of the table, hung by his hands on the table edge and let go. He landed on the floor beside the glasses, jumped up and ran to cover beside Mary and Steve.

Now, however, Dr. Thorkel was rising slowly to his feet. He realized, after hearing Mary's shout, that the little people were in the room with him. He was frantic with rage, but at the same time his quivering hands and knees showed that he was also possessed of a growing fear. These little creatures of his had become real handmaidens of Tantalus, and he felt much like the lion that is afraid of the rat, or the elephant that expects the little mouse to run up his trunk, and smother him to death.

His scientific mind told him that smart little people were likely to be more difficult than rats.

"So my fire didn't get you!" Thorkel roared. "So you've come back! So you are here!"

Anxious to cut off their escape, Dr. Thorkel stumbled across the room to the back door. He closed it, turned and rested his back against it. This movement on the part of their giant enemy was quite unexpected.

Bill Stockton's shoulders lumped. Mary held tight to his arm. The scissor-saber that Bill still held was pitifully inadequate in the face of the rage of the awakened doctor. Steve Baker was looking around the room, trying to discover some means of circumventing the infuriated scientist. None presented itself.

CHAPTER TWENTY-ONE

Again the fearful eyes of the little people returned to the colossus who stood at the back door. Dr. Thorkel had now quite lost control of himself. There was no denying the maniac strain that had gradually been taking possession of the scientific intellect. If Bill and Mary had been trying to excuse Thorkel's action on the ground of scientific ardor, they now saw that all claim to this exception had been washed away by his craziness.

Thorkel's glassless eyes were squinting, and it was obvious that he could see but dimly. Nevertheless he knew that the miniature humans were in the room, and might be as deadly to him as so many lurking vipers. Still he did not dare give them the opportunity to escape, since that might only postpone the danger.

Bill Stockton was the first one to sense that for once the little people had the upper hand, that Dr. Alexander Thorkel was now the one on the defensive.

"We've got him," Bill declared emphatically. His satisfied words reached the doctor's ears and goaded the frantic scientist to a new outburst. Mary laughed nervously. Steve cursed luridly.

"So you would dare attack me!" Dr. Thorkel roared. "Well, you have made a great mistake. You understand? You are shut up in this room. You will never get out, because first I will find you." His tone became frenzied, and his words ran up the entire pitch from bass roar to a high tenor crescendo. "I will find you! Do you understand? I will find you!"

With the bolt shot by his fumbling fingers, Dr. Thorkel moved away from the door. At first his advance was slow, menacing, but finally, when he could no longer restrain his motor muscles, he began rushing around the room, kicking things over, stamping here and there. One of the chairs fell on its side, and the half blind scientist stumbled over it and fell flat on his face.

His hands groped around him. Splinters of the broken chair cut into his cheeks and nose, and blood began dripping to the floor of the room. In his berserk rage, Thorkel was his own worst enemy.

Bill, Mary and Steve backed under the table. Now they were drawn up to their full height, ready to go out with chins up and chests out.

"I will find you!" screamed Thorkel, his livid face becoming even more horrible as a result of the clotting blood on his face. "And when I find you, I will destroy you. I will not wait for you to become a greater menace to me. I will destroy you now."

Bill, Mary and Steve left the shelter of the table as Thorkel bumped against it, caught by one corner, and threw it into a corner, scattering the specimen case, the papers, the half eaten sandwich and other articles that had been cluttering its top.

The chair that had served as a carriage for the improvised shotgun next came within Thorkel's path. He felt the barrel of the weapon. Closing his fumbling fingers over it, he snatched it up. By now, he had quite lost his head in his insane anxiety to kill the little people. He stood, wavering on unsteady feet in the middle of the wreckage he had wrought. There was dead silence in the room. Thorkel stood listening wit the shotgun ready to shoot. He could not see very well, not only because of his poor vision, but also because of the film of blood that had dripped down from his eyebrows and forehead.

Nonetheless, Dr. Thorkel was ready to shoot at the next sound. Bill Stockton watched the weaving motion of the rifle barrel, the quivering, nerve-ridden hands of the crazy scientist. The trio was hiding behind a small crate, through the cracks of which bits of wrapping paper protruded.

As Thorkel moved around to face them, Bill Stockton pushed back and brushed the paper. There was a rustling sound. It would scarcely have been audible under other circumstances. But with Dr. Thorkel's nerves on edge, and his ears pricked up, it was enough.

His finger tightened on the trigger, and he quickly shot in the direction of the crate without even bringing the gun to his shoulder. The entire room was shaken by the concussion of the discharge in the confined space. But Thorkel's lack of aim, and the kick of the loosely held gun, prevented the shot from doing any harm to the three little people.

The entire charge went through the bottom of the back door and left a splintered, gaping hole. As soon as the smoke and sound from the shotgun blast had died down, Mary and Bill took up their stand in the questionable shadow of the doctor's boots.

Steve was bolder than the others at the moment, and he was approaching the lower section of the back door, just beyond and to one side of the others. After examining the opening that had been blasted in the door, Steve waved reassuringly to his companions.

Holding Mary by the arm, Bill headed for the door. They looked back at Thorkel. Satisfied that he was not an immediate menace, they examined the new means of escape that had been fortuitously open to them. Then Bill said:

"I have a plan."

"I hope it's a good one," Mary replied. "My nerves are at the breaking point. If I go through another forty-eight hours like these last ones, I'll be no good for anything but the batty coop."

They were mumbling in low whispers that could not possibly carry to the bewildered scientist. Steve was busy picking splinter out of the door to widen their exit.

"If we can get Thorkel to chase us, and we head in the direction of the mine, he may fall in."

"Sort of like tricking African lions into the staked pit," Mary suggested calmly. "Let's try it."

With the din of the discharge finally dissipated, Dr. Thorkel was listening sharply, wondering if he had hit anything. Then he shook his ungainly figure, seemed to gain better control of himself. Addressing himself in a "whistling-in-the-dark" fashion, he said"

"You're acting like a fool—a blind fool!"

Mention of his blindness prompted a more reasonable course of action. He felt his way quickly toward the tray where he had kept his extra glasses. The discovery that these glasses were gone quieted him, because it gave him something tangible to deal with. He looked around, squinting pitifully.

"So—my little friends—" he gritted— "you really wage war on me, eh?"

He still held the shotgun in his hand, but, since he was unable to find the shells, the weapon was useless to him. Finally he broke the gun, cast aside the stock, and carried the barrel as a club.

During this interlude, Bill, Mary and Steve had again dropped out of sight in the piles of rubble around the floor. Thorkel found the upturned table, and, kneeling, felt around it for his glasses. Having no success there, he finally got down on his hands and knees to feel around the floor. The gun barrel was still in his hand.

Bill Stockton realized that within a very few moments the mad scientist would find his glasses where they lay in plain sight. With them, the advantage that the little people had held would be discounted, and Dr. Thorkel would again be a formidable adversary. Bill's bare feet made no sound as he shook off Mary's restraining hand and hurried forward.

Even as Bill approached him, Thorkel was on hands and knees, holding the gun barrel in one hand and groping for his glasses with the other. Bill ran in, snatched up the glasses and whacked them against the table leg, breaking one lens. Thorkel heard the crash of the glass. He swung at Bill with the gun barrel, and the mineralogist dropped the glasses and ran back to his place of concealment.

Thorkel's questing fingers moved along in front of him, he found the glasses, with one lens broken, picked them up and rose to his feet. As he straightened, he put the broken glasses over his ears, adjusting the single lens over one eye, and then roared in savage exultation:

"Now you *can* call me Cyclops, because I have but one good eye!"

The terrible sound coming from the mad scientist was enough to send shivers up and down the spines of strong men an woman. Crouching in their hiding places, the three little people stared, frozen, as the titan form of Thorkel rose above the table edge. Blood-stained, dirt-smeared and terrible, the giant towered there. His voice rose in a shout of laughter.

He placed the table upright once more. Then he began picking things up from the floor and piling them on the table, thus reducing the area in which they might be hiding. As he worked, he muttered softly:

"Soon there will be no place for my little cobras to hide from me."

Swiftly Dr. Thorkel strode forward. With methodical haste he began to search the room, overturning boxes, flinging the cot aside to examine the cases beneath it. Bill Stockton followed his movements with all the care and attention of an enemy general. Then he made a preemptory signal and Mary and Steve Baker dashed out from their hiding place between Thorkel's discarded boots.

"We've got him going," Bill declared. "Now to get him out into the mine yard."

Mary gritted her teeth. Steve nodded soberly.

Even with his one good eye, it was obvious that Dr. Thorkel had no idea where the little people were. The miniature trio scampered across toward the back door. The overturned cot and the bed clothes filled that end of the room. For the moment they were cut off from the vision of the one-eyed scientist.

As they stood in the doorway, Thorkel, discovering that they were not among the things that had been under the cot, began to rise. Since Bill's plan demanded that Thorkel see their escape and follow them, he shouted:

"Outside, quick! He can't see us. The cot's in the way."

Dr. Thorkel stiffened at the sound. As he tried to locate it, the three little people clambered through the gaping hole the shotgun charge had made. It was not easy. Mary's clothing caught on a sharp splinter. The cloth ripped as Bill jerked at it to free her. When the strip of linen was left behind them, Mary laughed and said:

"What with me parading in the cave in the nude while my Irish serape dried over the fire, and now losing an important part of my draperies on that splinter, you're going to have to marry me, Bill just to keep people from talking."

"We'll be a couple of angels with St. Peter officiating, if we don't get a move on," Bill declared.

Heavy footsteps thudded on the floor behind them. The door was flung open. As Bill had anticipated, the noise had attracted Thorkel's attention. He had looked over the cot. Seeing that they were escaping, he rushed to the switch panel by the radium room door. There he turned on the floodlight in the mine yard, then started after his quarry, convinced that he could easily trap them inside the bamboo fence.

Thorkel's shadow temporarily hid the three as they raced forward. The mouth of the mine shaft loomed up before them, a plank stretched across the pit.

"Down there!" Stockton gasped. "It's our only chance."

It was the only possible place of concealment, and it also brought Dr. Thorkel in the direction that Bill had hoped he would take. The doctor's one good eye did not miss the little people's movements as they scrambled over the brink and down the steep rock of the shaft walls.

The mad scientist rushed up, paused at the shaft, stopped and peered down after the miniature humans. Then, balancing himself precariously, and holding the gun barrel in one hand, Dr. Thorkel crawled out on the plank across the mouth of the mine shaft.

He skirted the windlass and, steadying himself with one hand on the rope that ran down into the black depths, again attempted to make contact with his midget tormentors.

Bill Stockton was the only one visible. He was on a ledge about two feet below Thorkel's piercing gaze. The floodlights lighted everything with the brightness of day, and Thorkel licked his lips as his gaze spotted the mining engineer. The gun barrel came down in a wide sweep.

Bill parried it momentarily with the tightly gripped scissor-blade. There was a splintering crack as Thorkel struck at his quarry. A wave of numbness went up Bill's arm as the gun barrel struck the scissor blade. Then the metal club clattered against the rock side of the mine shaft. Abruptly the weakened plank caved in with Thorkel's weight, and dropped into the black depths below.

The frenzied scientist still gripped the windlass rope with one hand, and that saved him temporarily. For a second he swung wildly, while the echoing crash of the falling wood and the gun barrel resounded up from the depths. Thorkel's grip became surer. Panting, he hung there briefly, his bald head gleaming with sweat. He began to climb back up the rope.

But Bill Stockton was not entirely inactive while the doctor was striving to right himself. He glanced around quickly. Mary was clinging to a sloping rock, her white face turned toward the giant. Steve Baker was looking at the mineralogist, his gaunt gray features twisted with hopeless fury.

The mining engineer made a quick gesture, pointed to his sward, and began to swarm back to the surface. Pulling away from Mary, he started up the ledge toward the rim of the mine shaft. Bill's route to the yard took him close to the point where Dr. Thorkel was struggling on the rope. Hanging on with one hand, the scientist reached out to grab Bill as he moved by. The mineralogist stabbed Thorkel's extended fingers with his scissor-blade cutlass. Thorkel jerked back his hand in pain.

Then Bill Stockton wriggled past the helpless scientist and, once on the ground, scrambled back to the handle of the windlass. With the sharp blade of the scissor he severed the small rope tying the windlass handle, freeing the windlass.

Realizing Bill's intention, Dr. Thorkel hastened his efforts to gain the edge of the pit. Afraid that Bill would not reach the windlass in time, Steve Baker decided to take a hand. He leaped out and gripped Thorkel's leg. The unexpected weight on his limb was enough to break the scientist's sense of coordination, and when he let go of the rope and leaped for the safety of the mine yard, he missed the edge by inches.

When Bill cut loose the rope at the windlass handle, Thorkel's weight on the cable was enough to start him downward toward the depths of the mine. Steve realized what had happened, and was lucky enough to release his hold on the doomed maniac in time to grip the ledge below the lip of the pit.

Before the scientist could understand what had happened, Thorkel lost his grip. Gasping with fear and rage, he shook his head violently. Then with a whine and a whir the windlass ran out as the severed rope whirled around it. A long, quavering cry broke from Thorkel's throat as he dropped away into the darkness.

Higher and higher it rose; it broke off abruptly. Then in changed to a long shriek—and ended.

Bill Stockton ran to the brink and peered over. Mary was clambering weakly up toward him. He reached down to help her the last few steps. Steve Baker was also dragging himself upward, thankful that he had not taken the long downward dive with the maniac scientist.

Dr. Cyclops was dead!

CHAPTER TWENTY-TWO

As the trio of little people walked cross the brightly-lighted mine yard to the back door of the house, Steve asked:

"What do we do now?"

"We'll have to get back to Iquitos some way," Bill replied.

"Think we can get back to our normal size?" was Baker's next question. Bill shrugged his shoulders, then looked toward Mary.

"You're the scientist, Mary," he said. "What about the machine?"

"It's no good," Mary replied despondently. "The device is only a condenser. It can't bring people back to their normal size. I guess we'll have to remain this size for the rest of our lives. But think of what Ringling Brothers will pay us. But now we've got to get back to civilization, somehow—"

"As we are?" Steve Baker's face fell. "That's impossible."

"Wait a minute!" Bill interrupted. "I've got a hunch. Do you remember when we first saw Thorkel, after he reduced us?"

"Yeah! So what?" Steve was skeptical.

"He wasn't trying to kill us then, even though he knew we suspected him of having murdered Mira, the native girl. He knew that we had little chance of ever turning him in, and we could hardly hope to overcome him, then—at least that was his line of reasoning."

"I still don't follow you," Mary broke in.

"What I'm driving at," Bill explained, "is that he was merely interested in weighing and measuring us. But after he examined Dr. Bulfinch he turned into a killer. Why do you suppose that happened?"

"He probably intended to kill us all along, for trying to steal his secrets," Steve Baker declared.

"Maybe," agreed Bill. "But he wasn't in any hurry at first. He knew he could dispose of us any time he wanted. Only after he examined Dr. Bulfinch he found out something that made it necessary for him to get rid of us in a hurry."

Mary caught her breath. Her scientific brain was again functioning. She was afraid to accept the explanation that leaped fullblown to her mind.

"Why? What?" she stammered.

"Remember the white pony we saw in the jungle when we were camping in the cove. Pedro thought it was Pinto, *but the animal was too big*. It was an albino pony, and they're rare. That pony *was* Pinto, and when we saw it, it was growing back to normal!"

"We're growing, too," Mary breathed solemnly. "That's it."

As they spoke they were approaching the back steps. Bill stood alongside the bottom step and said:

"Remember how these steps used to come up to our chests? Now they're down around our legs and we don't have half the trouble getting up and down that we used to have."

"You're right," Mary declared. Steve Baker was so fascinated at the prospect of regaining his full height that he was speechless.

"Sure," Bill continued. "That's what Thorkel found out when he examined Dr. Bulfinch, and that's why he tried to kill us before we grew back to normal size. I think it's a progressively accelerative process. In two weeks, or maybe even in ten days, we'll be back to normal."

"It's logical," the girl commented. "Once the compressive force of the radium has been removed, we expand—slowly, but elastically. The electron swing back to their normal orbits. The energy we absorbed under the ray will be liberated in quanta—"

"Ten Days,' breathed Steve Baker. "And then we can go down the river again.

But it was a month before the three, once more normal in size, reached the Andean village of Iquitos. The sight of human beings, no longer gigantic, was warmly reassuring Indians leaned against the huts, scratching lazily for fleas. Peering down the archway along the street a ragged Bill Stockton turn to grin at a disheveled Mary Phillips.

"Looks good, eh?" he asked with a grin.

Steve Baker was absorbed in thought, obviously pondering a difficult problem.

"We've got to decide whether we're going to tell people about what we've been through," he declared. He scratched his stubbled cheek. "One way we get our pictures in the paper and tanks of free *pulque*. But it's just as likely we'll end up in a padded cell if we tell the truth. If we don't tell the truth—"

He paused, stiffening. A mangy cat had appeared from beyond the arch. It did not look anything like the well-fed Santanas. Nevertheless Steve Baker's muscles tensed; his breath burst out in an explosive "Scat!" as he sprang forward. The cat vanished quickly, shocked to the end of its tail.

Baker's chest inflated several inches.

"Well," he said, with the quiet pride of achievement, "did you see that?"

"No," murmured Stockton, who was seizing the opportunity to kiss a willing Mary. "Go away. Quietly. And quickly."

Baker shrugged and followed the cat, a predatory gleam in his eye.

Bill lead Mary into the shade of one of the tile-covered porticoes. As they settled down on a rustic bench, he said:

"I'll get Fred Harper to fix things up so that we can operate the radium mine. It will mean a lot to your clinics and sanatoriums and laboratories. But you're not going to have anything to do with it until you've spent a couple of years just riding around on boats and trains with your new husband, looking at the sun and the moon and stars, and realizing that, compared to them, you're not so big after all."

"Sounds like a good idea, as long as science is going to get some good out of all the suffering we're been through. We'll establish a radium research foundation, name it after Dr. Bulfinch, and I'll have his name in lights all over the place!"

"I though all that stuff was phony once upon a time," Bill admitted, "but now I can see that it's the real stuff."

"We might even tell Steve that, if he wants to tell the story about Dr. Thorkel's notes, we can substantiate it. With Thorkel's notes, my experience, and the radium from the mine, I think I could make some little people myself." She cocked an eye at Bill inquiringly.

"I don't ever want to see anything small like that again," the mining engineer insisted.

Mary laughed musically. Then she took hold of his lapels, drew his lips to hers again, and her hands went up and over his shoulders to clasp behind his neck.

"You big, bad he-man. I can think of a time when you'd be delighted to have some little people scampering around. Well?"

Growing understanding brought a flush to Bill's face, and he said:

"Well, maybe! If you say so."

They kissed again.

THE END

DR. CYCLOPS

A Novelet of
Men in Miniature
by
Henry Kuttner

CHAPTER I

Camp in the Jungle

Bill Stockton stood in the command gate, watching Pedro driving the mules down to the river pasture. The swarthy half-breed's face was split by a broad grin; he twirled his black mustache and sang loudly of a *cantina* in Buenos Aires, thousands of miles to the east.

"How the devil does he do it?" Stockton moaned, shaking the perspiration out of his eyes. "I can hardly drag myself around in this heat. And that guy actually sings—"

Yet it wasn't only the heat, Stockton knew. There was more to it than that. A feeling of sombre menace—hung heavy above this wilderness encampment. During the weeks of jungle travel from the Andes, through tropical swamp and pest-infested jungle, the feeling had grown stronger. It was in the humid, sticky air. It was in the sickly-sweet. choking perfume of the great orchids that grew outside the stockade. Most of all, it was in the actions of Dr. Thorkel.

and she had a face that belonged on the silver screen rather than in the lab. She also had a hell of a temper.

"He's supposed to be the greatest scientific wizard of the age," Stockton thought skeptically. "But for my money he's nuts. Sends a message to the Royal Academy demanding the services of a biologist and a mineralogist, and then asks us to look into a microscope. That's all. Won't even let us get inside that mud house of his!"

There was reason for Stockton's bitterness. He had been literally forced into this adventure. Hardy, the mineralogist, had been taken ill at Lima, and Dr. Bulfinch, his colleague, had sought vainly for a substitute. None was available. None, that is, save for a certain beachcomber who was going rapidly to hell with the aid of a native girl, bad gin, and rubber checks

Bulfinch's assistant, Dr. Mary Phillips, had solved the problem. She had brought up the bad checks, threatened Stockton with jail if he refused to come along. Under the circumstances, the one-time mineralogist had shrugged and acceded. Now he was wondering if he had made a mistake.

There was menace here. Stockton sensed it, with the psychic keenness of a professional adventurer. Secrecy was all around him. Why was the mine yard generally kept locked, if the mine actually was worthless, as Thorkel contended? Why had Thorkel seemed so excited when Stockton had mentioned the iron crystals, crystals Thorkel had been unable to see because of his weak vision?

Then, too, there was the matter of the Dicotylinae—certain bones Mary Phillips had found. They were the bones of a native wild pig, but the molar surfaces had proved it a species of midget swine entirely unknown to science—four inches long at maturity. That was odd.

Finally, only an hour ago, Thorkel had blandly said good-bye, only twenty-three hours after the arrival of his guests. Bulfinch had, Stockton mused with a chuckle, thrown a fit. The goatish face had gone gray; the unkempt Van Dyke had bristled.

"Are you attempting to intimate that you summoned me—Dr. Rupert Bulfinch—ten thousand miles just to look into a microscope?" he had roared.

"Correct," Thorkel had answered, and went back to his mud house.

So far, so good. But there was trouble ahead. Neither Bulfinch nor Mary would think of leaving, even though that meant defiance of Thorkel. And Thorkel, Stockton felt, was a dangerous customer, cold-blooded and unscrupulous. His round face, with its bristling mustache and bald dome, could settle into grim, deadly lines.

Moreover, from the first a quiet, unspoken sort of conflict had arisen between Thorkel and Baker, the guide who had accompanied the party from the Andes. Stockton shrugged and gave it up.

Dr. Bulfinch came up behind Stockton and touched his arm. There was repressed excitement in the biologist's goatish face.

"Come along," he said softly. "I've found something."

Stockton followed Bulfinch into a nearby tent. Mary Phillips was there, mounting the bones of the midget pig. She was, Stockton thought, much too pretty to be a biologist. A wealth of red-gold hair cascaded over her shoulders,

"Hello, beautiful," said Stockton.

"Oh, shut up," the girl murmured. "What's the matter, Dr. Bulfinch?"

The biologist thrust a rock sample at Stockton.

"Test this."

The younger man's eyes widened.

"This isn't—hell, it can't be!"

"You've seen pitchblende before," Bulfinch said with heavy sarcasm.

"Where'd you get it?" Stockton asked, excited.

"Baker found it near the mine shaft. It's uranium ore," he said quietly, "and it's a hundred times richer than any deposit ever discovered. No wonder Thorkel wants to get rid of us!" Mentally Stockton added, "And I'll bet he wouldn't stop at murder to shut us up!"

"Good God!" Bulfinch whispered. "Radium! Think of the medical benefits of such a find—the help it can give to science!"

There was an interruption. A black streak shot into the tent, followed by a gaunt, disreputable dog, barking wildly. The two circled a table and fled outside again. There was the sound of a scuffle.

Hastily Stockton raised the tent-flap. Pedro, Thorkel's man-of-all-work, was holding the dog, while a cat retreated hastily into the distance.

The half-breed looked up with a flash of white teeth. "I am sorry. This foolish Paco—" He pulled the dog's tail. "He does not know he can never catch Santanas. He just wants to play, though. Since Pinto went away, he is lonesome."

"Yeah?" Stockton asked, eyeing the man. "Who was Pinto?"

"My little mule. Ah Pinto was smart. But not smart enough, I suppose." Pedro shrugged expressively. "Poor mule."

A man came out of the gathering twilight—a tall, rangy figure, with a hard-bitten, harsh face—a Puritan gone to seed.

"Hello Baker," Stockton grunted.

"Bulfinch told you about the radium?" Baker said, without preamble. "It's valuable, eh?"

"Yeah. Plenty valuable." Stockton's eyes narrowed. "I've been wondering about that. Wondering why you were so anxious to come along when you could have sent a native. Maybe you'd heard about this radium mine, eh?"

Baker's harsh face did not change, but he sent a glance of sheer black hatred toward the house.

"I don't blame you," he said under his breath. It does look screwy. But—listen, Bill, I had a good reason for wanting to come here. If I'd come alone, Thorkel would have been suspicious—shot me on sight, maybe. I'd have had no chance at all to investigate—"

"Investigate what?" Stockton asked impatiently.

"I used to know a little native girl. Nice kid. Mira, her name was. I—well, I thought a lot of her. One day she went off to act as Thorkel's housekeeper. And that was the last I ever heard of the girl."

"She isn't here now," Stockton said. "Unless she's in the house."

Baker shook his head. "I've been talking to Pedro. He says Mira was here—and disappeared. Like Pinto, his albino mule."

The swift tropic night had fallen. A bright moon silvered the compound.

And suddenly the two men heard the faint, shrill neigh of a horse, from the direction of Thorkel's house.

Simultaneously the figure of Pedro appeared, running from behind a tent. He cried, "Pinto! My mule Pinto is in the house. He has come back!"

Before the half-breed could reach the door of the house, it opened abruptly. Thorkel appeared. In the moonlight his bald head and gleaming, thick-lensed spectacles looked oddly inhuman.

"Well, Pedro?" he asked quietly, in a sneering voice.

The other jerked to a halt. He moistened his lips.

"It is Pinto, *Senor—*" he whispered.

"You are imagining things," Thorkel said, with cold emphasis. "Go back to your work. Do you think I'd keep a mule in the house?"

A new voice broke in.

"Just what do you keep in there, Doctor?"

It was Bulfinch. The biologist emerged from the tent and approached, a lean, gaunt figure in the moonlight. Mary was behind him. Baker and Stockton joined the group. Thorkel held the door closed behind him.

"That is nothing to you," he said, icily.

"On the contrary," Bulfinch snapped, "as I told you, I intend to remain here until I have received an explanation."

"And as I told *you,*" Thorkel said, almost whispering, "you do so at your own peril. I will not tolerate interference or prying. My secrets are my own. I warn you: I shall protect those secrets!"

"Are you threatening us?" the biologist growled.

Thorkel suddenly smiled.

"If I showed you what I have in my house, I think you would—regret it," he observed, a suggestion of subtle menace in his silky tones. "I wish to be left alone. If I find you still here tomorrow morning, I shall take . . . protective measures."

His eyes, behind the thick-lensed spectacles, included the group in one ominous glance. Then, without another word, he reentered the house, locking the door behind him.

"Still staying, Doc?" Stockton asked. Bulfinch growled.

"I certainly am!"

There was a brief pause. Then Pedro, who had been listening intently, made a commanding gesture.

"Come with me. I will show you something—"

He hurried around the corner of the house, trailed by the dog Paco. Bulfinch, his lips working, followed and so did the others.

A tall bamboo fence blocked their way. Pedro pointed and applied his eye to a crack. Stockton tested the gate, which had previously been open. It was barred now, so he joined Pedro and the others.

"Wait," the half-breed whispered. "I have seen this before."

They could see the mine-shaft, with a crude windlass surmounting it. And then a gross, strange figure entered their range of vision. It resembled, at first glance, a man in a diving suit. Every inch of the stocky body was covered with the rubberlike fabric. A cylindrical helmet shielded the head. Through two round eye-plates could be seen the heavy spectacles of Dr. Thorkel.

"Uh-huh," Stockton whispered. "Protective suit. Radium's dangerous stuff."

Thorkel went to the mine and began to turn the windlass. Abruptly Stockton felt a hand touch his arm. He turned.

It was Baker.

"Come along," the other said softly. "I've opened the door. Cheap lock—and Mary uses hairpins. Now we'll be able to see what he's got hidden in that house."

"*Si!* The doctor will be busy in the yard for a long time—" Pedro said, nodding.

Silently the group retraced their steps. The door of the mud house was ajar. From within came the sound of a shrill neigh, incredibly high and thin. . . .

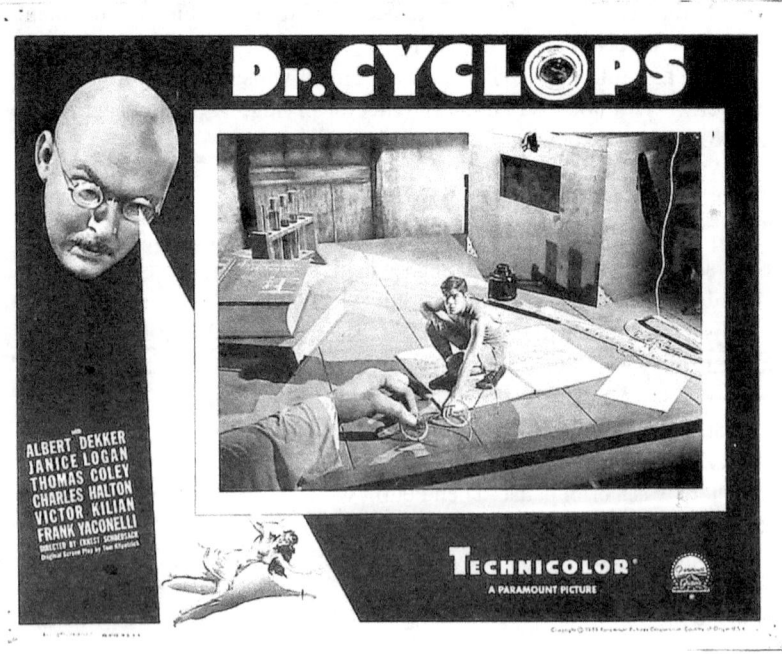

CHAPTER II

The Little People

The room was disappointingly bare. Across from the front door was another, apparently leading to the mine yard. Another door was in the right-hand wall, and a small mica window was let into it.

There were heavy wooden chairs, a work-bench, and a table bearing microscope and notebooks. On the bench were several small wicker baskets. Littered carelessly about the floor were a rack of test-tubes, books, a beaker, two or three small boxes, and a dirty shirt or two.

Pedro pointed to the floor.

"Hoof prints—Pinto was here, yes!"

Mary bent over the microscope, while Bulfinch examined the notebooks.

"Thieves!"

Thorkel stood in the doorway leading to the mine yard, his eyes glaring behind the glasses. He was whitely livid with rage.

"So you would steal my discoveries. You have no right here! You are merely my employees whom I have discharged and instructed to leave!" He saw the notebook in Bulfinch's hand, and his voice rose to a scream of rage.

"My notes!"

Stockton and Baker seized him as he sprang at the biologist. Bulfinch smiled coldly.

"Restrain yourself, Dr. Thorkel. Your actions are not reassuring."

Thorkel relaxed, panting.

"I—you have no right here."

"You are behaving irrationally. For your own good, and for the benefit of science, I must demand an explanation. To leave you here in the jungle would be nothing short of criminal. You are grossly overworked. You are not"—he hesitated—"not in a normal state mentally. There is no reason to be suspicious or to fear persecution."

Thorkel sighed, removed his glasses, and rubbed his blind eyes with a weary gesture. "I am sorry," he murmured.

"Perhaps you are right, Doctor. I—I am experimenting with radioactivity." He went to the mica-paned door and opened it, revealing a small closet, plated with lead. From the ceiling hung a projector, resembling the type used medically to treat cancer by radium rays.

"This is my condenser," Thorkel said. "You may examine it, Dr. Bulfinch. I must trust you—I have shown this to no one else in the world."

Bulfinch entered the closet. The others were at his heels, intently scrutinizing the projector which seemed the heart of the mystery.

Pedro paid no attention. He was opening, one by one, the boxes on the bench. And abruptly, he paused, transfixed with astonishment. His lips form the word, "Pinto!"

A white mule was within the box. An albino mule, no more than eight inches high!

"Pedro!" Thorkel called sharply. The half-breed sprang up. His elbow overturned the box, which clattered to the floor.

The midget mule was flung out. Only Thorkel and Pedro saw the beast as it struggled up and raced across the floor.

The door was still ajar. The mannikin animal fled out into the night.

For a second Thorkel's eyes clashed with Pedro's.

"Come here," the scientist said tonelessly. "I want you to see this, too."

The half-breed went toward Thorkel, his face blank with amazement. "What—what happened to—"

Thorkel smiled. He pointed to the closet where the others were still examining the projector. Pedro turned to look.

Thorkel moved with the swiftness of an uncoiled steel spring. He struck at Pedro. Caught unawares, the half-breed was hurled into the closet. The door slammed shut behind him.

Thorkel locked it with a swift movement. His hand closed on one of the switches nearby; he pulled it down. Instantly there was a low hum, which rose swiftly to a sibilant crackling buzz.

Green light blazed through the mica window.

From a shelf Thorkel took a heave helmet and donned it. He leaned forward to peer through the mica pane.

"Thieves!" he whispered. "I told you to go! I could not force you—but if you insist on staying, I must be sure that you will not interfere with my experiments or try to steal my secret. So you wished to help me, Dr. Bulfinch? Well, you shall—but not quite as you expected!"

Thorkel's laughter rose above the crackling snarl of the condenser. . . .

The infra-red lamp suspended from the ceiling sent down a rich, warm glow. Beneath it was a glass dish, containing a colorless liquid that was boiling gently, warmed by an electrode. From the dish streamed a whitish vapor which shrouded the floor, almost hiding the dim outlines nearby.

One of these figures writhed and sat up, tearing away the silken wrappings that bound it. The face of Pedro appeared. He sprang up, knee-deep in the white vapor, coughing and chocking for breath.

Beside him another form stirred. Bill Stockton rose shakily, breathing in great gasps.

"Air—air's better up here . . . what the hell!" Discovering that he was naked save for the silk shroud, he adjusted it, looking rather like a Roman, with his harsh eagle face and keen eyes.

Mary and Baker were the next to appear. Then came the grim face of

Bulfinch. For a moment each was busy adjusting their makeshift garments.

"Where are we?" Pedro gasped. "I cannot see—" He choked and coughed.

"Calm down," Bulfinch said curtly. "We won't be asphyxiated." He sniffed and glanced at the light above. "Ozone, ammonia, humidity, temperature—calculated to revive consciousness."

"Where are we?" Mary asked. "In the mine?"

They could not see beyond the small circle of light. Stockton gripped Pedro's arm.

"You know this place better than we do. Where are we? What's Thorkel done?"

"Suddenly horror grew in Pedro's eyes as he remembered something. "Pinto," he gasped. "He has made Pinto—*little!*"

"Nuts," Stockton grunted. "Let's grab hands and feel our way around. Come on!"

"He has made me little like my mule!" Pedro whispered.

Without warning the faint red glow of the lamp faded and died. It was almost utterly black. Stockton saw that they were in a cellar, at the foot of a flight of stairs that led up to an opening door. On the threshold stood Dr. Thorkel, looking down at them. Santanas, the cat, crouched by the scientist's feet.

"He has made us little!" Pedro screamed.

And it was true! Thorkel was—a giant! A thirty-foot titan towered over them! The cellar door seemed as big as a two-story house; Santanas was a sabre-toothed tiger!

Bulfinch was chalk-white. He sprang back suddenly as Santanas spat down at the tiny group. Thorkel hastily bent down and picked up the cat. His voice was booming thunder. "No, no—you must not frighten them," he told the cat. Thorkel stepped down into the cellar, and the others shrank from this colossus. Mary's voice rose in a scream.

"Good," said Thorkel. "Vocal cords unimpaired, eh? You have no temperature? Dr. Bulfinch, will you be good enough to take the pulse of your companions?"

Pedro broke and raced for the stairway. Thorkel nodded, smiling.

"Little creatures—their first instinct is to escape. Run if you like, then. And the wee folk ran. . . .

Climbing those stairs was a feat. Each tread came up to their breasts. But, pushing, pulling, scrambling, the miniature humans swarmed up toward the light. Soon they were gone from sight. Thorkel put down the cat and followed, shutting the cellar door. He turned to glance around the room. The little people had hidden themselves.

"Come out. You have nothing to fear," he said smoothly.

Thorkel waited, and then sank down into a chair.

"Where is your scientific spirit, Dr. Bulfinch?" He smiled. "Did you not wish to join me in my experiments?" He mopped perspiration from his bald head and slid the chair away from the patch of sunlight that slanted in through the windows fronting the mine yard.

Bulfinch's head appeared cautiously from behind one of Thorkel's discarded boots. He walked toward the giant.

"Come closer," Thorkel urged.

Bulfinch obeyed, staring up at the other.

"What is the matter?" Thorkel said fearfully. "Can you not speak?"

The biologist's voice was thin and high.

"Yes, I can speak. What have you done—and why?"

Thorkel leaned forward, his huge hand reaching toward the tiny figure on the floor. Bulfinch retreated in alarm.

"I only wish to weigh you," he said softly. He rose and settled back in his chair. "Come out. I won't eat you. As you can see, I have reduced your size."

His pale eyes behind the thick glasses, watched intently as, emboldened, the others appeared one by one. Pedro had been hiding behind a chair leg, the others behind a stack of books on the floor. They advanced until they were in a group with Bulfinch.

"You should be proud," Thorkel said. "You are almost the first successful experiment—Pinto was the first, Pedro. Too bad you let him escape. Again I thank you, Mr. Stockton, for identifying the iron crystals. They gave me the last clue."

He blinked down at them. "Till you came, I could reduce organic substances, but life could not be preserved in them. It is a matter of electronic compression of matter under ray bombardment. The radium in the mine gave me unimaginable power. Look." He lifted a sponge from the table and squeezed it in his fist. "That is it. Compression. But energy is required, rather than brute force—"

Baker spoke up suddenly. "Did you do this to Mira?"

"The native girl—my housekeeper? Why yes,. But I failed—she was reduced in size, but she was dead. How do you know her? Thorkel did not wait for an answer. He rubbed his eyes wearily. "I am very tired. It has taken days to reduce you, and I have not had one moment's sleep . . ." His voice trailed off wearily. Sleep smothered him.

Stockton was staring around.

"We've got to get out of here. Do you realize that this fiend intends to kill us all?"

Bulfinch looked a question. "That scarcely—"

"He told us he murdered the native girl, didn't he? He's a cold-blooded devil."

Instinctively they glanced at the door. The bar that locked it from the inside was thrice the height of Stockton's head.

Human beings—scarcely more than half a foot tall!

On the floor nearby a boot stood on end—"Human Physiology," by Granger. Stockton went to stand beside it. His head scarcely came to the top of the volume.

"Well?" he asked bitterly. "Any suggestions?"

Bulfinch nodded. "Yes. Books are handy things. If we can pile them up and reach the door-latch . . ."

It took time, but Thorkel did not awaken. A pencil, used as a lever, opened the door a crack. And then the little people were outside in the compound. Strange sight! A cactus patch not far away was taller than the tallest tree. The camp tables were fantastically high. A chicken was moving jerkily in its quest for food—and its bobbing comb rose higher than Stockton's head!

If it saw them, it made no hostile move. Slowly the tiny group moved forward, toward Bulfinch's tent. Each box and crate was a mountain to be skirted. The rough ground hurt their bare feet.

Pedro was glancing around nervously. Abruptly he cried out and pointed. Stockton whirled with the others, and he showed his panic.

Out of a crumbling hole in the mud hut's base Santanas, the cat, was crawling. The creature's eyes were intent on the little people. More formidable than a tiger, it wriggled free and bounded toward them, sharp fangs bared!

CHAPTER III

Death in the Jungle

Stockton seized Mary by the hand and dragged her toward the shelter of the cactus clump. The others were not slow in following. Baker paused to hurl a pebble at the car, but the gesture was futile.

Snarling, Santanas came on. The cacti were too far away for safety. Hopelessness tore at Stockton as he realized that none of them could reach the clump. He could almost feel sharp fangs sinking into his flesh.

The cat spat viciously. There was an uproar of furious barks. As the little people miraculously found concealment amid the cactus spines, they turned to see Santanas fleeing from Paco, Pedro's dog.

"Whew!" Barker gasped. "That was a close one."

Bulfinch regarded him somberly, tugging at his Van-dyke. "There will be more 'close ones,'" he said with grim meaning. "Every creature larger than a rat is apt to be a deadly menace."

"What can we do? Mary asked.

"First—food, weapons," Stockton said. "Then we'll deal with Thorkel and find some way out of this."

The day dragged on, and Thorkel still slept. Santanas did not reappear. Mary engaged herself in making sandals, a difficult task at best, and worse when the knife is larger than you are.

As for Stockton, he managed to take the screw out of a pair of scissors, and one blade provided him with a serviceable weapon, about the size of a sword.

Thorkel's voice startled them when it came. He was leaning out the window, like a giant in the sky, regarding them.

"You are resourceful, my small friends," his voice boomed out. "But now come back. I must weigh and measure all of you."

The group drew together. Thorkel laughed evilly at them.

"I won't harm you. Come Dr. Bulfinch," he said silkily.

"I demand that you restore us to our normal size," the biologist snapped.

"That is impossible," the other said. "At present, anyway. All my energies have been devoted to the problem of atomic shrinkage—compression. Perhaps, in time, I can find the antidote, the ray that will turn men to giants. But it will take months of research and experiment—perhaps years."

"Do you mean we must remain like this—"

"I shall not harm you." Thorkel smiled. "Come—" He leaned forward. Bulfinch drew back, and, with an impatient grunt, Thorkel disappeared from the window. His feet thudded across the floor. Bulfinch hastily fled back to the others.

"The cactus," he gasped, panting. "Let's hide!"

But already Thorkel was emerging from the door. His figure loomed gigantic. A few quick strides, and he had cut off the retreat of his quarry. He crouched down, spreading his fingers wide.

Escape was impossible. Mary and Baker were gathered up in one titan hand. With the other Thorkel reached for the fleeing Bulfinch.

Pedro had secured a fork from somewhere, and held it like a spear. He thrust at the huge hand.

Chuckling, Thorkel brushed the weapon aside, knocking Pedro headlong. Contemptuously he stood up, still gripping Mary and Baker.

"Dr. Bulfinch!" His voice was thunderous. "Listen to me!"

The biologist was peering out from the depths of the cactus. "Yes?"

"I wish to weigh and measure you. You are a scientist; your reactions will be more valuable than those of the others. I am conducting an experiment for Germany—my fatherland. If my reduction method proves successful, we will be able to reduce our armies to miniature size. Our men will be able to steal into enemy territory, sabotage industrial centers. And no one will suspect the destruction due to—men in miniature. You will not be harmed. I promise you that. Will you come out?"

Bulfinch shook his head stubbornly. His whole being revolted at the ruthless plan outlined by this sinister genius. A plan that might mean the death of thousands of innocent civilians.

"No? Then, perhaps, if I apply a little pressure—a very little—to these tiny people I hold so gently in my hand—"

The constricting fingers tightened. From Baker's lips came a grunt of pain. Mary's voice rose in a scream.

"Oh, damn!" Bulfinch snarled. "All right, Thorkel. You win. Put them down." He emerged from the cactus as the scientist gently deposited Baker and Mary on the ground. They were unharmed, but so giddy from the rapid descent that they could scarcely stand.

Calmly, Thorkel picked up Bulfinch's tiny figure. The biologist made no resistance. The others were left staring as Thorkel walked back to the mud house; the, swiftly they fled into the cactus. There was silence.

"He won't hurt him," Pedro said, without conviction.

Stockton stepped out from the protection of the cactus. "I'll just make sure. Wait here." He started toward the house, gripping his scissor-blade harder than was necessary.

It was minutes later when he reached the door, still slightly ajar. He peered through the crack, just in time to hear Bulfinch's cry and witness the murder of the biologist.

Thorkel was seated at his table. With one hand he gripped the tiny Bulfinch; with the other he pressed a wad of cotton down over his victim's face.

Then, swiftly, he dropped the limp body into a glass beaker. Stockton drew back, sick with horror, and his improvised sword made a noise against the door. Thorkel glanced down and saw the small watcher.

"So you would spy on me? he asked quietly, and without haste picked up a butterfly net from the table. As he rose Stockton fled.

Thorkel got to the door just in time to see him disappear into the cactus. Nodding, he found a shovel and followed his quarry.

It took ten minutes to clear and break down the cactus bed. And then Thorkel realized that he was looking at the outlet of a tile drain pipe that extended to and under the compound wall. He straightened, staring nearsightedly across the barrier.

"You had better come back!" Thorkel shouted. "You cannot live an hour in the jungle—and there is a storm approaching!"

Storm in the jungle—the greatest rain forest in the world. Bear, deer and monkey fleeing from thunderbolts and unchained devils of the lightning. The screaming of parrots clinging to their wind-buffeted perches.

The black hell of night closed upon the jungle.

Through that madness fled the little people. And, by sheer luck, they found a cave in which they cowered through the eternal, dragging hours of shaking fury, helpless, hopeless beings in a world of gigantic menace. . . .

It was dawn. Chilled, dispirited, and shivering, the little people emerged from their refuge. In the dawn light they examined each other.

"We look like hell," Stockton said.

"I'm glad you include yourself," Mary told him, trying to adjust her tangled hair. "I wish I had a few pins."

"They'd be as big as you are, about . What now?

Baker had been talking to the half-breed. Now he turned to face the others.

"Pedro has an idea. If we can get to the river and find a boat, we can float downstream to civilization. They'll be help there."

"That's an idea," Stockton nodded. "Which was is the water, Pedro?"

The half-breed pointed, and without delay they set out, plodding through the rain-wet jungle. Once a monkey, larger to them than a gorilla, swung down uncomfortably close, and once the inconceivable ferocity of a bear crossed their path, luckily without seeing them. They kept to a well-trodden path, but on all sides the monolithic trees stretched up, higher than skyscrapers.

The weedy grass rose above their heads. It was a world of stark fantasy and lurking menace.

Once Stockton, lagging behind the others, saw Paco, the dog. He was frisking about an albino colt which was diligently cropping grass. For a second Stockton considered the idea of catching and riding the colt, but gave it up immediately. The beast was much too large. He shrugged and followed the rest of the band.

The river bank did not prove an insurmountable obstacle, though it took time to descend. They went upstream to a little cove, where Pedro, he said, had moored his canoe. Peeking their way around a thick patch of weeds, they reached the craft. It was gigantic. Beached on the sand, it remained immovable no matter how they strained and pushed.

"Great idea," Stockton grunted. It's like trying to move a steamship."

"Well, even that can be done," the girl told him. If you use rollers."

"Isn't she smart?" Pedro said with naive admiration. "We can cut bamboo—"

"Sure!" Baker joined in. "We can rig up a lever and windlass—it'll take time, but that's all right."

It took even more time than they had thought. With their crude tools, and the unexpected toughness of the plant-life to tiny hands, it took hours, and the morning dragged on with little accomplished.

Pedro lifted his head and dashed sweat from his dripping mustache. "I hear—Paco, I think," he said doubtfully.

"Never mind Paco," Baker told him. "Lend a hand with this windlass."

"But Paco—he is a hunting dog. Dr. Thorkel knows that. If he—"

"Time to rest," Stockton decreed, and straightened, rubbing his aching back. Mary, who had been toiling with the rest, sank down with a groan. She tossed her red-gold hair back from her tired young face.

Stockton made a cup out of a tiny leaf and brought the girl water from the river. She drank it gratefully.

"No use to boil it," the man explained. "If ther're any germs in the water, we can see 'em without a microscope."

Pedro and Baker flung themselves down full length on the sand and lay panting. "This is devil work," the half-breed observed with conviction. "If I live, I shall burn twenty candles before my patron saint."

"If I live, I'll kill twenty bottles, Baker said, "But there's one guy I'd like to kill first." His face darkened. He was remembering Mira, the native girl, whom Thorkel had murdered so casually. And poor Bulfinch.

"What about you, Bill?" Mary asked.

He glanced at her. "I know what you mean. Well—I wouldn't even make a good beachcomber now. I might go native with the field mice."

Abruptly Stockton turned to face her. "No I didn't mean that. This is pretty terrible, but it's shown me something. All this—" He flung out an arm toward the towering grasses in the background. "Wonder and strangeness, which we never quite realized—until we're small. I—I was a good mineralogist once. I could be again. Remember those checks I tore up, Mary? I'm going to pay you back every cent they cost you. That's rather important to me now. . . ." He frowned. "If we come out of this alive—"

In the distance Paco barked again. Pedro stood up, shading his eyes with a calloused palm. "It is Dr. Thorkel," he stated. "He carries a specimen box, and Paco leads him."

"Damn!" Stockton snapped. "We've got to hide. Take to the water, to break the trail."

"No," Pedro said. "There are alligators." He nodded toward the tall patch of grass near them. "We can hide in—" He stopped, and horror grew in his eyes.

Mary, following his glance, gave a little gasp and recoiled.

For something was coming out of the high grasses. Dragonlike and hideous it slid forward, cold eyes intent on the little people. The sunlight gleamed on rough, warty scales.

Only a lizard—but to Thorkel's victims it was like a triceratops, a dinosaur out of Earth's ferocious past!

Stockton barely had time to snatch up his scissor-blade sword before the reptile rushed. He was bowled over by that blind charge. Gasping, still clinging to his weapon he scrambled to his feet.

Mary was backed up against a tell weed-stem, her eyes abrim with fear. Before her Pedro had planted his squat form.

He gripped a bit of wood, holding it like a cudgel—a matchstick in the hands of a mannikin!

The lizard came back, jaws agape, hissing. Baker had found a sharpened splinter of bamboo, and held it as a spear. He thrust, and the point glanced off the reptiles armored flank.

The barking of Paco was thunderously loud. A shadow fell on the group. Something seemed to swoop down out of the sky—and the vast face of Dr. Thorkel stared at them as the man crouched down.

"So there you are!" he boomed. "What's this? A lizard? Wait—"

In his left hand he gathered the struggling forms of Mary and Pedro. They struck vainly at the huge, imprisoning fingers. He reached toward Stockton.

Simultaneously the lizard rushed again. Stockton drove his blade at the gaping jaws; Baker thrust at the wattled throat. The creature gave back, writhed aside. Thorkel's hand reached out—

The reptile's jaws closed upon it! Thorkel screamed in pain as he jerked back, cursing with agonized fury. Mary and Pedro dropped unnoticed from the scientists's other hand.

Stockton fled toward them. "The bushes! Quick!"

Habit made him say that. Actually, they darted into the concealing stems of the high grasses, thicker than a forest of bamboo. Behind them they heard Thorkel cursing; then fell silent.

Paco barked.

"That damn dog of yours," Baker growled. "He's a hunter, all right."

Thorkel's voice sounded. "Come out! I know you're in the grass. Come out or I'll fire it."

Stockton glanced at Mary's white face, and whispered an oath. Baker's thin lips were grim. Pedro rubbed his mustache.

"Paco—he will follow me," the half-breed said. "You stay here."

And he was gone, racing through the grass forest.

There was a moment of silence. Then Stockton, galvanized into activity, crept forward, parting the fronds till he could see Thorkel. The scientist was holding a match-box in his fingers.

Blood dripped from one hand to the ground.

Paco's bark came from further away. Thorkel hesitated, looking around, and then extracted a match.

From downstream came Pedro's voice.

"Paco! *Fuerra! Fuera!*"

Thorkel, lighting the match, looked up.

Abruptly he dropped it and snatched at the rifle he had laid down. He took steady aim,

The boom of the gun was deafening thunder.

Pedro screamed once. There was a faint splash from far away.

Sickness tugged at Stockton's stomach as he saw Thorkel go striding off. He went back to the others.

"Pedro's done for. That leaves three of us."

"Damn Thorkel! Baker ground out. Mary said nothing, but there was both pity and sorrow in her eyes.

They heard Paco go racing past, to leap into the river and swim out.

Then the first coiling tendrils of smoke drifted through the grasses.

Instantly Stockton remembered the lit match that Thorkel had dropped. He seized Mary's hand and urged her forward.

"Come on, Steve, he said urgently to Baker. "He's trying to smoke us out. We can't stay here—"

"Come out! roared the bellowing voice of Thorkel. "Hear me?" His huge boots stamped through the grass patch.

And the fire spread, remorselessly, hungrily.

Mary was gasping with strain. "I can't—go any further, Bill."

"That's right," Baker seconded. "If we come out in the open, he'll see us. We're trapped."

Stockton stared around. The flames were closing in upon them. Black smoke billowed up. Abruptly Stockton saw something that made his eyes widen.

The specimen-case.

Thorkel's box, lying at the edge of the grasses!

Without a word Stockton raced toward it. He still had his improvised sword, and, leaping to a rock beside the box, he used it as a lever to pry the lid open. Instantly the others saw his intention.

Awkwardly, frantic with the need for haste, they clambered in. The lid had scarcely fallen before a jolt and a sense of swinging movement told them that Thorkel had remembered his property.

Through the small ventilators, covered with copper-wire mesh, daylight slanted in vaguely.

Would Thorkel open the case? They wondered.

CHAPTER IV

The Cyclops

It was night before Thorkel gave up the search. Wearily he pushed open the door of the mud house, put the shotgun on a chair, and dropped the specimen case on the table.

"They must be dead," he groaned. "But I must be sure. I must!"

He polished his spectacles, peering at them vaguely. His watery eyes blinked in puzzlement. Then he went to the door of the radium room and peered through the mica panel. Something he saw there made him turn to the mine-yard door. He flung it open, switched on a floodlight, and went out, leaving the door ajar.

As soon as he had left the lid of the specimen case lifted. Three tiny people emerged. Fearfully they clambered to the eat of Thorkel's chair. They gained the floor, and went toward the open door.

"He's busy with the windlass," Mary whispered. "Hurry!"

Stockton halted suddenly. "Okay," he said. "But—I've stopped running. You two go on. I'm going to stay and—kill Thorkel, somehow."

The others stared at him. "But Bill!" Mary gasped. "It's impossible! If we reach civilization—"

Stockton laughed bitterly.

"We've just been fooling ourselves all along. We can never reach civilization. If we launched a boat, we could never get ashore. We'd starve to death, or crack up in the rapids. We're imprisoned here, as surely as though we were in jail. We can't get away."

"If we—" the girl began. Stockton cut her short.

"It's no use! We can't live long in the forest. Only luck has saved us so far. If we were savages—Indians, perhaps—but we're not. If we go out in the jungle again, it means death."

"And if we stay here?" Baker asked.

Stockton's smile was grim. "Thorkel will kill us. Unless we murder him first."

"All right, suppose we manage to kill Thorkel," Mary asked quietly. "What then?"

"Then? We live." Stockton nodded, a queer look in his eyes. "I know. The projector only works one way. We can't regain our normal size, ever. Even if we were large enough to operate the machines, if we could work out the formula for returning us to our normal size. There's not much chance of his doing that."

Baker said slowly, "If we kill Thorkel, we'll have to remain—like this—forever?"

"Yeah. And if we don't—he'll get us, sooner or later. Well?"

"It's a—a hard choice," Mary whispered. "But at least we'd be alive—"

Baker nodded, and pointed to where Thorkel's discarded gun lay across the chair.

It was aimed at the scientist's cot.

"By God!" Stockton grunted. "That's it!"

Having come to a decision, the three acted quickly. They climbed the chair, and using books as props and the scissor-blade as a lever, adjusted the shotgun.

"Sight it at his pillow," Stockton told Baker, who was looking down the gun barrel. "Up a little . . . there! Right at his left ear!"

Mary was tying a piece of thread to the gun. "Can you cock it, Bill?"

"Yeah." He was straining with the lever. "Okay." But, despite Stockton's apparent assurance, he was feeling slightly sick. The choice was—horrible! To die at Thorkel's hands, or else to remain in this world of littleness forever.

"Thorkel's coming back!" There was panic in Mary's voice.

The three scurried to cover. Stockton managed to capture the thread's dangling end, and ran with it around a box, out of sight. Mary and Baker found shelter beside him.

The scientist's shadow fell across the threshold. He entered, yawning wearily.

Carelessly he scaled his hat on a corner and sat down on the cot, unlacing his boots.

Stockton's hand tightened on the thread. Would the titan notice the altered position of the shotgun?

Thorkel dropped his boots to the floor and started to lie down. Then, struck by a thought, he rose again and went to a cupboard, taking from it a dish of smoked meat and some cassava bread.

Placing this on the table, he drew up a chair and began to eat.

Apparently his eyes ached. Several times he polished his glasses, and presently discarded them entirely, substituting another pair which he took from a tray on the table. He ate slowly, nodding with weariness. And at last he removed the new pair of spectacles and slumped down, pillowing his head in his arms.

He slept.

"Oh damn!" Baker said with heart-felt fury. "We can't use the gun now. We couldn't prop it up at the right angle. It looks like the jungle, after all—unless maybe we can use a knife on him."

Stockton looked speculatively at the scissor-blade. "Wouldn't be sure enough. We've got to kill him, not disable him."

"Disable him—That's it!" Mary said suddenly.

"Bill, he's blind without his glasses!"

The three stared at each other, new hope springing to life within them. "That's it! Stockton approved. "We can hide them, and bargain with him, perhaps—"

"We must be quiet," Mary warned.-

But Thorkel slept heavily. He did not stir when the little people climbed up to the table, and, one by one, handed down the spectacles till they could be thrust out of sight through a hole in the floor.

"That's the last pair," Mary said with satisfaction, peering down into the depths. "He won't find them in a hurry."

"The last but one," Baker denied. "Bill—" He stopped. Stockton was gone.

They saw him back on the table-top, tiptoeing toward the sleeping Thorkel. He skirted the specimen-box and approached the spectacles, gripped in the scientist's huge hand.

Gingerly he attempted to disengage them. Thorkel stirred. He mumbled something, and his head lifted, slow with sleep.

Fear tightened Stockton's throat. On impulse he jerked the spectacles from Thorkel's hand and fled behind the specimen-box.

Blinking, Thorkel felt around for the glasses. His pale eyes stared unseeingly.

There was a little thud. Stockton, crouching at the table-edge, saw the spectacles hit the floor, without breaking. He did not see Thorkel rise and fumble toward the specimen-box.

Mary's voice was ice-shrill.

"Jump, Bill, jump!"

Hastily, Stockton slipped over the edge, hung by his hands, and dropped. The floor rushed up to meet him. He landed heavily, but sprang up and fled before Thorkel could see the movement.

The scientist said, a curious tremor in his voice,

"So you've come back. So you are here, eh?"

There was no answer. Thorkel stumbled to the back door, closed it, and put his back against it.

And for the first time, Thorkel knew fear.

Thorkel tugged at his mustache. His voice shook when he spoke.

"You would dare attack me? Well, that is a mistake. You are shut up in this room. And i will find you—" He whirled at a fancied movement or sound, glaring blindly, swinging his bald head from side to side with a slow, jerky motion.

"I will find you!"

Stockton pulled Mary back farther into their place of concealment behind a crate. "He's crazy with fear. Keep quiet!"

Thorkel began to stumble around the room, kicking aside apparatus, boxes, clothing.

He fell, and when he rose there was blood trickling from the corner of his mouth.

His hand closed on the shotgun. He snatched it up, and stood silent, waiting.

Without warning Thorkel flung up the gun and fired. The crashing echoes filled the room. Stockton peered out, saw that there was a gaping, splintered hole in the bottom of the back door.

Thorkel waited. Then a grim smile twisted his lips. He felt his way to the table and sought for the tray of extra glasses. His hand encountered nothing. The room was utterly still. "Then—this is war? Thorkel asked slowly. With a sudden furious motion he broke down the shotgun and gripped the barrel, holding it like a club.

He dropped to hands and knees and felt beneath the table. Slowly he advanced. In a moment, Stockton realized, he would find the glasses where they lay.

Stockton's sandaled feet made no sound as he raced forward. Before Thorkel could react, the geologist had sprung beneath his nose, snatched up the glasses, and smashed them against the table-leg.

Thorkel swung viciously with the gun-barrel.

Stockton, perforce, dropped the glasses and fled. The huge metal club missed him by inches. He vanished into the shadows.

Crouching in their hiding-places, the three little people stared, frozen, as the titan form of Thorkel rose above the table edge. He was donning his glasses. One lens was splintered and useless.

Blood-stained, dirt-smeared, and terrible, the giant towered there. His voice rose in a shout of laughter.

"Now!" he roared. "Now you can call me Cyclops!"

Swiftly he strode forward. With methodical haste he began to search the room, over turning boxes, flinging the cot aside to examine some cases beneath it. Stockton made a peremptory signal. Mary and Baker dashed out from their hiding-place between Thorkel's discarded boots. They followed Stockton swiftly toward the back door.

"Outside, quick!" he whispered. "He can't see us. The cot's in the way."

They clambered through the gaping hole the shotgun charge had made. It was not easy, and Mary's clothing caught on a sharp splinter.

The cloth ripped as Stockton jerked at it.

Footsteps thudded across the floor. The door was flung open. Thorkel switched on the floodlight.

His shadow momentarily hid the three as they raced forward. The mouth of the mine-shaft loomed up before them, a plank stretched across the pit.

"Down there!" Stockton gasped. "It is our only chance."

It was the only possible place of concealment. But Thorkel's one good eye did not miss the little people's movements as they scrambled over the brink and down the steep rock of the shaft-walls. Skirting the windlass, he fell to his hands and knees and crawled out upon the plank, steadying himself with one hand on the rope that ran down into black depths.

Stockton, climbing to a rock, realized that he still held his scissor-blade sword.

He lifted it in futile threat.

There was a splintering crack as Thorkel struck at his quarry. The gun-. barrel clashed on rock. And, abruptly, the plank caved in and dropped.

Thorkel still gripped the windlass-rope with one hand, and that saved him.

For a second he swung wildly, while the echoing crash of the falling wood and the gun-barrel echoed up from the depths. Then his grip became surer. Panting, he hung there briefly, his bald head gleaming with sweat.

He began to climb up the rope.

Stockton glanced around quickly. Mary was clinging to a sloping rock, her white face turned toward the giant.

Baker was looking at the mineralogist, and his gaunt gray features were twisted with hopeless fury.

Stockton made a quick gesture, pointed to his sword, and began to swarm back up to the surface.

Instantly Baker caught his meaning. If the rope to which Thorkel clung could be cut—

But it was thick, terribly thick, for a tiny man and a scissor-glade!

Thorkel pulled himself slowly upward. In a moment Baker saw, he would reach safety. The trader's lips drew back from his teeth in a mirthless grin; he abruptly rose and edged forward a few paces.

Then he sprang.

Out and down he went, and his clutching hands found Thorkel's collar. Before the scientist could understand what had happened, Baker was clawing and snarling like a terrier at his throat. Thorkel almost lost his grip.

Gasping with fear and rage, he shook his head violently, trying to knock his assailant free.

"You dirty killer!" Baker snarled.

He tossed about madly, once almost crushed between Thorkel's chin and chest. And then, suddenly, Thorkel was falling. . . .

With a wine and a whir the windlass ran out as the rope was severed. A long, quavering cry burst from Thorkel's throat as he dropped away into the darkness. Higher and higher it rose—and ended.

Stockton ran to the brink and peered over. Mary was clambering weakly up toward him. And, behind her, was Baker.

Bill was standing beside an upright book, a curious expression on his face. He looked around vaguely.

"The machine—" he old Mary. "Can you work it?"

Mary was pouring over Thorkel's notebooks. She said despondently, "It's no good, Bill. The device is only a condenser. It can't bring people back to normal size. We'll have to remain this size the rest of our lives. And now, we've got to get back to civilization, somehow—"

"As we are?" Baker's face fell. "That's impossible."

"Wait a minute," Stockton interrupted. "I've a hunch—do you remember when we first saw Thorkel, after he reduced us?"

"Yeah. So what?"

"He wasn't trying to kill us then. He just wanted to weigh and measure us. But after he examined Dr. Bulfinch, he turned into a vicious killer. Why do you suppose that happened?"

"He probably intended to kill us all along. For trying to steal his secrets," Baker suggested. "He was probably afraid that we would warn the Allies of his plans."

"Maybe. But he wasn't in any hurry at first. He knew he could dispose of us any time he wanted. Only after he examined Dr. Bulfinch he—found out something that made it necessary to get rid of us in a hurry."

Mary caught her breath.

"What?"

"I saw a white mule in the jungle a while ago. A colt. Paco was playing with it. At first I figured it might be Pinto's colt, but mules are sterile, of course. That meant two albino mules here—which isn't very probable—or else it was Pinto. Remember, Pedro said the dog used to play with the mule."

"How big was the mule?" Baker asked abruptly.

"The size of a half-grown colt. Listen, Steve, when we first came out of the cellar I measured myself against that book—'Human Physiology.' It was just higher than my head. But now it only comes up to my chest!"

"We're growing!" Mary whispered. That's it."

"Sure. That's what Thorkel found out when he examined Dr. Bulfinch, and why he tried to kill us before we grew back to normal size. I think it's a progressively accelerative process. In two weeks, or perhaps ten days, we'll be back to normal.

"It's logical," the girl commented. "Once the compressive force of radium power is removed, we expand—slowly but elastically. The electrons swing back to their normal orbits. The energy we absorbed under the ray will be liberated in guanta—"

"Ten days," Baker murmured. "And then we can go back down the river again!"

But it was a month before the three, once more normal in size, reached the Andean village that was their first destination. The sight of human beings, no longer gigantic, was warmly reassuring. Indians leaned against the huts, scratching lazily for fleas.

Peering down the archway along the street, a ragged Bill Stockton turned to grin at Mary.

"Looks good eh?"

Baker was absorbed in thought," he said, scratching his stubbled cheek. "One way, we get our pictures in the paper and tanks of free *pulque*. But it's just as likely we'll end up in a padded cell if we tell the truth. If we don't tell the truth—"

He paused, stiffening. A mangy cat had appeared from beyond the arch. Baker's muscles tensed; his breath burst out in an explosive *"Scat!"* as he sprang forward.

The cat vanished, shocked to the core.

Baker's chest inflated several inches. "Well," he said, with the quiet pride of achievement, "did either of you see *that?*"

"No," murmured Stockton, who was seizing the opportunity to kiss Mary. "Go away. Quietly. And quickly."

Baker shrugged and followed the cat, a predatory gleam in his eye.

THE END

Note the clapboard and giant glasses in the grip's hand.

OUR NEXT ATTRACTION